Elizabeth Morgan is a writer, playwright and actor from Llanelli, Wales. She has had four books published, including two non-fiction volumes on France, a novel and a guide to drama. Thirty-four of her plays plus several of her short stories have been performed in the theatre, on television and on BBC Radio 4. She has worked as an actor in theatre, film, television and radio in a variety of diverse roles ranging from the French concierge in the iconic sports comedy film *Grand Slam*, to Dylan Thomas's *Under Milk Wood*, which she performed with Anthony Hopkins, and the voices of Destiny and Rhapsody Angel in Gerry Anderson's much-loved *Captain Scarlet*. She toured the USA for over five years with her two one-woman plays and has taught and directed in several of Britain's major drama schools. She divides her time between Cardiff and the South of France.

TICKET TO PARADISE

ELIZABETH MORGAN

PETER OWEN
London and Chicago

PETER OWEN PUBLISHERS
81 Ridge Road, London N8 9NP

Peter Owen books are distributed in the USA and Canada by
Independent Publishers Group/Trafalgar Square
814 North Franklin Street, Chicago, IL 60610, USA

Published in Great Britain 2015
by Peter Owen Publishers

PAPERBACK ISBN 978-0-7206-1861-7
EPUB ISBN 978-0-7206-1862-4
MOBIPOCKET ISBN 978-0-7206-1863-1
PDF ISBN 978-0-7206-1864-8

A catalogue record for this book is available from the British Library.

Typeset by Octavo Smith Publishing Services

Printed and bound in the UK by CPI Group (UK) Ltd, Croydon, CR0 4YY

To the memory of my dear feisty mother
who told me I should write it.

ACKNOWLEDGEMENTS

Heartfelt thanks to my friends Sir Derek Jacobi, Miriam Margolyes, Nicholas Parsons, Prunella Scales and Timothy West, CBE, who took time out of busy schedules to wade through pages of text and write such supportive comments. And to other friends and family who have suffered my endless enthusiasm about the Patagonian story.

*This is a novel based on historical fact.
The personalities in it are purely fictional,
as are their family stories. But the major disasters that
befell this extraordinary band are fact.*

PREFACE

A traveller passing through this Welsh valley in 1860 would have been struck immediately by its contrasts; rural beauty on one side and industrial dedication on the other. Sheep, smallholdings, cultivated strips, a few cottages, looked down over serried ranks of miners' dwellings, huddled together, as if for protection, sometimes in the valley, sometimes halfway up the mountain. These villages, newly created, ran breathless through the terrain, with no pause for air between them; and industrial growth was spreading. A growth propagated not by the native population but by wealthy foreigners – English, who had been sharp enough to recognise an outcrop of coal when they saw one; and the location was perfect. The nearby Bristol Channel, with its fishing villages, easy to expand, was an excellent outlet. As for labour, take away a farmer's land and he is out of work. Training was all that would be required. But would the farmer willingly part with the land? A problem certainly, but if legal proceedings were to be conducted in English – and, after all, that was the law – it was simply unfortunate if the farmer could not quite comprehend.

It was inevitable that industry should come to this land so rich in mineral resources. First there was iron ore, then coal, and, with the new railways replacing the old canal system, expansion and profits were assured. There was nothing to stop the greedy talons of money and power from scavenging even further and deeper into the rural landscape. Acknowledgement of the human condition in this industrial maelstrom was secondary to the industrialists' master plan. Justice had twice come out of her corner and led the Chartists at Newport and the Daughters of Rebecca in the south-west. But physical success was minimal, and the life of a worker was still cheap. For a Welshman with blood in his veins, what did the future promise; a struggle that could last perhaps two or three generations? Some were already thinking of more immediate options.

GLOSSARY OF WELSH WORDS

Arglwydd Mawr	God Almighty
bach/fach (f)	little, dear
bara	bread
bara brith	currant bread
cymanfa ganu	group sing-song
carthenni	woven Welsh wool blankets
cwtching	snuggling
chwarae teg	fair play
cachu	shit
cawl	Welsh lamb stew
cariad	darling
Duw	God
Duwedd Mawr	good God
dadcu	grandfather
eisteddfod	festival of song, poetry and music
ffradach	pandemonium
fy nghariad i	my darling
hiraeth	longing
hwyl	enthusiasm
Iesu bach	dear Jesus
Iesu Mawr	great Jesus
teisen lap	fruit cake
twp	stupid
ychafi	yuck

I

It was warm and dry and promised to be a good September. You could see the valley and the mountains; there was no mist, unusual for this time of year. Grass was very green, pools and waterfalls brimming over after the particularly wet summer months.

The school, on the rural side of the valley, lay in a hollow cupped out of the surrounding mountainside. It was a small grey unsympathetic building. The blue sky did nothing to enhance its appearance, for even the sun did not so much as glance the walls with a ray.

In the corner of the school playground stood a little girl, quite alone. Her eyes were shut to stop the tears that were about to run down cheeks, burning now with shame and embarrassment. This was only the first day of her punishment; there were to be three more of being sent outside to stand in this corner just before playtime, morning and afternoon. Around her neck was a short length of rope from which hung a piece of slate. Long flaxen curls fell about her shoulders and her new cotton smock, which she wore to keep her dress clean. She hated the teacher. He was a big bully, just come from England. She couldn't understand him anyway.

Suddenly the moment she had been dreading arrived. The school door opened, children spilled into the playground, skipping and running, but her little body, rigid with fear, tried to shut out all sounds of the awful ritual that was about to take place.

The teacher blew a whistle. Despite tightly shut eyes she could feel the others gathering around her in a semi-circle. Another blast on the whistle, and all was silent.

The humiliation was complete.

'Now!' he boomed. 'You all know why Bethan Rhys is here?'

'Yes, sir,' they chorused.

'Then let this be a warning to you all. Next time,' he paused, narrowing his eyes as they swept over the apprehensive semi-circle.

'Next time it will be *five* days – outside – all day!' He smiled. 'Five days perhaps of rain, of thunder, of lightning!' He spat out the words while his pupils silently digested the full horror of his threat.

Bethan shuddered and made a private pact with God about the next couple of days.

'Are you ready?' he continued.

'Yes, sir,' they trilled.

He raised his stick like a baton. 'One, two, three.'

A few hesitant voices, barely above a whisper, mouthed the words 'Welsh not. Welsh not.'

'Stop!' he yelled. 'I want everybody, if you please. *If* you please! Anyone who does not shout out these words with vigour and with all of their strength will be joining this disobedient girl tomorrow. Is that clear?'

It was abundantly clear. Obeying, the voices shrieked and bellowed. 'Welsh not! Welsh not!'

On and on they chanted until at last the teacher, satisfied he had made his point, blew the whistle again. 'Enough! Now you may play – in English.'

Obligatory taunting over, Bethan slowly opened her eyes, sticky and swollen, and looked up at the mountains. They were spinning like tops, and her thin legs were trembling. She was forbidden to move, and the slate rested uncomfortably on the buttons of the Welsh wool bodice her mother had made for her only last week. Her mother knitted vests and bodices for all of them, but the wool was oily and coarse next to her skin and to Bethan still smelled of sheep.

Out of the corner of her eye she espied her best friend Elin Morgan. Her family lived in a nearby farm cottage, and the two little girls were the same age. Elin was as dark as Bethan was fair, with large brown eyes like saucers and black curly hair cut to her shoulders. A large brown saucer winked at Bethan. Winking was Elin's speciality. Despite hours of tuition by her older brother Tomos, Bethan simply could not master the art. Elin's wink always made her laugh – but not this time, for not a word was allowed to be spoken, not a glance acknowledged. At the end of the day, as Bethan was picking up the linen bag, which had contained an apple and a piece of *bara saim* bread and dripping, the teacher called her to him.

'Now, girl,' he growled. 'No more of that tribal language. You will speak only in the tongue of all civilized people the world over: English! Is that clear?'

The trembling child had understood but two or three words.

'*English!*' he bellowed.

Nodding her head, 'English,' she whispered.

'And you, too, Elin Morgan. Don't think I haven't been watching you.'

Elin, who had been standing behind her friend, stared at him like a startled gazelle, grabbed Bethan's hand, and together they ran out, not daring to look back lest this Bastille and its gaoler should hold them for ever.

These two were inseparable, and, though they both had older sisters, it was to each other they told their secrets.

Breathless, they scrambled over a stile into a field that would lead to home on the other side of the mountain. Here Bethan threw herself down on a bank and began to sob. All day she had saved her tears of shame and her frail little body rocked, wretched with anguish. Elin, watching mutely, stretched out her hand, gathered a small bunch of buttercups, daisies and forget-me-nots and thrust them into Bethan's small damp fist. Standing over her, Elin raised the corner of her school smock and dabbed her friend's tears. She knew this time she had been lucky that it was Bethan the teacher had heard speaking Welsh. For, even in the playground, under his eagle eye all secrets were whispered in their mother tongue. Playing in English wasn't the same. It was so difficult to remember to speak this foreign language. Besides, they barely understood it, and this made school lessons much harder.

Tears dried, flowers and bag in hand, Bethan jumped up and ran down the bank into the field to join Elin who was gathering more flowers to take home to her mother. Looking up at her best friend, Elin winked and grinned.

'Gummy. That's what you are!' Bethan laughed, pointing to the gap where Elin's front teeth used to be.

'Don't care. I'll have my grown up teeth before you.'

'Mine are loose. Honest. Feel.'

'No they're not.'

'They are. Go on. Feel.'

And so with conversation ranging from teeth to socks and sisters, the two little girls, cotton smocks bouncing over red flannel dresses, skipped their way home to mams who loved them and who tried to protect them from the harsh realities of their world as best they could. The future would have to take care of itself.

Dafydd Rhys crouched over the dark furrowed soil where he had been working since early morning, flexed his shoulder muscles and stood up. With aching limbs he strode to a nearby patch of grass, dense and short, and sat down. Despite his weariness he smiled with gratitude at the beauty that surrounded him. The majestic mountains were etched against the blue sky. He loved his native soil, his language and for this brief moment shut out gnawing fears of the blight that threatened to destroy everything he held dear. His eyes scanned the length of the mountain range, beyond to the Brecon Beacons and still further, until all disappeared in a warm September haze. He turned his head and glared at the valley below. No smiles for this, only bitterness and anger. Smoke belched from the chimneys of the ironworks as ore was smelted and the molten lumps hammered into tracks for the new railways.

He hated the iron. How many children had it killed and maimed as they stood innocently in the path of its lethal river of fire? He was thankful that his firstborn, fifteen-year-old Lisa, was an ironstone girl, who broke up lumps of the rock for smelting. Safer but tough work, and he had wanted her to stay at home, help her mam, but that was impossible now with the rent doubled. A few yards away from the smoke were the rotating wheels of the two new coal pits sunk only a few months ago. Young Tomos was there, somewhere underground, working in Llysfawr Mine. He would willingly have changed places with him, but how could a thirteen-year-old boy run a farm, even a small one, and the farm was vital to their survival? Each day, he prayed that Tomos would come home safe from the shift, for the pits' sirens announced disasters with sombre regularity.

Death and tears were slowly becoming a way of life in this new

Wales. A man of lesser faith than Dafydd Rhys would have crumbled. Many had, but when there is so precious little, when every day there is so much at stake, what is there left but faith in God? Only the continuing hope of divine intervention can lighten the heart and ease despair.

Down in Merthyr they were saying the iron would be a thing of the past in ten years; from now on it would be the coal pits. It was true. Welsh coal for English fires had become the fashion, and with railways coming into the valley everyone was making money; everyone but those who did the work. When the iron started rich men from the English Midlands were content to use the dozens of outcrops of coal scattered over the rural landscape, but domestic fuel was another matter. These new seams were found deep inside the earth, and boys such as Tomos risked their lives daily to pull up hods of the precious mineral.

Dafydd was a handsome man, with a strong muscular frame, tall for a Welshman, with strikingly dark blue eyes and black hair that now lay flat against his head, damp with sweat.

His brown weatherbeaten skin gave him the look of a person of Latin origin, a foreigner. Certainly he was a foreigner to the dozens of English who had migrated to the new industries. But they were the foreigners, and Dafydd resented the effect their arrival was already having on the Welsh way of life, its language, its people and its history. He pulled a rag from his pocket and wiped the drops of perspiration that the hot sun had drawn from his face.

What was to become of his young family? The small farm barely supported them. Bess the cow produced enough milk for butter and cheese but just for themselves, nothing to sell. Pity he had to sell her last heifer. No chance now of building up a small herd. Three-dozen sheep grazing on the mountain supplied wool, which they sold in Merthyr or Carmarthen, together with an occasional lamb to the butcher. Since the enclosures, grazing land was hard to come by, but Glyn Morgan, a neighbouring tenant farmer, had left agriculture for the iron and had given Dafydd the use of his fields.

The farms, only two fields apart, had been worked by their forebears for a century.

Glyn and Dafydd were very close, like brothers; both playmates and schoolmates. Their children, too, had grown up together. Glyn's daughter Bron worked with Lisa in the iron, and his son Huw with Tomos down the Llysfawr. As for the two youngest, they had been born within months of each other and were becoming as inseparable as their fathers had been.

Of course the two men were only tenant farmers, for the farms and the mountain with its thousands of acres were owned by a wealthy family from London. They may have been Welsh originally, but they were so far removed from home soil they might as well have been French. In fact Dafydd was convinced they would have been better off if Lord Gwilym was French, then he might have held a few revolutionary ideals. His Lordship was rarely seen apart from election time, for he represented the constituency in Parliament; though what a London Parliament would do for them, even given their financial interest, was a sick joke.

Rumour had it that Lord Gwilym was about to sell, or at any rate lease his acreage to an industrialist, for the rich soil on the lower slopes, which though producing abundant fields of grain, was black, so there could be no doubt as to what lay beneath. What would happen then? Dafydd like Glyn would be pushed into industry, receive no compensation for the farm and be forced to find a hovel for his family in Dowlais or Cyfarthfa, where disease ran riot through stinking refuse swilling streets. Even religion was dictated by London. Be Anglican – or else!

When Lord Gwilym's agent, a snivelling Englishman, came to collect the rent from Maldwyn Roberts and one of his kids let slip they had been to chapel Sunday school the rent was doubled. Then his wife died in childbirth, and that was that. The children were put in Carmarthen workhouse and Maldwyn dispossessed.

Frustration and anger streaked Dafydd's face again. This was no way to live. How could a man look after his family? Where was the sense working in a powder keg for the cigar-smoking rich and their profits?

He was an intelligent man, a homebred political philosopher, largely self-taught. The three Rs had come easily to him during his few years of formal education, and he could speak English well when required. Under his father's influence young Dafydd had grown up on the principles of the French Revolution and the sermons of Richard Price.

By fifteen he had read every political pamphlet in the house, including Thomas Paine's *Rights of Man*. As a young man he dreamt of setting to rights the wrongs of a political system controlled by pernicious class divisions. Politics coursed through Dafydd's veins with his life-blood, and in Wales they were now inextricably bound to the new Nonconformism that believed in the preservation of language and national identity. Dafydd knew the work of William Williams, Howell Harries, Robert Owen and John Frost. With such impossible political horizons, how could he ever be content with his lot? At the age of thirty-five he was already a maverick, a potential leader, who saw himself as a man of the people, determined to exploit the qualities that nature and a radical father had given him.

His cheeks burned with indignation at the chains that bound and gagged him into political impotence. If he became an outspoken opponent, what then? Dispossession for sure, then imprisonment, transportation or hanging to follow? There had been some inching progress with the Chartists and the Rebecca Riots, but it was all too slow for Dafydd. He sensed that one day the force within him would be too powerful and would have to break out, even if it meant losing everything for the greater good.

All this contemplation turned his stomach into a knot of aching discontent, and right now there was the harvest to get on with, another field to reap. He rose, stretched his aching back and looked up at the sky.

'*Annwyl Iesu* – dear Jesus,' he whispered. 'Help us, please.'

He picked up a stone and, raising a powerful arm, hurled it into the smoking valley below.

Myfanwy Rhys picked up the wooden palette knife Dafydd had made her and turned over the last batch of Welsh cakes sizzling on the griddle. Cakes were a treat these days, especially for young Bethan who would be coming home from school soon. The heat from the fire was overpowering on such a warm day, and her cheeks glowed. On the big kitchen table dough for the week's bread was laid out on a piece of white calico, before being put aside in a big earthenware tub. Though small, Myfanwy was strong and wiry. A woman had to be. Childbirth was strenuous and you had to have good muscles to run a home.

A black iron kettle of boiling water hung on a chain suspended from a spit over the fire in the black-leaded grate. She poured water into a large tin pan, splashing red coals that hissed in reply, and carried it to a trough in a corner of the kitchen, big enough to hold all their dirty dishes. It had been Dafydd's idea. She had a good man, she knew that, thoughtful, gentle, too, even when he loved, for he had never once forced himself on her, like the shocking tales she had heard about other men. No better than animals some of them, especially with a drop of beer in their bellies. She shuddered at the thought.

Myfanwy was from Dowlais and had worked as a doorkeeper for tuppence a day at the four-foot level. It was a hard beginning for an eleven-year-old, twelve hours in the semi-darkness. Consequently her skin had retained a disconcerting pallor. A small blue crescent scar on her forehead remained the only evidence of her banishment to the underworld. After three years, unlike Persephone, her mother brought her up to work in the iron. By fourteen she had witnessed accidents that had left children blinded, burnt or dead. She moved on to become cleaner to a manager's wife in Merthyr, where she was obliged to learn English.

She had met Dafydd at an open-air *cymanfa ganu* on a Sunday. They were standing next to each other, and he thought he had seen an angel. Girls around these parts were usually short, dark and dumpy, but this one was slim and delicate-looking, her fair auburn hair tied back in ringlets off her face. She thought he was the most handsome boy she had ever seen.

After four weeks of courting, they were kissing each other with a passion that left them weak, but chapel and the Bible forbade them to go further.

It was a strange time for morals. Death was in attendance day and night in the pits, and cholera and typhus rampaged through Merthyr, Dowlais and Aberdare, so with precious few expectations, and possibly so little time, why stem the surge of passion? Why not taste all the fruits of love, for by now Dafydd and Myfanwy were so in love they barely ate nor slept. She thought of nothing but Dafydd, he thought of Myfanwy and politics. One warm Sunday evening after chapel, sitting on a soft patch of grass halfway up the mountain, and hidden from view by a lush copse of woodland, Dafydd used his powers of polemic and persuasive argument to their utmost, explaining why they should now do what all adults in love do, and, quoting the Bible, that they should cleave to each other and become as one. He wrapped her Bible in her shawl and placed it under her head. 'There we are – a holy pillow.'

Though she was ready to agree and obey her own physical stirrings of passion, she said, 'So long as you are sure I'm not sinning.'

Gently undoing the buttons of her chemise he whispered, 'Sure. No problem with the scriptures, my lovely.' He nestled his lips in her breasts.

'But, Dav,' she gasped, 'we're not married.'

He was barely able to speak for the desire and passion that clogged his throat. 'Marriage is an invention of capitalism, *cariad*. Nothing more.'

'Why's that?'

'To be sure the millions are kept in the family.'

'So?'

'So we aren't capitalists, are we?'

'Oh, Dav, I don't care what we are', and Myfanwy, breathless from desire that raced around her head and body, prodding into life fierce urges she could not resist, curled her slender frame around her beloved's firm loins, all resistance blown to the four winds the moment flesh met flesh.

They were both virgins, and Dafydd knew instinctively he had to be very gentle, overcoming the wild passion that possessed his body the moment he touched her. This he had learnt from older men always ready to give sound advice on sexual matters to a growing lad, noting carefully how to give pleasure to a woman. Frissons of inexplicable sensations swirling through Myfanwy's stomach caused her to moan softly. 'Oh, Dav, my lovely boy, I want to touch you, too, all over,' she whispered.

He raised himself up on his elbow and smiled down at her. 'I'm all yours, my darling Myfanwy, body, head, soul – for ever and ever.'

And so their union was truly consummated. All that was left now was the mere formality of marriage.

Dressing again took a long time as they stopped for a kiss, for an embrace, for another declaration of love.

'So long as we haven't sinned,' Myfanwy repeated.

'No! What we have done we have done through love. Not like the aristocrats and the royals with their lives of loose morals. No love there'

'How do they get on with their church then?'

Dafydd smiled. 'Easy. Their money supports their church, so the church shuts up about their morals.'

'But we're chapel, Dav.'

'Aye, but same God, isn't it? He must be quite used to the antics of the rich by now. Anyway God doesn't know about class.'

'So we aren't going to suffer because we have – you know.'

Dafydd grinned. 'Of course we aren't. Are the dukes and duchesses struck down dead every day because they spend nights in debauchery and drink with loose men and women?'

Myfanwy giggled. 'No, or there'd be none left.'

'There we are then. And what did you have under your head?'

'My Bible.'

'What did my elbow lean on?'

'Your Bible.'

'So we have become as one with the full support of the Bible.'

'Dav, you'd convince our cat he could fly.'

Exploding into peals of laughter they walked hand in hand back into town on a cushion of love, having crossed their Rubicon into adulthood.

They married before Christmas, and exactly nine months later Lisa was born. Dafydd remained with Myfanwy, holding her hand through all those hours of difficult labour and even helped the nurse at the moment of birth. In order to plan future offspring, Dafydd exercised restraint and withdrawal. How she loved to feel his body close to hers in bed, the smell of his skin, his roughened hands as they gently touched her breasts and her thighs, the sweet words he whispered when the youngest was asleep in the stump bed beside theirs. Sometimes even now she had only to look in his eyes to feel something stirring deep in her stomach, and she would long to touch him.

But these days Myfanwy couldn't help thinking about Dafydd as he used to be, before politics and anger with each new outrage tightened the coils of fury within him and imperceptibly distanced him from his family.

If a man's spirit is crushed, anger will fester and, one day, explode.

It had been a bad year for them. When Hawkins the agent found out Dafydd had not voted for Lord Gwilym he doubled the rent. That was the reason why young Tomos and Lisa had to work. If Hawkins ever found out about Sunday chapel he had the right to increase it yet again. Myfanwy wondered who Dafydd hated more, Hawkins or himself – for having to shut up and say nothing.

She heard the familiar sound of her father's stick tapping on the cobbled yard. Most of the time Dadcu, as the children called him, kept to himself in the front parlour, with his bed and the rest of his few possessions. After Myfanwy's mother died, Dadcu continued working in the iron until the accident when he lost an eye. He was no trouble, fair play, and he doted on the children, carving strange and wonderful toys for them out of any old piece of wood.

The moment Bethan arrived home and saw her mother she ran headlong into her arms, sobbing loudly again. Elin, like a little guardian angel, explained the events of the day. Myfanwy tried not to make too much of her punishment lest it provoke another outburst from Dafydd. Tears dried, and with a Welsh cake for comfort, Bethan set about her daily task of collecting eggs from the six layers.

At the pit head in Llysfawr thirteen-year-old Tomos Rhys stood in line with his pal Huw Morgan, who was a couple of years younger. They were doorkeepers on the fifth level. Not much danger there, except for trams, but the manager had told them only this morning it would be picks next week for them and down to the pit bottom. They were getting too old for doorkeeping.

You had to work in the dark down at the bottom, the men said, because of the gas, and if you got out in time, when it was bad, you could count yourself lucky. The line shortened, and the two boys, black with coal dust, moved nearer the desk where two English clerks sat, one handing out wages the other filling in paperwork. Tomos and Huw understood English well, and there seemed to be plenty of it around them today.

'Lot of English come in this week,' whispered Huw.

'From where?'

'England.'

Tomos grinned at his friend. 'I know that, daft.'

One of the clerks, smiling malevolently, pointed out their names on the list, speaking slowly as though addressing the mentally impaired and making loud remarks to the other foreigners about the stupidity of the locals.

Both boys could read and write well in Welsh and had no difficulty in writing their signatures, the same in any language. With a chorus of mocking guffaws to see them off, the boys took their coppers and hurried out. They walked in silence for several yards up the path that led to home.

'Funny – all those foreigners in Wales,' said Huw.

Tomos, dark like his father, glowered. 'Aye, it's like they've taken us over – like they owned us.'

'But they do, don't they?' observed the younger boy quietly.

Lisa Rhys placed the heavy pick on the ground and straightened her back. Ten hours a day breaking up lumps of ironstone for the smelters across the other side of the big yard was hard.

Though they worked under a half roof, the girls were cruelly exposed to the elements. Often one of them would pass out with fatigue, excessive bleeding or stomach cramps. Miscarriages were common, sometimes welcomed, sometimes not. Whatever the cause, the unfortunate girl had to keep on working for the pittance at the end of the week if she wanted to survive.

Lisa looked over at her friend Bron Morgan doing battle with a stubborn lump.

'Come on. Leave that. You've done enough for these buggers today.'

Bron smiled and obeyed.

At fifteen Lisa had a woman's figure and a maturity beyond her age, for the years of childhood were cut short here. The pit manager, recognizing this, put her in charge of a gang of twelve girls. Dark-haired, she had her mother's fine-boned face and frame. Even now with the sweat trickling from her forehead, cotton petticoat and skirt clinging to damp thighs, she looked defiant. Lisa was her father's daughter.

Halfway home they flung themselves down on a tump of soft grass, dried by the day's heat. Bron breathed deeply and turned her face to kiss the sun full on his lips. 'I hate it down there. No air – the stench.'

'Me, too.' Lisa stretched out beside her, chewing on a piece of grass.

'But what else is there? Get married?'

A year younger than Lisa, Bron was a pretty little thing, small, round and brown as a berry. 'No fear. Don't want babies,' she giggled.

Lisa smiled slyly, rolling over to face her friend. 'You don't have to have babies. Didn't you know?'

'No.'

Snorting at Bron's ignorance Lisa continued. 'True! I'm telling you. Haven't you ever heard your mam and dad – doing it?'

'No! Well, don't know really.'

'Well, you listen, girl. Mine do it. I can hear them, and Mam's not having babies every whip stitch, is she?'

The younger girl's eyes opened wide, perplexed. 'No, I suppose she's not.'

Lisa rubbed her eyes. 'Still sharing a bed with your brother?'

Bron nodded.

'I threw our Tomos out when he was thirteen. He sleeps with Dadcu now.'

'And your Bethan?'

'She sleeps in Mam's and Dad's room – for now.'

Bron got up, brushed the dry grass off her skirt. 'That's why your mam doesn't have any babies – Bethan's listening, like you,' she laughed.

They ran home, giggling, sharing confidences, laced with the salacious observations of adolescents on the brink of finding out for themselves.

Lisa was stripped and sitting in the tin bath in the kitchen when Tomos burst in. Flinging her arms across her breasts, she yelled, 'Gerrout, Tomos Rhys, or I'll thump you!'

Tomos's black face vanished as quickly as it had appeared. His sister was not to be trifled with.

Myfanwy filled up the bath with more hot water. Already a handful was this daughter of hers. 'He won't bite. No need to get so het up.'

'So? I don't bust in on him.'

Myfanwy poked her head out of the kitchen door.

'Tomos! Candles, if you please.'

Tomos had two after-work tasks.

During the day his grandfather, Dadcu, collected rushes, which Tomos peeled to a strip, enough to support the pith. Later Myfanwy pulled them through hot grease – too dangerous for the boy. They made good cheap lights. Proper candles were for Sundays.

'Tell our Lisa to hurry up then, or I'll never get this black off.'

The boy's second task was to round up the sheep with their border collie, called Gors because she came from Dafydd's parents' village, Gorseinon. He loved being out with the dog and running on the mountain after working underground – it was was better than the helping make candles.

Around the table at suppertime, the children took it in turn to recount the day's events; something Dafydd had always encouraged them to do, provided their mouths were empty. When Lisa knew Tomos was going to be sent down to level ten she was furious and begged her father to do something.

'All right, all right, my girl! You've had your say. Now Bethan *fach*, it's your turn.'

The little five-year-old enjoyed recounting her saga, relishing especially the kisses and sympathy she received from her older siblings.

Myfanwy's eyes never left Dafydd. Without a word, he quickly rose from the table and strode outside into the yard. A brief nod to his daughter, and Dadcu followed him. Dafydd was leaning on the gate, head bowed. The wise old man took out his clay pipe and filled it with baccy that he pulled out of a worn leather pouch in his pocket.

'What's eating you, boy?'

Dafydd shook his head. 'I want to blow up the bloody lot down there.'

Dadcu lit his pipe. 'Get you far that will – Botany Bay or a noose in Newport.'

'Aye aye – don't worry. I won't do anything stupid.'

In the momentary silence Dadcu spat into the twilight. 'Ever thought of moving away?'

'Where to, North Wales?'

'No no, right away – you and the family – abroad.'

'America?'

The old man shrugged. 'Myfanwy's cousins went there a couple of years ago. Good life by all accounts.'

Dafydd straightened up. 'Dadcu, I love Wales, our language, our culture. I want to preserve it. D'you know what's happened in America?'

The old man quietly puffed on his pipe and shook his head. His son-in-law was about to tell him.

'They go there thinking they're going to keep themselves to themselves, but they have to work, so they speak English. Kids come along, and that's it. They're American, not Welsh any more. Wales is forgotten.'

'But you could always have your own shops, your own patch.'

'Dadcu, they've already done that. What's his name, the Reverend Michael Jones, hasn't he tried to start a Welsh colony? Wisconsin it was, then Oregon.'

'No good was it?'

Dafydd shook his head. 'The last failure was Tennessee.'

A resounding spit from Dadcu flew over the gate with deadly accuracy.

'Pity. Big country America! Pity they can't find you a corner somewhere.'

Dafydd ran his fingers through his hair. 'What do they want with us when they're having a civil war?'

Somewhere on the mountain Tomos could be heard whistling instructions to Gors, who was barking with canine delight as she rounded up the sheep.

'What choice have you got, boy?'

Dafydd sighed impatiently. 'Think I'll go for a stroll – see Glyn.'

The old man grunted approval. Clutching his pipe, his kindly old face creased with worry, he stared into the gathering half-light of evening, even at this moment far brighter than the future.

The Morgans' cottage, two fields higher up, was a home from home for Dafydd. Here Glyn lived with his wife Rhiannon, a bright round Llanelli girl who had worked in the tinplate, and their children. Glyn was not a political animal like Dafydd and, though slower to see the exploitative tentacles of capitalism, was just as much a Welshman and abhorred industry's increasing threats to the landscape, their way of life and Westminster's slow strangulation of the mother tongue.

As Dafydd rounded a corner of the path that would take him up the mountain, he saw Glyn coming down.

'Hey! Just coming to see you. On my way to night shift I was.'

'Everything all right?' Dafydd asked.

'Oh, aye. Fine.'

The two men greeted each other with a friendly cuff on the shoulder.

'Come over by here – sit down for a minute.' Glyn pointed to a rocky outcrop a few feet away. 'Got something to show you.'

He pulled out a newspaper from his jacket pocket. 'Look, Welsh Emigration Society. Reverend Michael Jones, Liverpool.'

Dafydd took the paper, printed in Welsh, and glanced at the front page.

'Aye aye, I know. Not America again, is it?'

'No, Patagonia.'

'I thought the Argentinians didn't want us there.'

'According to this,' said Glyn, pointing to the paper, 'they've changed their minds. A Welsh colony this time, boyo. Independence, language – the lot! And something else, too.'

Glyn pulled a pamphlet out of his trouser pocket. It announced a talk to be given on Sunday in their chapel by a Mr Lewis, representative of the society, who had had 'talks with and assurances from the Argentine government concerning the setting up of a self-governing Welsh colony in the fertile Chubut Valley'.

Dafydd studied the pamphlet for a moment and whistled through his teeth. 'Patagonia, is it?'

The summer sky was darkening. Trees were tinged with deep crimson rays. Down below, Tomos, Gors beside him, was making his way back to the farm. Wasn't this what Dafydd wanted for the boy, fresh air and freedom, not ten hours a day with a wager on his life? In a few years it would be Bethan. Unthinkable.

Evaluating every word, Dafydd said slowly. 'Glyn, do you think, honestly now, it would be possible, we – you, me, our families, others like us – could make our own country so far away? Another Wales?'

Glyn smiled. 'Anything's possible if you have enough faith, Dav. Got to have faith. See what he says on Sunday, is it?'

Glancing at the valley below, Dafydd shrugged. 'Has to be better than this.'

2

'Mam! Come and see our Bethan,' Lisa called from upstairs.

Myfanwy, wearing her Sunday chapel frock protected by a large apron, was in the kitchen clearing up breakfast.

'Tell her to come down here. I'm busy.'

She heard the treble tones and giggles as her youngest pattered down the wooden staircase. The door at the bottom opened to reveal Bethan decked out in a new cream smock; her hair dressed by Lisa in bows made from leftovers. Shy and smiling, the child stood still for a moment, head lowered.

'Oh! You look a treat, *cariad*,' said Myfanwy, pleased with her handiwork. 'Turn around – go on.'

Delighted, the child obeyed then ran to her mother, snuggling into the slippery starched apron.

Bethan didn't care for chapel, because all the grown-ups looked so stern. Sunday school was much better, because you could talk, sing and ask questions. Once in chapel Minister Jenkins stared at them very hard and asked who would join him to fight the Devil. Immediately she had put up her hand because she knew the Devil would look just like her teacher, and she was ready to fight him any time. But Lisa tugged at her sleeve and started to laugh. Tomos coughed, Mam went red, and Dadda looked at her and winked. She had to stare at her fingers for the rest of the service and wondered what she had done wrong. Chapel was never the same after that, but today the new smock would make up for sitting still as a stone.

The Rhys and Morgan families met up as usual at the junction of two narrow lanes that led to the chapel hidden in a copse. The two little ones pirouetted around their fathers immersed in earnest conversation while Myfanwy and Rhiannon, Glyn's wife, chatted domestic practicalities, neither daring to raise the subject of Patagonia.

Chapel was unusually full. Families squeezed into pews already overflowing. At one end of this simple whitewashed building, was a rostrum on which stood a table and two impressive chairs. The Reverend Jenkins sat in one, giving a brief smile and a nod to his flock as they took their places. Sitting beside him was a bespectacled grey-haired man, well dressed, clutching a folio of documents.

After they had sung 'Aberystwyth', a new hymn with plenty of harmony – 'to clear troubled minds', the choirmaster always maintained – the Reverend Jenkins addressed his eager congregation, in his practised stentorian eloquence.

'Dear brothers and sisters, we live in a confused age. Everything we hold precious is being taken from us. We are standing upon a fragile edifice that is being battered and eroded by the winds and storms of political change. Soon our proud land and its people will be a memory, a mere passage in history books. Is this what we want?' he declaimed, scanning the pews.

'Would we reject the possibility of a new Wales, in a new country, where our heritage would be preserved? Would we reject the possibility of earning an honest living from the land? Would we reject the possibility of living each day without the fear of death from iron a nd coal?' With voice ever rising he asked, 'Would we reject the possibility of never – *never* – more hearing that awesome blast from the pit summoning mothers and wives to collect their dead?' He paused again. 'Would we?' he thundered.

The congregation sat mesmerized as he dabbed the perspiration on his forehead and upper lip. No one moved. Not a throat was cleared.

His eyes sought out the children.

'And our children, my friends, our precious investment. Do we not owe them a better life, a safer life, where we no more will see them walk into the fiery furnaces of industry or be struck down by disease?'

He stopped, bowing his head for a brief moment of personal recollection. Only last year his five-year-old, a winsome little girl, died of typhus, contracted from him, so they said, after he had been visiting the sick in Cyfarthfa.

The Reverend Jenkins next turned to the grey-haired man at his side, a Mr Lewis, the representative of the Welsh Emigration Society and the expert on Patagonia.

Within half an hour Mr Lewis had painted a very attractive picture of the country – uninhabited, an ideal location, and, furthermore the Argentinian government had agreed that Patagonia should eventually be self-governing. The climate was perfect, as was the crop potential.

That a government was prepared to treat them like human beings was no less than stunning, unbelievable. A hundred acres per family it would be, with corn, wheat, timber, horses, cattle and sheep.

A euphoric congregation filed out that evening. This was too good to be true; too good an opportunity to miss.

No one had thought of asking Mr Lewis whether he had personally visited this earthly paradise.

Both families agreed to wait for three weeks before making a decision, but, even so, the very fact that Patagonia existed as an escape route had an immediate effect, particularly on Dafydd. Those chains of impotence, which for so long had nourished his festering anger, were slowly loosening. Patagonia was restoring his dignity.

Sitting round the supper table a few days before the arranged decision meeting, Bethan piped, 'Is it true you can speak Welsh all the time in Patagonia, even in school?'

Tomos grinned. 'No schools, Bethan.'

The child squealed with delight, though not quite sure whether to believe him. She turned to her father. 'Dadda, what'll we do with the chickens?'

'Leave them with me, *cariad*. I'll look after them,' replied her grandfather.

There was a moment of cold shock. All eyes turned to the old man. He was part of the family.

Bethan tugged at his hand. 'If Dadcu's not going, I'm not going, even if there is no school, so there!'

Myfanwy looked at her father, stupefied. Leaving him behind had never been part of the family agenda. 'But, Dad,' she said anxiously.

'Dad, surely that's not true, is it? You are joking, aren't you? I mean, we're a family. You're part of it – and you'll come with us if we go?'

Stroking his little granddaughter's hair, the old man said, 'Listen now, all of you. I'm seventy-five next birthday, so what do I want with a long old voyage? Don't like boats anyway. Patagonia may be fertile, but it's overgrown, isn't it? Able-bodied men and women you want there, not old one-eyed Dadcus. No! Patagonia is for you, not for me.'

Bethan snuggled her blonde head into her grandfather's grey whiskers.

'I'll look after you, Dadcu.'

'No, Bethan, you look after your mam for me, is it?'

Many sacrifices would have to be made for this Utopia, and while Myfanwy was distraught at the very idea of leaving her father, let alone her country, it made no sense forfeiting young lives for old. She had to close the door on her own feelings, say nothing and pray she would be able to give Dafydd the strength and support he would expect from her.

Sitting with her mother the following evening repairing shirts, Lisa asked, 'Why don't you want to go to Patagonia, Mam?'

'Who said I didn't?' Myfanwy replied sharply.

'Obvious, isn't it? You've never got anything to say when we all talk about it.'

'What d'you want me to say, girl?'

Lisa shrugged her shoulders. She knew from her mother's tone she should not press the point.

'Look, Lisa, we only know what they tell us. We've asked a hundred questions, but how do we know it won't be a hell on earth? D'you think I want to leave my dadda – for ever? Might as well bury him. You, all of you, your father, too, hear only the golden promises of these strangers. They, those Argentines, are not men of God – they are politicians out for themselves!'

'And what about our politicians, Mam? Who are they out for? Will they care if we are dispossessed when they find coal under our kitchen? Will they care when one of us gets killed down the iron or coal? What compensation will you get for us?' She watched her mother, head bent over a shirt repair. 'At least the Argentinian government will give us land, not take it away.'

Myfanwy said nothing, but Lisa hadn't finished. 'Look, I don't want to leave Dadcu, Mam, but he's got his own butties after all, and he'll have the house to himself, won't he?'

A smile flickered about Myfanwy's mouth. She had to admire her daughter's efforts.

'And anyway, Mam – you'll have us.' She paused. 'You won't ever have to worry that Tomos and me aren't ever going to come home, or come home with no eyes or no legs like Eira Pugh and Owen Williams. Or that Bethan will have to go down the iron or pit. Fields and farms in Patagonia.' She touched her mother's arm. 'There's lovely it'll be, Mam.'

Myfanwy sat very still clutching the shirt on her lap. Their eyes met. Nothing was said. Then she gently drew her daughter to her and, stroking Lisa's hair, said, 'My girl, my precious girl.'

Myfanwy decided to make a start on the weekly baking, knowing it would take her mind off tomorrow when the four adults would be meeting to make a decision. Though, it seemed to Myfanwy, Dafydd's mind was already made up.

The fire was hot, so she opened the kitchen door for some fresh air. The wind was coming from the east, blowing autumn through the valley. She fancied she heard a pit siren, but sound never carried accurately up the mountain, especially when the wind blew.

Minutes later clogs clattered into the yard, a perfunctory thump on the kitchen door, and two farm neighbours, women from further down the valley, stood in the doorway.

There was no need for words. Myfanwy's throat tightened as she recalled the sickening sound she had heard.

'Accident! Down the Llysfawr.' The fearful words, breathless, half sobbed, pierced Myfanwy's stomach like a knife.

The second woman, a softly spoken widow, a look of terror on her face, said, 'My Bryn – he's with your Tomos and Rhiannon's boy, somebody's gone to fetch her. On the lower level the boys are.'

A grim silent crowd had already gathered at the pithead. Whispered rumours about the size of the explosion, and where it had taken place, were already flying.

Gas, at pit bottom, one of the managers said. Rescue teams had been sent down, but so far no one had surfaced. The crowd grew as news spread through the town. Fear, like a freezing band, clutched the heart and curdled the stomach. Older women, pregnant women, women with dishcloths still in their hands and old men who remembered huddled together.

Some muttered prayers, but nowhere was a voice more than a whisper, lest the slightest vibration of sound or movement should disturb the already shattered honeycombs of underground galleries. Myfanwy and Rhiannon stood together, shawls pulled tightly around shoulders.

It was colder now and beginning to rain. The wind soughing through the trees swirled clusters of dead leaves about the feet of families in torment, waiting, staring unblinking at the motionless wheel, preparing themselves for the ghastly hauls that they knew would be discharged before their eyes.

Dafydd arrived with Glyn. They all embraced silently and stood, hand gripping hand. There was nothing to say. There were no words of comfort that could calm the agony of watching and waiting for the slightest shudder of that wheel. This was the new way of living and dying in a once pastoral landscape, and there was no turning back.

Suddenly the wheel jolted into life. The cage rose from the scorched underworld and shivered to a standstill. There was a moment of utter silence; even the breeze held its breath. Slowly rescue workers carried out the recognizable dead on stretchers and placed them side by side. Some were limbless and horribly gashed. All were drenched in the colour of the earth's black bowels. One by one the corpses were claimed. A young pregnant woman fainted, another, sobbing, cradled her beloved in her arms. An old man stood helpless by the body of his son.

'My boy, my boy,' he repeated as tears filled the runnels of his wrinkled cheeks.

Forty bodies lay waiting to be taken off to the makeshift mortuary.

Forty homes had been destroyed, and love lay in pieces.

Two long hours passed, wind and rain biting into the numbed living, waiting, still as stone, willing the motionless wheel to spring into life. The injured had been taken to the local hospital. Tomos and Huw were not among them. Myfanwy was preparing herself to accept the certainty that Tomos was dead.

A manager, with red eyes, black with grime, stood on a raised mound of slag facing the families. In his hand he held a piece of paper.

'The list, by here, of those still down.'

His voice was barely audible. 'No chance – they had no chance at all.'

He drew a black hand across his cheek and read out names. His own son was one of them. Tomos, Huw and several other youngsters were not. Frantic parents exchanged glances, and as he returned to the hut Dafydd and Glyn caught the manager.

'Our boys,' Dafydd demanded, 'in God's name, where are our boys?'

'All accounted for now. Sorry, sorry.'

Glyn flared. 'They've got to be in there somewhere!'

The manager shook his head. 'They weren't on pit bottom – for sure. New north seam, level two started today. I think some of the children were drafted down there.'

'So where are they then?' Dafydd asked.

'Haven't been brought up – still searching they are. Been a bit of a fall there, too, but no casualties.'

'Gas! What about gas?' Glyn asked the question, dreading the answer.

The manager threw up his hands in despair 'I don't know . . . I don't know.' He was on the point of tears.

'Then get us a list, will you. Please.' Dafydd could see the enormous strain the man was under.

'Impossible. Sion Lewis, only one in charge of level two, and he went down to pit bottom halfway through the shift. Took my boy with him.'

Tears streaked down the blackened cheeks. Dafydd put his arm around the distraught manager's shoulder in a silent human gesture of understanding.

He turned away from them and stumbled back into the hut, weeping as he went.

Everyone waiting at the pithead knew that after so many hours of incarceration the smallest gas leak could have disastrous consequences.

Another hour passed, then slowly the wheel trembled. An audible gasp could be heard as tension among the waiting families reached breaking point. The cage, like a lumbering beast rose to the surface and stopped with a judder. There was no sound from anyone. With each silent second, desperate parents prepared themselves to claim a small, blackened corpse.

The cage door groaned open, and children, huddled together, stood blinking in the dusky light, half afraid to step into the world they had left hours before. Glyn shouted, 'Huw!' More names followed, and out they tumbled, little girls and boys, stunned, some crying, all in shock, as they were swept into the arms of weeping parents who rushed to envelop this most precious delivery. Tomos and Huw staggered from the lift supporting each other. It was nothing less than a resurrection. Myfanwy gathered her lost boy to her body, his black face wet with tears.

The two families walked away from the horror, exhausted and silent; Dafydd's hand like a protecting claw gripping Tomos's shoulder.

The light from the oil lamp shone in the cottage window. Dadcu opened the door, and Tomos threw himself into his grandfather's arms, burying his head in the comforting familiarity of the tobacco-stained waistcoat.

Bethan touched Tomos's arm to make sure he was alive. 'Tomos was nearly dead, wasn't he, Dadda?'

'Nearly – but God gave him back to us.'

'So where did God take him then?'

'He didn't take him anywhere, *cariad*.'

'Then how could he give him back?'

'Later. Questions later.'

Bethan had the ability to make her father laugh – and never more than at this moment. He picked her up and hugged his little blonde daughter in gratitude.

Huw and Tomos walked trembling into the kitchen where their older sisters Bron and Lisa were waiting for them, faces tear-stained and blotchy. Lisa glanced at her mother, wondering whether she would now still be unwilling to commit herself to Patagonia.

The two families shared supper, and afterwards the men went outside to talk, the older man to puff on his pipe. It was a chilly evening but dry, as they leant on the five-bar gate. The sounds of their children laughing filtered from the cottage.

'Makes you realize how quickly life can be – snuffed out – as delicate as a candle flame,' Dafydd said quietly.

Like a punctuation Dadcu aimed spittle into a far corner of the hedge.

'And that's why you'll go, isn't it? To make sure they won't be – snuffed out.' The old man turned to Glyn. 'How does Rhiannon feel about it?'

Glyn smiled. 'Can't wait to get out of this hell hole.'

The old man nodded. 'So it's only Myfanwy then. Only my daughter is the problem?'

The men said nothing.

'She doesn't want to go because of me.'

'Come with us then, Dadcu,' said Glyn.

'Glyn boy, you'll not be wanting an old man who can't plough a furrow, can't dig a trench. Now listen, both of you. Leave my daughter to me. Good God, it makes no sense to stay here – not after this.'

Dafydd stared silently into the chill dusk and hoped that if there were to be a change in his wife's heart it would come in time.

Myfanwy was putting away the last pots in the kitchen. The children were asleep; Tomos in Dadcu's bed and Bethan with Lisa just for tonight. Dafydd had already gone upstairs.

Her father called her from outside. She slipped on a shawl and went to him. 'What is it, Dadda?'

'Come here,' he said, stretching out his hand. 'Think I don't know why you don't want to go? Why you won't give that man of yours a straight answer?'

She avoided his eyes. 'What on earth are you talking about?'

'Patagonia!' he snapped. 'Now listen to me. I don't want any more of your nonsense. You must go – all of you – for your children. You owe it to them. I shall stay by here, and that's final!'

She knew how stubborn he could be. There was nothing she could say.

'If you don't go because of me, do you realize you'll be putting responsibility on to my shoulders. Good God, girl – how d'you think I'd be feeling every time they went on a shift? I couldn't live with that. Who could? And I won't! It's not fair.' The old man spat loudly. 'If you want to finish me off before my time – stay! If you want me to die a happy old man in my native land – go! I can hear your mother. Saying the same thing she is.'

He tapped out his pipe and said quietly, 'Go you now, *cariad*. Listen to your old dadda – and no more doubts, is it?'

Myfanwy's eyes filled. She put her arms about him and kissed his gnarled old cheeks. 'Thank you, Dadda. Thank you,' she whispered.

Upstairs Myfanwy crept between the crisp white sheets. Dafydd was already in bed. He kissed her forehead. 'Thank God today is over.'

She turned to face him. 'Dav, I've been so – so selfish – about Patagonia. I've been unfair to everybody, the children, Dadda – most of all you. I'm sorry.'

He stroked her cheek.

'And I love you, Dafydd Rhys. No more doubts, I promise. Patagonia it shall be.'

Dafydd took her in his arms. 'Myfanwy, *cariad*, the only wife for me you are – in Wales, Patagonia – the world! You know that.'

His hand slipped down to caress her breasts and thighs. Her cheeks burned, as they always did, like that first time on the mountain. Now, lying beside him, she only wanted to make him happy. She was never as excited as he seemed to be, especially when his seed came, burning hot. She often wondered about that feeling – what it must be like. After all she was only a woman, and a woman was quiet and modest in the marriage bed. If God had meant them to feel a man's passion he would have made men and women the same. A few women she had heard of in Merthyr, went wild, but they were loose and immoral, with not a shred of decency. She was happy with the way things were. Dafydd only had to touch her and the pit of her stomach took leaps; sometimes gentle, sometimes so strong she wanted to cry out. Maybe that was the same thing.

She loved feeling him inside her, immodest though it probably was, and best of all when he spilled his seed inside her. But on those three occasions, she had fallen pregnant. Some women said you could never fall right after the monthly flow, but Dafydd did not believe that any more, not after Bethan was conceived, so he had taught her how to bring it forth on her stomach. She liked this, for she wanted to touch him and to share that final moment when he seemed to lose the world and be with her alone.

His hand stroked between her thighs. Her sighs and moans told him this gave her pleasure, and he found the place that made her cry out.

Myfanwy thanked God for this husband of hers, for she had heard of the way some men, even good men, treated their wives in bed.

Their need for each other tonight was never so great. They sought comfort and love in each other's arms. The tensions of this terrible day had wound nerve ends into tight coils that had to be unravelled. Now inside her his pace increased, her cheeks were hot and damp. Suddenly, instead of withdrawing he went on, stronger, faster, until finally the floodgates were released in an explosive fusion of passion and tension. They clung to each other and sobbed.

'I want to be with you for ever and ever,' she whispered.

'Unless you are, my darling wife – I won't live – won't want to.'

He wiped away her tears with his hand.

Today had been a catharsis. It had seen a resurrection, a realization and now a resolution. Tonight they were stronger than they had ever been. Tonight a new life began in Myfanwy's womb. They were not to know how important it would be.

3

It was a cold December, with the first fall of snow settled comfortably on the higher slopes above Merthyr and the surrounding valley. By now each family had been given a list by the emigration society of farming implements and tools deemed necessary for their new life.

There was little point in any winter farming – not now. The land around the cottage was cold and hard, furrows like corrugated tin. However desolate the landscape appeared, Dafydd's heart was not. The latest emigration circular had promised tall strong forests along the riverside surrounded by luscious pastures, where herds of their very own animals could feed. Temperatures, it assured, were mild and perfect, a promised land indeed.

Two weeks before Christmas there was a heavy snowfall. Myfanwy looked out of the window. She felt quite giddy watching large flakes tumbling like feathers. Myfanwy liked snow, not for itself but because it could disguise. Even ugly industry in Merthyr took on a sort of enchantment, shrouded in white and tipped now in glancing moonlight. Snow turned back the clock, with landscape rural and beautiful as it used to be, as it never would be again.

'What'll he do with the fields, Dav – Lord Gwilym?'

'Coal. See the soil over there?' He pointed through the window,

'All round that gorse hedge – black it is, black as jet. Aye, there are outcrops all right and not far below the plough either. I know, I've turned some up.'

'It will all go, won't it? And no one will remember, only us. And we'll be in Patagonia. They'll never know what it was like – before. Makes me sad.'

'Come on. It'll all be here in a hundred years.' He smiled. 'But we won't! Cup of tea will cheer you up.' He was clearly not prepared for another Patagonian session with his wife.

She sat down remaining silent while he poured out two cups from the teapot on the hob.

'Dav,' she said quietly, 'I – I haven't seen for over a month. Next one is due now really – but no sign.'

'Are you sure?' He thought for a moment. 'P'raps it's all this upheaval.'

She took the cup and looked at him with mild irritation. 'No. And I am sure. I've been feeling a bit sick as well – same as the others.'

He looked out of the window. 'Must have been – the night.'

'I know when it was,' she said quickly.

Dafydd could see she was on the verge of tears again. He put his arms round her. 'Be happy, *cariad*. I am! This one will be born in Patagonia. Maybe the first Patagonian Welshman!'

'Or woman,' she corrected.

He laughed. 'Another woman? God help me! I've got three of you as it is. And if she'll be anything like our Bethan I'm done for.'

No secret how he idolized his youngest.

'When?'

'August. Second or third week. Couldn't be a worse time could it? Winter.'

'Nonsense! A perfect time! Look, we're sailing beginning of May – take us four weeks. That's the beginning of June. Two full months to get our home together and fields ploughed before our little Patagonian arrives.'

'But how much help will I be giving you? None at all.'

'Don't you worry about that, my lovely. We've got two able-bodied children.' He pecked her cheek. 'And their father!'

On Christmas day Myfanwy told the children, 'You are going to have a new brother or sister.'

Dadcu chuckled. He already knew. Tomos went bright red and shifted uncomfortably, looking directly at his mother's stomach, puzzling how it could be the same girth as yesterday. Lisa smiled and looked slyly at her father. Bethan, meanwhile, shrieked with delight.

Later that evening the two teenagers, Lisa and her friend Bron, stole into a corner of the yard, where under cover of their heavy woollen shawls they whispered adolescent secrets.

'So – so it's true – your mam and dad are still . . . doing it then.'
Bron's round face glowed in the semi-darkness.

''Course they are. Told you, didn't I?' retorted Lisa sharply.

She was angry with her parents. It would be embarrassing walking
out with a mother the size of a house. Far better the other way –
with herself pregnant. Pregnant? The very notion caused a delicious
contraction somewhere in the pit of her stomach and a sharp intake
of breath, as her imagination raced wantonly over that much-talked-
about sequence of preceding events.

'But you said you don't have to have a baby,' Bron insisted.

'Not if you don't want one, but they must have wanted one – so
there.'

Lisa was impatient with her friend. She was such a child at times.

The younger girl fell silent for a moment. 'Did you – did you
really – *hear* – them?' she whispered.

''Course I did – the night Tomos and Huw came out of the pit.
They were all over each other, remember? Well, Mam cried. I could
hear her. Then I heard Dadda say something.'

'What?'

'Couldn't hear through the wall, could I, daft! But then . . .'

'Then, what? Hurry up!' Bron's voice was hoarse with
anticipation.

'Then a lot of breathing – noisy like.'

'Never!' Bron, eyes large as saucers, was not giving up yet. 'Well,
go on.'

Lisa tucked her blouse deeper into her woollen skirt, showing off
her round breasts and small waist. Her hair was piled in curls on top
of her head, the way rich ladies wore their hair. She laughed.

'God, you're terrible, Bron Morgan! That's all! No more.'

Bron was clearly disappointed. 'So you can't tell for sure then,
can you?'

Lisa giggled. 'Oh yes I can', and she inched her head nearer her
friend.

'It's the bed; it creaks – bounces up and down, see!'

At last a truth had been revealed, and Bron smiled conspiratorially.

'So that's what's going on then, is it? I'm always hearing that up
in our house.'

'There we are then. I told you, didn't I? Your mam and dad are doing it as well – no different.'

'There's awful,' replied the younger girl, trying to come to terms with the incomprehensible.

''Course it's not, silly. It's natural.'

'Maybe for some – but not for my mam and dad!' she added vehemently.

Lisa put her arm round her friend's shoulder. 'It's natural for all of us, Bron – honest. Look at me, I'm sixteen nearly. Half the girls in Merthyr are married by sixteen.'

Bron smiling sheepishly, whispered, 'Do you want to – do it?'

'Yes,' Lisa whispered back. 'Can't wait really.'

'But you have to be married, don't you?'

'So the chapel says. But I'll tell you something – I'm not going to wait. Just till Patagonia, that's all!'

They collapsed into pubescent mirth and went to bed dreaming of a night when they would be clasped in the arms of some handsome lad who would cover their trembling eager bodies with kisses, passion and love.

It was up to Patagonia now.

The sailing date was fixed – 3 May. Emigrants were to convene first in Bala. The next day they would take the new train to Liverpool. Thereafter it would be one night on board the *Halton Castle* in Liverpool docks ready for sailing on the early morning tide.

On the eve of their departure Myfanwy slipped quietly out of the back yard and on to the mountain. The moon shone brilliantly; the short grass cool to her feet. She walked barefoot up to the familiar piece of rock that seemed to have burst through the mountainside like a chair and sat.

Below, the sights and sounds of industry; in the distance, lights from scattered farms; around her, peace, calm and silence. There was a slight breeze blowing from the summit, fresh and fragrant. Still dusk, she could see the clumps of foxgloves, gorse and ferns, totems of her childhood and of her children's; too late to turn back now.

She looked up at the sky and whispered, 'Dear God, why does

it have to be like this? Why can we not live in peace, here – in Wales?'

By six o'clock next morning the carts were piled high with pieces of furniture, farm implements, tools and luggage. The horses were harnessed, and wheels rumbled into action. Carts, with Glyn and Dafydd at the helm, led the way, followed by Dadcu and the family wagon.

Dawn had broken, and the sky, clear and blue, promised a fine day. Never had the mountains and valley looked so beautiful. No one spoke, save the youngest, who chattered and giggled, oblivious to any sense of occasion.

'Goodbye, door!'

'Goodbye, windows!'

'Goodbye, saucepan!'

'Goodbye, kettle, goodbye – *slugs*!' shouted Elin.

And they shrieked loudly, their mothers too wrapped in their own thoughts to control them. Tomos, red-eyed and miserable, sat with his arms about Gors, who licked him affectionately. Lisa and Bron sat together and gazed into a hazy future. Myfanwy, hands in lap, felt the stirrings of the child within her. From time to time she shut her eyes committing vistas to memory, to recall for the unborn child who would never know the motherland.

By the time they reached Machynlleth the horses were exhausted. They found a coaching inn, with a couple of rooms for the women.

Myfanwy was never so thankful for the comfort of a bed and hot water to wash, for herself and the girls.

Dafydd and Glyn, finishing off quarts of ale in the tavern's large kitchen, noticed a thin young man of about thirty carrying a fiddle in a satchel. He was obviously hungry, for he set about the plate of bread and cheese laid before him with vigour. Dafydd watched as he picked off every loitering breadcrumb left on his plate. 'Hungry were you, boy?'

The thin young man laughed. 'Aye, that I was.'

Looking at him carefully, it was obvious he was wearing his Sunday best.

'Going far?' Glyn asked.

'Bala,' he said and wiped his upper lip with a large white handkerchief.

'Cost plenty to take a coach – all I could spare, like. I'll have to spend the night by here, on this bench.'

'What's your trade?' Dafydd asked.

'Bit of farming.' He smiled and patted his fiddle, 'and this. Will Jones, fiddler, at your service, sirs! Fairs, weddings, funerals and merrymakings, whatever – no odds.'

'Going to fiddle in Bala, are you?'

'Oh no, sir – a steam locomotive – to –'

Glyn interrupted. 'Not Liverpool?'

The young man raised his eyebrows.

'That's where we're going,' Dafydd added.

'Well, well.' The young man smiled. 'But after Liverpool, sirs, I am going where few men have ever been – raw but beautiful. Where there is equality and freedom enough for a solitary voice, even mine, to be heard. Patagonia it is called, sirs. A land of milk and honey.'

Dafydd held out his hand to the young fiddler. 'Welcome to the new Welsh brotherhood, Will Jones.'

That night Will Jones shared the wagon with the boys, their fathers and Dadcu. He was a skilled musician, playing songs, merry and soulful, until eyelids closed. Dafydd thought how fortunate they were in counting Will Jones the fiddler in their number. With him the melodies of Wales would be kept alive in their unknown patria.

In Bala, emigrants convened at the chapel. Dozens had already gathered outside the chapel hall. Tethered horses and carts, piled high with belongings, filled the small square. They were a motley collection of people of all ages. Women and children were to be taken into local homes, and paillasses were already positioned on the chapel-hall floor for the men.

Lisa and Bron surveyed the boys and young men.

'Not much here,' Lisa mumbled.

'What'll we do then? Nobody else in Patagonia, only us! God, Lisa – we're stuck!'

Lisa grinned. 'You'll have to marry our Tomos!'

Bron grimaced. '*Ych!* There's a terrible thing to say, Lisa Rhys!'

The very thought sent them into paroxysms of giggles.

An important-looking and very well-dressed man stood on the chapel steps holding a handwritten list of names. This was Goronwy Pugh, a deacon, his hands as white and delicate as a lady's.

'How many are we, Mr Pugh – all told?' asked Glyn.

'One hundred and fifty-three, sir.'

Myfanwy raised her eyebrows. 'It will be a big ship then, won't it?'

'Indeed, ma'am – a very large vessel it is, and plenty of room for everyone to live in comfort and space.'

'Is the Reverend Michael Jones coming with us to Patagonia?'

'Er – no, sir, but his son will be,' the deacon replied.

With women and children taken off to comfortable beds, the men began to talk and exchange information. They were, for the most part, miners, Dafydd being one of the few farmers. Medicine was represented by Dr John Williams, a single man in his thirties, and God by Evan Jenkins, the minister, who with his wife had decided to join the emigrants. Will Jones represented music, though many of them had fine voices, and with the addition of a harp and a harmonium the Reverend Mr Jenkins was truly thankful.

The next morning, very early, Dafydd, Glyn and Dadcu took the carts and wagon to the new railway station. The slatted wooden seats of closed compartments offered little comfort, but the sheer excitement at the speed with which cottages, farms and villages disappeared out of sight was breathtaking and an experience of such wizardry that the notion of comfort was forgotten.

At the end of the day, they arrived at Liverpool Lime Street Station trembling with nerves and vibrating bodies. They took directions for the trek across the bewildering, alien city to the Welsh chapel in Prince's Street, where they were given food cooked by the chapel women. Later, all women and children were billeted in chapel-goers' homes. The men remained in the hall and slept on mattresses. The next day the great man, the Reverend Michael Jones, was to address them.

No one moved in the crowded hall as the Reverend Jones climbed up to the small podium. At last, here was the thinker, the designer behind this grand plan. He walked to centre stage, an impressive commanding figure, the fronds of his long beard sweeping across the lectern as he surveyed his congregation. His voice was strong and clear as he bade them first stand to join him in prayer, hymn and psalm. The congregation seated, he addressed them.

'Dear friends, you are all, I know, anxious to start your journey – your voyage of a lifetime. How proud we are of you – brave, courageous men and women who love their God, their culture, their language, their country; who are prepared to start again in a foreign land for the sake of preserving that which they hold dear. Wales will never forget you! History will never forget you, for you are the makers of history!' Punching the air, with passion he declaimed, 'You, are the makers of our new Wales! But I fear you will have to be patient. Our ship, the *Halton Castle*, is not quite ready. I am truly sorry about this,' he continued; 'we are in the hands of the shipping line. Meanwhile, you will all be looked after by members of the chapel. You will not go hungry.'

There was no sound, not even a ripple of movement from the assembly. Dafydd glanced first at Glyn. Sitting near the front, he caught the minister's eye and rose to his feet.

'Where exactly is our ship? Where is the *Halton Castle*, minister?' he enquired.

The Reverend Jones looked ill at ease, uncomfortable. 'I am not – not – absolutely sure. Not sure at all.'

There was a stunned silence.

'Should not you of all people know, be absolutely sure, minister?'

The assembly came to life, stirred by Dafydd's directness. Whispers became mutters of concern.

'We have,' the man of God intoned loudly, 'we have arranged to take you to Patagonia, and take you we will. Another ship is being looked at for this purpose. A matter of days – I do assure you, my friends. Remember this is God's will. Have faith. Have no worries!'

Still on his feet Dafydd continued, his voice as clear and commanding as the Reverend's, 'Despite our faith, we are worried, minister, for our women and children and our limited financial resources.'

There was rumble of assent from the assembly.

'Yes well, Mr – Mr . . .?'

'Dafydd Rhys, sir.'

'Er, yes, Mr Dafydd Rhys, from . . .?'

'Merthyr, sir.'

'Merthyr – I see. Well, we shall keep you informed each day and every day, and I can assure you no one will suffer unnecessarily. I now call upon Almighty God.'

Dafydd remained on his feet. 'Excuse me, minister, there is something else.'

The Reverend huffed, clearly put out at yet another interruption. 'And what is that, Mr Rhys?'

'Minister, we have all of us here made sacrifices in the last year and, because of our limited means, planned very carefully, day by day. You will appreciate that most of us have nothing left. We are dependent upon the Emigration Society. And what happens to us when our personal resources have run dry while we wait for a ship?'

Once more a louder ripple of support for Dafydd's words rose from the congregation.

'I have told you, Mr Rhys, no one will suffer unnecessarily.' With speed to forestall yet another embarrassing question, he intoned loudly, 'Now let us ask Almighty God for his blessings and to hear our prayers, after which we shall sing hymn number twenty-five.'

Dafydd sat down. Any continuing discontent would now be conveniently silenced in prayers and hymns, after which God's man made a propitious exit to his waiting coach.

After his commendable performance on the emigrants' behalf, it was clear that Dafydd Rhys of Merthyr not only had their welfare at heart but could express himself with thought and intelligence. Therefore it was no surprise that a small crowd of anxious men gravitated towards him the moment the Reverend Jones had left.

'What in God's name can we do?' was the question on everyone's lips.

'Well,' Dafydd began, 'we'll have to call at the shipping office without fail, morning, noon and night.'

'I'll have to find work. Spent out we are,' a man shouted.

'Try the docks – bit of labouring,' opined Trevor Trehearne from Swansea.

Glyn volunteered to collect the lists of casual navvying jobs that the shipping companies distributed daily. At least it would be some–thing.

From now until they sailed, families would meet only at mealtimes in the chapel hall, so Dafydd suggested a pooling of information every night after supper.

The city and its lifestyle were completely unknown to the Welsh. They had been exposed only to the elemental experiences of birth, work, industry, death and God. Real corruption had been perceived usually in political terms. But here in the city for the first time they were rubbing shoulders with evil. Troublemakers roamed too freely in these airless streets, and with so much time on their hands the older girls from the emigrant group could barely avoid contact with undesirable influences.

'Make sure Lisa has enough pennies in her pocket,' Dafydd urged his wife. 'I have seen and learnt too much. This city is Sodom and Gomorrah, I swear it, Myfanwy – full of dishonourable men that would take advantage of a young Welsh girl with no pennies in her pocket. So you make sure she has. Remember now!'

It was inevitable that there would be a victim.

But it was not a girl.

Defenceless Will Fiddler, playing his violin at a busy street corner, upturned cap on the ground with just a few coins to show for the day, was set upon by thugs. They pinned him against a wall, emptied his cap and, despite the frightened half-hearted entreaties of the crowd, was kicked and punched until he groaned in pain, his body hunched, his head gashed. He was left a bloody heap on the pavement. When he was brought back to Myfanwy's lodgings by passing emigrants Dr Williams bound his broken ribs, dressed his wounds and gave him a few drops of laudanum to kill the pain. This incident was frightening, and impatience with the false promises of the Welsh Emigration Society was turning to anger. The emigrants were helpless, and they knew it. They had paid up months ago for their passages. How could they return with nothing, to nothing?

Dafydd attempted to meet the Reverend Mr Jones and was told by a deacon that their leader sent best wishes but was too busy at present to see him. Rumours were flying now. Too busy, was he? Why? Perhaps there was no ship – never would be.

Surely the man of God, in whom they had placed such awesome trust, would never let them down? Or would he? Each day the Black Mast shipping office had the same reply: 'No emigration ship.'

Early on the morning of 25 May, as Dafydd and Glyn turned into Chapel Square, they heard the strident raucous voice of Emmanuel Price, a loud-mouthed redhead from North Wales who had an evil temper, it was said. Standing on the chapel steps, he was plainly inciting the men to take over one of the empty ships in the dock.

'Is there not one that resembles in shape and size our emigration ship, that phantom of the high seas, the *Halton Castle*?' Emmanuel Price was a skilled orator. 'I'll tell you, my friends – I'll tell you what we do. Have we not paid for an emigration ship? Are we animals to be pushed around – herded in pens?'

The men were tense, excited now, anticipating the command for action.

Price continued. 'We have a right to take what is ours, have we not? Patagonia is ours – we have been given it! A ship is ours – we have paid for it! Patagonia awaits us – the ship we have paid for does not. So I ask you, one and all, let us march now – to the docks – and *take* what is ours by right! By tonight we could be sailing on the tide!'

The crowd was agog. Voices exploded in a clamour of support.

But the proposals on offer had to be stopped. Quickly Dafydd placed himself alongside Emmanuel Price. 'Listen, all of you,' he shouted. 'Before you do anything – and no one has got more reason to get out of this place than I have – please listen! We all feel the same frustration, but Emmanuel Price here is asking you to commit a crime; to steal a ship – for which we will all be punished. All of us! Then nobody will be going to Patagonia. It'll be prison or the noose!'

No one knew precisely how it started, but a fair sprinkling of moderates who listened to Dafydd's restraining words tried to stop the warmer bloods from following Price, who was already out of the square and bound for the docks and a frigate. It was only the arrival of wives and children at the chapel that halted the punch-happy combatants, forcing them into a hesitant truce.

An hour later Emmanuel Price and two or three followers were escorted back to the chapel by special constables. They were charged with breaking and entering a ship in dock and for trespassing on another's property. Through the influence of one of the deacons, charges were dropped.

Price had been humiliated. Had they all marched with him, he claimed, instead of listening to that 'holy voice of God, Dafydd Rhys', the constables would have been powerless. They could have been sailing in an hour. Damn Rhys! But vengeance was sweet, and he could wait.

Dafydd realized something had to be done and quickly. Tempers were smouldering. The *Halton Castle* was part of the Black Mast shipping line where Glyn collected daily worksheets. The boss, a Captain Vaughan, had just come back from his travels.

'He'll be in the office tomorrow so they say. Go and see him, Dav.'

'Aye, Davvy Rhys,' said Trevor Trehearne, 'Go direct, like. Ask about our bloody ship.'

Ever cautious about taking direct action, Dafydd suggested they should try yet again to seek out the Reverend Jones.

'Bugger the Reverend,' was the general retort. 'See the Captain!'

Dafydd was ushered into a back office, simply furnished with pictures of ships and a large map of the world completely covering the third wall.

On a bureau were several bottles of rum and whisky with accompanying tumblers. In front of a bow window was a carved black armchair and the biggest desk Dafydd had ever seen.

The door opened and in strode Captain Vaughan. By any standards he was a big man, but for a Welshman he was a giant. Six foot four, with a broad frame, bushy black beard and eyebrows, he looked capable of building an entire navy single-handed. Dafydd perceived a twinkling warmth beneath this intimidating exterior.

'So how may I help you?'

His voice boomed with the accents of North Wales, with which Dafydd was not too familiar.

'The *Halton Castle* – your ship, sir, is it not?'

'Correct.'

There was no time to be less than blunt. 'Then where is it, Captain Vaughan?'

The big man sat down heavily behind his desk and nodded briefly in the direction of a chair at Dafydd's side.

'Sit you down, Mr Rhys.' He took a long ruler and pointed to the map of the world.

'Somewhere in the Pacific Ocean. She's about . . . there.' The ruler came to rest just south of Ceylon.

Dafydd was too stunned to speak. The implications were shocking. They had been duped!

'But it could take weeks, sir! We have already been in Liverpool twenty-six days – summoned here in the first instance to sail aboard your ship on 3 May. We have paid up! Our life savings, sir! So – so where is that money, Captain Vaughan? Where is it?'

'Calm down, Mr Rhys,' said the big man quietly. He rose and stood at the window, his black eyes darting between Dafydd and the sea. 'Your money is safe. But it's not with me.'

Dafydd was about to question this second revelation, but Vaughan continued, 'It is with the Reverend Mr Jones.'

'But – why?'

'Because I refused to take it.'

His words came like a punch in the solar plexus. 'What?'

'Do you want the truth, sir?'

Palms sweating, throat dry, voice paralysed, Dafydd gave a perfunctory nod.

Vaughan looked at the man sitting before him. Good, strong, honest, nobody's fool. He deserved no less than the truth. 'Very well, I shall not mince my words, Mr Rhys. What I am about to say may come as a surprise.'

Dafydd sat rigid, waiting.

'I have been a sailor all my life – know the world – its rogues, its saints.' He smiled. 'I know where to find paradise on earth. Where melons are as large as pumpkins and where grapes are as round as oranges. Where olive-skinned people gather their daily sustenance with as much ease as we hold out our hands to catch a raindrop. Where young women weave garlands of bougainvillea and oleander blossoms to adorn their bodies and hair. Where the men find fish aplenty in an azure sea and lithe slender women splash in lagoons of crystal blue – breasts like ripe lemons.' Carried away by memory, his eyes embraced the sea. Jolting back to the present, he added sharply, 'But I have seen places where the Devil himself would not care to loiter.'

Dafydd could not quite comprehend the point of this peroration.

'I can understand,' Vaughan continued, 'why our working people wish to emigrate. Our far-flung empire is in need of our own countrymen to work and to govern. Each week, from this very dock, my ships carry them away in their hundreds – America, Australia, Van Diemen's Land, South Africa.'

Still utterly perplexed, Dafydd could do nothing but listen. There was more to follow, that was obvious.

The Captain leant on the desk. 'Something else you do not know.'

Dafydd felt a lump of lead settle in the pit of his stomach. His mind raced, not knowing how to react to these appalling new revelations.

'Some months ago,' Vaughan continued, 'the Reverend Mr Jones wished to charter an emigration ship for you. I agreed, until – until I was told the destination of my ship. Not America – not Australia – not South Africa but', he paused, cheeks livid with anger, 'but – Patagonia!' He spat out the word. 'And that fellow Jones knew nothing of that God-forsaken continent. I asked him to show me on paper these promises made by the Argentinian government. There is nothing written,' he shouted. 'They are mealy-mouthed promises, Mr Rhys. And their government changes its mind like a woman every few weeks.'

Dafydd's heart pounded. This could be the end for all of them. 'But, sir,' he countered, 'we were given written assurances by the Welsh Emigration Society.'

'Poppycock,' Vaughan boomed. 'Absolute poppycock!'

With trembling hand Dafydd drew out of his pocket a folded leaflet on which these promises were clearly written and handed it to the Captain.

'Lies, Mr Rhys,' Vaughan snorted. 'And I have told him so!'

'But – but men have been sent out, sir, to see the quality of the land – its climate. We have promises, sir, of autonomy from the Argentinian government.'

Vaughan could see Dafydd Rhys was a desperate man. He wished with all his heart he could put Jones before the emigrants. He would need wings and God to get out of that.

'Mr Rhys, I give your autonomy two years. Look, the Argentine government wants that wild land tamed. You are ideal fodder. They want to colonize – like Jones and his cronies. They want to protect the Argentine from any Chilean aggression – and . . .'

Dafydd rose from his chair ashen-faced and in despair. 'I'm not sure I want to hear any more, sir,' he mumbled.

For his part Vaughan was aggrieved that he should have to explain the truth to this good fellow who had put his trust in idiots. He sighed. 'So what did they tell you?'

'That the climate was extremely fine; that the soil was rich – we have all taken farm implements at their request – and each household shall be given dairy and farm animals, plus a generous acreage of land. Furthermore –'

Vaughan interrupted 'I know that coastline. A good friend was an officer on the *Beagle* with Charles Darwin – you've heard of him, I suppose?'

'Oh yes, sir. The atheist. Believes we come from apes, does he not?'

Morris snarled. 'In the case of the Welsh Emigration Society I believe that theory to be indisputable! They did not tell you of the hundreds upon hundreds of arid miles, where man and beast can disappear never to be found again? Of the lashing storms along a barren coastline?'

Dafydd stood quite still and said not a word.

'An earthly paradise they promised, eh?'

'Kind of, sir – kind of.'

The Captain sat down again.

'Well, this is one paradise to which I categorically refuse to transport my countrymen. Convicts, perhaps. My own kith and kin, never!'

'But our money, Captain Vaughan – the money we've paid up. Nothing left for most of us. Nothing!'

'At this very moment the Reverend Mister is fitting up a tea clipper, using his wife's inheritance, I believe. A good woman – not like him.' He turned to look at the sea. 'We had a very angry exchange here in this very room.'

'I take it you refused again, sir.'

'I did indeed, Mr Rhys.'

Dafydd was in a hopeless situation. He was now party to a vital disclosure, which should not have to be a confidence and yet had to be or there would be a riot.

'Do you know anything more about the new ship, Captain Vaughan? I mean – how long do you think it will take to get her fitted up?' Dafydd had to give them some positive news.

'May be ready in a few more days. He has a captain and crew – not any of mine – but they are capable enough.'

Dafydd turned to leave. 'Thank you for your time, Captain Vaughan'

'Don't thank me for shattering your dreams, but – I had to tell you.'

'Of course. But I'm very perplexed. I have a responsibility to the group. Hard to know what to say to them.'

The big man sighed. 'Tell the men if they want to know anything about Patagonia – they can ask me. I'll be here for the next couple of weeks.' Vaughan smiled wearily. 'Perhaps even Patagonia will be better than the life you have left, eh?'

Dafydd, his head lowered like a wounded animal, his face creased with worry, looked at the Captain. 'My children in coal and iron – son very nearly killed last year.'

'Then it will be better, Mr Rhys.' The Captain shook his head. 'Forgive me – I wish I could have taken you to a ready-made paradise, that's all!' His voice was gentle now.

Dafydd shrugged, exhausted and sick with worry. 'We wouldn't know what to make of an easy life, sir.'

Vaughan cupped Dafydd's hand in his. 'You are a good man – and may God bless you!'

With door ajar Dafydd asked, 'The tea clipper, Captain. Would you know her name? Be nice to give them a name. Real evidence, you know.'

'*The Mimosa,* I believe. Yes, that's it – *The Mimosa.*'

That evening the emigrants received news of their impending departure aboard *The Mimosa.* Sailing time was fixed for 7.30 Sunday morning. Tomos was grieving bitterly at having to leave Gors with Dadcu. Others were taking their dogs, but Myfanwy insisted Dadcu needed Gors for company. By six o'clock the emigrants had assembled at the embarkation point.

The Mimosa was a three-mast, square-rigged clipper, about a hundred and fifty feet long. It was a bright crisp morning, her white sails impressive against the blue sky. Seven o'clock and the quayside, though clear of last night's mountain of luggage, was crowded with emigrants and the families they would be leaving. Myfanwy stood silently with her father holding his hand.

It was a subdued gathering, everyone in a state of limbo, apart from squealing children clamouring to run up the gangway. The past weeks had taken their toll on energy and patience. It was only to Glyn that Dafydd disclosed the details of his meeting with Captain Vaughan, but for the sake of everyone they had resolved to put his pronouncements out of their minds.

The Reverend Mr Jones arrived with a bearded man in uniform, whom he introduced as Captain Willoughby.

Standing on the raised gangway, the Reverend addressed them. 'Soon you will be boarding this fine ship *The Mimosa,* but now let us sing together.'

The harmonium and voices rang with beauty, passion and emotion. The Reverend Mr Jones then invited the emigrants' own minister, the Reverend Mr Jenkins, to lead them in prayer. It was a thoughtful gesture, as this was the man who would be their link with the Almighty for the foreseeable future.

Prayers over, the Reverend Jones addressed them once more.

'The time has come for us to say goodbye. I, too, am saying goodbye – for the present – to my own son, Edward'

Edward Jones, a slim young man of about twenty, stood shyly on one side with his mother who looked as though she could not bear to part with him.

'Do not be sad,' he urged. 'Think of the new Wales you are going to build. Be happy in that thought.'

Myfanwy stood before her father.

'Well, my girl,' he said, 'you are doing the right thing. Never doubt that – not for a minute, d'you hear?'

'Yes, Dadda,' she whispered, clasping him tightly, tears flowing down her cheeks.

'Come on now. I'll come to see you next year – all right?' he smiled.

She, too, smiled but knew it would not be so. She would never see him again. She kissed him, hugged him once more, then quickly turned away and started up the gangway, unable to look back at the slight, solitary figure.

In turn the children bade their goodbyes. Lisa wept. Bethan could not see why people were crying. They could all come back again soon for a holiday, just like that girl in school who went to live in Bristol. Tomos had two goodbyes, one for his grandfather and one for Gors. It was difficult to know which of the two was more poignant. As he clasped the old man Dadcu whispered, 'I've got something for you, *bach* – here, take it.'

He put into his hand a beautifully carved wooden bone.

Tomos was surprised but said; 'Thanks, Dadcu. In case I get hungry, is it?'

'No, boy. In case Gors gets hungry – on the ship!'

Tomos opened his eyes wide. 'But, Dadcu, Gors is staying with you.'

The old man chuckled. 'No, she's not. Go on – take her!'

And he handed Tomos the plaited rope lead attached to the dog's leather collar.

Tomos's eyes filled up. 'Oh! Oh! Thanks, Dadcu – thanks.' He sniffed and wiped a wet cheek with his thumb.' But what about you?'

'I'm having a pup from Johnny Edwards in Merthyr. Go you now. Go you.'

The old man, hands in pocket, kept his eyes fixed on the ground, as the last of his family boarded the ship that would take them from him.

All goodbyes said and wept over, families stood together against the rail. As the gangplank was raised, the Reverend Michael Jones on land, and the harmonium on deck, led them in an emotional rendition of the Welsh National Anthem. On the penultimate line *The Mimosa* pulled away from the dockside.

Handkerchiefs fluttered until they faded from sight. This was the moment they had been waiting for. The long journey into the unknown was about to begin.

Dafydd had lost his faith in man.

Would his faith in God be strong enough? A nightmare of uncertainty descended upon him and gnawed in the pit of his stomach like an incubus, as he replayed in his head the words of Captain Vaughan: 'I have seen places where the Devil himself would not care to loiter.'

It was now up to the Almighty. He only hoped the Almighty would be up to it.

4

Captain Willoughby was a squat little man sporting a neatly clipped beard around a weatherbeaten chin. Everything about him was neat; stiff starched collar, shining buttons, a knife crease in his trousers and not a speck to blemish his uniform. His eyes, blackcurrants squeezed into small sockets, bored coldly into the assembly gathered between decks while he waited for absolute silence, from passengers and animals alike. A glance from the eagle-eyed Willoughby ensured rapt attention despite a capricious sea.

'Welcome aboard,' he boomed. 'We shall have a pleasant voyage to Patagonia, I am sure, provided you all know, understand and obey the rules of my ship. The first and most important rule is cleanliness! You will devise punishments for those who disobey!' he barked.

Dafydd leant down and whispered in Myfanwy's ear, 'This fellow would be happier sailing without any passengers. Look at that scowl on his face.'

Already the Captain was visualizing his scrubbed decks and polished rails fouled with emigrants' vomit and excrement. His lecture continued. '"Man overboard" is a particularly onerous cry for me and my crew. Therefore all animals and children will be kept tethered and within sight when we are in a high sea, and to ensure this rule is obeyed the crew will, in the event, lock all passengers in their quarters.'

No one dared move.

'Of course,' thundered the Captain, 'we sincerely hope it will not come to that. Thank you.'

So saying he turned sharply away from the white-faced passengers. Death by drowning had not been part of anyone's agenda.

★

Quarters were assigned; single women in the prow and single men in the bow. In between was the married quarter, with communal tables and slatted benches running like a spine through the centre. The Captain took the view that married men, used to regular sex, needed to continue the habit.

He prided himself on his knowledge of men's needs. Had he not been at sea for thirty years? Even at this moment he felt a frisson of pleasure at the thought of that nut-brown charmer waiting for him in Bermuda, their port of call on the return voyage.

A class divide pertained even on board an emigrant ship, for Dr Williams and the Reverend and his lady were given cabins. It would not do for a man of God to be heard taking carnal pleasures like other men.

Objections to anything were never expressed, as it was generally supposed the Captain knew best.

Myfanwy and Dafydd were given a married bunk next to Glyn and Rhiannon.

'Comfortable enough for you?' Dafydd grinned as his wife hauled her seven-months pregnant body on to the thin mattress.

'Aye aye. It'll do till we get there.' She looked at the row of married beds facing them across the dining area. 'But we'll have to put a curtain up. I'm not undressing in front of all those strangers.'

Lisa and Bron, delighted to be away from their parents if only by the length of the ship, took charge of the young ones, who for the most part were equally pleased to be herded together in a dormitory.

Tomos and Huw were the youngest in the group of young men and boys, who by now knew each other reasonably well. A few had that gruff crude speech heard all too often down the Llysfawr. They boasted and bragged of their female conquests and talked about the secret parts of a girl in a detail that rendered the younger and more sensitive boys speechless and blushing. One eighteen-year-old, Dai Jones from Merthyr, frequently stunned the inexperienced youngsters. Taking great care he was not overheard by older men, and just before the midday meal, Dai Jones gathered a few innocents around him. They included Tomos and Huw.

'Now listen here, you boys. We got six weeks, right? Six weeks, and I bet most of you'll get off with one of the girls.'

The young ones looked at each other wide-eyed.

'Not me,' said Huw.

'Me neither,' rejoined Tomos and several others.

Dai Jones laughed. 'How can you be sure, boy? You don't know, do you? We're here for six weeks. Right? And I'm only trying to give you a bit of advice, like. But o' course if you don't want it ask your mam and dad instead.'

The very idea of discussing anything of a sexual nature with their parents was beyond comprehension.

'Come on, Dai Jones – tell us then,' whispered a boy from the North with a broken voice.

'Aye – just in case,' piped a short-trousered twelve-year-old.

A chorus of sniggers made the boy blush.

'Quiet! And listen!' Dai Jones growled. 'When you fuck . . .' He used the English word. In Welsh it would have been too shocking. 'When you fuck a girl, she don't come – not like us.'

'Not never?' asked the boy with the broken voice.

'No! Well, I've never known one that did.'

'Don't they like it then?' asked a quiet pimply youth.

'They love it, mun – harder and faster the better. Honest! But – but you got to be clever, see. If they likes it too much they might come. And then – then . . .'

Nearly falling off their bunks now, necks craning forward to catch every pearl.

'Then what, Dai?' someone rasped.

'She could – fall!' the ominous voice of the oracle intoned.

There was a moment's silence.

'Good God! That a fact, Dai Jones?'

'On my mother's life, so remember, now – when you fuck – be quick, then she won't enjoy it too much.'

During this lesson of instruction the tall gaunt figure of Emmanuel Price had appeared. Deliberately concealing himself behind a pillar, he sought out Dafydd Rhys's boy. He had already noticed the daughter. A real beauty she was. Early days yet. He could wait.

Price pushed into the wide-eyed group. 'A load of nonsense he's telling you, boys.'

Dai Jones flushed with anger and embarrassment. This man was at least twenty-five; sure to have done it more than once.

'When a woman comes full she's like a tiger – screaming for more. They don't all, it's true, but you can learn, boys, which of 'em do – and which of 'em don't.'

There was no doubt in the minds of his young audience which of the two instructors spoke with authority. Price bent his tall figure and settled on a bunk. He was a compelling man, as the incident in Liverpool had illustrated.

A shock of red hair fell across his bony forehead, fringing bulbous green eyes that at times had a manic stare. Attention was rapt.

The boy with a broken voice said, 'Dai Jones says they fall if they come.'

Price threw his head back and laughed. 'They fall if you leave it all go inside them! I know, don't I?' He smirked.

They didn't, but they nodded as if they did.

A little lad, sitting on his own, barely able to speak with shyness, his voice hoarse, asked, 'Manny Price, how can you tell which of 'em are tigers – like you say?'

Price stretched his legs and smirked. 'Easy. Take our girls on the boat. For a start, there's a few John Thomas by here wouldn't get out of his seat for!'

He patted his crotch affectionately to subdue the embarrassed laughter and regaled the boys with remarks about the girls on board – their breasts, backsides, private parts and his assessment of their ability to be tigers. Tomos and Huw were the only boys who had sisters of the right age. Finally Price said, 'And there's that little fat pudding Bronwen Morgan.'

Huw reddened. 'My sister, Emmanuel Price – so shurrup.'

The tall man laughed. 'You don't know what I'm going to say! She's got a great pair of eyes – a great pair of tits. You could get lost in them for a week, mun. An arse like the side of this ship – and next year . . . she'll come like a tiger!'

Huw, scarlet, clenched his fists, 'Shurrup!' he yelled. Everyone except Tomos laughed.

Price glanced at Tomos. 'But every group has its queen bee – and we've got one, boys.' He lowered his voice conspiratorially. 'She's got breasts like firm pears, a waist to get your hands round, a backside like two bouncing balls, thighs as soft as a horse's nostrils.'

'How do you know about her thighs, Emmanuel Price?' Dai Jones sneered, anxious to get his own back.

'You can tell the way she flaunts herself – tosses her head when she looks you up and down. She's dying for it, mun. She's dying for a length of John Thomas – and she'd come like a tiger. Wild. Take my word for it. I can spot them a mile off. And somebody's going to do it, aren't they? Somebody's going to get up between Lisa Rhys's thighs . . .'

He got no further. Tomos shot out of his bunk, flung himself on the big man and landed a hard fist on his chin. Towering over Tomos, with one easy movement Price threw him off and dangled the boy in mid-air. His large left hand crashed against Tomos's face, spinning the youngster's head round in a half-circle, and hurled him, dazed, to the floor. Slowly Tomos staggered to his feet. The other boys stood silently watching.

Rubbing his chin, red from Tomos's blow, Price snarled, 'You bloody try that again – just try it, I'm warning you, Tomos Rhys. You won't bloody well get up – ever! D'you hear?'

Turning to leave the group of boys, he looked at Tomos who was still dazed. 'I will say this – you got more guts than that pathetic father of yours.' He turned on his heels and left.

In their hearts most of the boys were pleased at the thought of a prayer meeting after supper. For however hard they tried they were not grown men; they were boys. Their upbringing for the most part was God-fearing and circumspect. Emmanuel Price had shocked and embarrassed them. But he was a powerful man, and few doubted he was not telling the truth.

Winifred Howells, an unmarried school teacher in her late twenties, started a morning school for children up to twelve, and extra help was enlisted from all teenagers and adults who could read and write.

Blod Trehearne heaved her sixteen stone off a bench and addressed the women. 'I don't know what you women think of the food so far, but it don't suit me nor my family.'

'Nor us,' they agreed.

'And I'm not too keen on having a man cook for me neither! Never had one cook for me yet, and I'm damn sure I don't want to start now. So how about us taking over?'

Within twenty-four hours the women between them had organized life on board *The Mimosa*, from schoolroom to laundry.

The men, led primarily by Dafydd, focused on the political shape of their new colony. Democracy they would have, with free elections and one vote for all men and women over eighteen. The colony would serve as a model of true democratic government, with a Senate of ten members, one of whom would be the Chairman. That the Argentine government could be involved, even remotely, in Welsh Patagonia was never considered. Autonomy had been promised.

It was the Reverend Jenkins who suggested they should select the Senate there and then. Thus several were chosen and voted for. The ten members included Dafydd and Glyn. Emmanuel Price was another, but it was Dafydd who overwhelmingly won the Chairman's vote. To loud cheers, he addressed the assembly. He was nervous, for never before had he stood alone before so many.

'Brothers and sisters,' he began. 'As they told us in Liverpool, we are the makers of history. Our small colony, our republic, will be even more democratic than the French!' There were loud cheers. 'No more shall we Welshmen and women be exploited by the English colonists; those leeches of Westminster who have grown fat from our labour; trampling underfoot, our traditions, our language, our beliefs. We are about to gain a precious freedom. Let us use it!'

Devotion to their cause and idealism burnt in every breast.

Assisted by an accordion playing sailor, Will Fiddler started off the celebrations that followed the colony's first election day on board ship. His nimble fingertips chased each other up down the strings, while the company swirled, stamped feet, clapped, formed arches, twirled partners, made circles.

As the festivities continued, it became increasingly hot. Bron, cheeks flushed, sidled up to Lisa. 'Hey, don't tell our mam – Dai Jones has asked me to go for a walk, up on deck.'

Lisa grinned. 'Careful, girl, he's eighteen.'

'So what?'

'Fancy him?'

Bron blushed. 'No.'

'What are you going for then?'

Bron gave an embarrassed half-smile. 'Well – p'raps I do – a bit.'

'Better to be honest about it – to me anyway!' Lisa laughed. 'Go on then, girl, five minutes. I'll tell your mam you're in the privy if she asks. Watch his hands, and don't be long.'

Lisa was glad for her friend that she had found a boy she liked. She was the lucky one.

Meanwhile Lisa's face and figure, as she pirouetted daintily from one partner to the next, caused twinges of conscience in the breasts of many married men and surges of passion in the loins of several bachelors. She took innocent pleasure from being admired and responded by being flirtatious and coquettish, quite unaware of the effect she was having.

However, her general demeanour did not pass unnoticed by the women, married and unmarried.

Ten minutes later Bron returned, her cheeks red.

'How d'you get on?' Lisa asked.

'Tell you later.'

'Tell me now.'

'He's – all right.'

'Good.'

Bron lowered her voice. 'Bit *ych a fi* though.'

Lisa's eyes opened wide. 'Never! Did you?'

Shocked, Bron retorted vehemently, 'God no! What d'you take me for?'

Lisa smiled. 'Only asking, girl! Anyway I'm going up for a spell – too hot down here.'

'Nice moon,' said Bron. 'Sea's like glass.'

Lisa shrugged. 'Who cares – on my own I am.'

Moonlight splashed the deck with a cold illumination. The dark sea, striped with silver rays, was a millpond. There was only a slight breeze blowing to nudge them nearer Patagonia. The sky was navy-blue, stippled with a million stars. Lisa leant on the rail and breathed deeply. She thought of Dadcu, the old house and Merthyr. There had been so much to look forward to; a new life, finding a boy to love, to marry, to have children with. But there was no one for her, no man, young or old. And Patagonia was a country with no population. It was an empty land, as empty as she would be, for she would certainly be on her own until the day she died. What a future! Perhaps she could go back home next year.

Despite the moon, there were large areas of deck in deep shadow, with coils of rope, rigging, lifeboats, sailcloth, water butts and lockers full of provisions.

As Lisa carefully picked her way across to the other side of the deck a hand suddenly shot out, grabbed her waist, while another was clapped over her mouth. She gasped, tried to free herself, but she was held in a vice grip. She kicked wildly.

Her assailant laughed. 'Got you, bitch!'

It was Emmanuel Price. He swung her round to face him, keeping a hand over her mouth.

She could not move.

'Nobody's going to hear you, so don't try anything.'

His powerful frame towered over her.

She gasped for air, as with one swift movement he pushed her down on a tarpaulin behind a water butt, well hidden from the infrequent watch patrol. Taking his hand from her mouth, he threw his body on top of hers, making breathing difficult and therefore impossible to call for help.

He forced his lips on hers. She spat and turned her face away. He grabbed her chin in his large hand, pulled her face toward his and leered.

'Got you at last, Lisa Rhys, daughter of Dafydd Rhys – the King!'

'Let me go,' she pleaded. 'Please!'

'It's please now, is it?' he leered. 'Dying for it, aren't you?'

She attempted to bring her knees up to his groin, but they were pinned by his weight.

He tore open her bodice. His hands grabbed her breasts, pummelling flesh, until they ached. 'I've been waiting to get my hands on these for weeks.'

'Leave me be – for pity's sake,' she begged.

'Not before I've given you what you're dying for, princess!'

He grabbed at undergarments and threw flannel skirt and petticoat over her head, muffling her cries. Forcing her legs apart, he pushed into her. The pain was excruciating. She sobbed under the skirt still enveloping the upper part of her body. Again and again he pushed, his panting breath gathering momentum. She felt faint.

The weight of his foul body was suffocating. She could barely breathe. At last he gave a gasp and stopped, heaving his bulk off her crushed body.

'Let that be a lesson to you and that father of yours. See what happens when you go flauntin' yourself, you little whore! Better pull your skirt down, brazen bitch, or you'll have the boys queuing up.' Emmanuel Price laughed quietly to himself.

It was Tomos who found his dazed sister curled up behind the bilge buckets and rigging. She was whimpering quietly, hugging her knees, face buried in folded arms. He had seen Price slip out on deck soon after he noticed his sister leave the party. When Price returned, Bron told him Lisa was still on deck, and Tomos had the good sense to go in search.

'Lisa, Lisa, what's happened?' he whispered.

Seeing her brother, Lisa threw her arms about his shoulders and began to sob.

'Tell me,' he implored. 'Lisa, tell me.'

'I . . . I . . . f-fell over,' she wept, choking for air, her head still hiding in the skirt.

His sister's face was crumpled and wet with tears. When he saw her ripped bodice he shook his head. 'No, Lisa, you didn't fall. Tell me the truth. I won't say. Honest. Come on.'

Lisa began to sob again and hid her face.

The truth suddenly clicked in the boy's head 'God! Was it Manny Price? Did he chase you up here?'

'Yes! Yes!' she spluttered, gasping through her sobs.

Tomos was ready to kill. He remembered the pummelling he had with Price.

'He tried it on, but I fought him off, so don't say anything, Tomos!

You mustn't – too dangerous. Think of Dadda.'

Manny Price was on the governing Senate. He had supporters. There couldn't be a split in the camp now – and only halfway to the 'promised land'. Tomos was aching to ask his sister whether she had been forced to do it with Manny Price and, if so, could she have 'fallen', but he was far too shy. The thought of Lisa having a redheaded baby looking like Manny Price was too awful to contemplate. He assumed therefore that Price had tried it on and Lisa had fought him off, as she said. Otherwise he would just have to pray, non-stop, that God would take pity and forego procreation this time.

It was only Bron who knew the truth of what really happened.

Tomos told Huw that Price had tried it on. Myfanwy knew nothing, but the change in Lisa's demeanour did not go unnoticed.

'That girl is in a funny old mood, Dav. Anything wrong, d'you think?'

'Fed up most probably, having nothing to do.'

The secret could be contained, at least until they landed, for that was the youngsters' plan. However, they had not accounted for the *bragadoccio* Manny Price.

It took just a few days before every young man on the ship nudged and winked whenever Lisa appeared. Some of the older men gave her sidelong glances, privately wishing they had been Manny Price, if his story was true. Many doubted it and thought he was bragging; that he'd only tried it on that night on deck. Lisa's humiliation was complete when it filtered through to the women, and some of them began avoiding her as if she were some sort of leper.

'So what's all this then, Lisa – this business with Manny Price?'

Rumours had finally caught up with Myfanwy who was determined to get the truth out of her daughter.

Lisa tossed her head 'Nothing, Mam. He made a grab for me – tried it on, you know, and I kicked him, sent him packing. That's all.'

Myfanwy looked carefully at her girl. 'That's not what he's saying.'

''Course not. Bragging is second nature to him and his bunch of cronies.'

'Do you want Dadda to have a word?'

A look of shock momentarily crossed Lisa's face. That was the last thing she wanted, her father knowing the truth. 'What for, Mam, for trying it on? I'm not a child any more, am I? All men try it on, don't they? I'd be a laughing stock, running to my dad. So please, Mam, please,' she implored, 'just make sure Dadda says nothing.'

'But I want to punch the bugger.' Dafydd was furious.

'No, Dav – listen to me, will you? Our Lisa's a pretty young woman – we know that. Is this going to be the last time some bloke tries it on with her?'

'But he didn't just "try it on", did he? Not according to what he's telling his cronies?'

'Well, he's not going to tell them she kicked him away, is he? Come on, use your sense. Everybody knows he's a bragger – from the start of this voyage he's been telling the young lads God knows what.'

Dafydd said nothing.

She tried a new tack. 'Look, Dav, it's not like she's a baby any more. You've got to let your precious daughter grow up and be a woman, Dafydd Rhys. We'll always be there for her, but she must learn to handle the Manny Prices of this world herself. I'm telling you.'

Dafydd could see his wife meant business.

She put her hand on his arm. 'After all, you came courting after me, didn't you? Nasty piece of work he may be, but you can't blame Manny Price for fancying your daughter, can you? So the least said the better.'

Dafydd grunted and put his clenched fist in his pocket.

A few days after the event Bron ran to Lisa breathless, quivering with anger. 'They're saying you asked for it.'

'Who are?'

'Them chapel hags. They're saying you've been flauntin' and he couldn't help himself! Don't you worry, I've just had a terrible row with a few of them, gave them what for, I did. Narrow-minded bitches.'

Tears spilled from Lisa's eyes. 'I've got no future now, have I? You are the only one who knows the truth, Bron.'

'What about your mam? You haven't told her then?'

'God no! She heard the rumours, but I've convinced her Price just made a grab and tried it on and I sent him packing. And now he's trying to get his own back by spreading all these lies.'

Bron put her arms round her distraught friend. 'Come you, Lisa. Come you! They are never going to know the real truth, not from me they're not. And all men try it on if they think they can get away with it, so what's new? Let those bitches talk – let them – if it hasn't happened to any of them it's because they're too bloody ugly!'

They were the words Lisa needed to hear. It was the first time she had laughed in days, and she loved Bron for it. The humiliation she had suffered at the hands of Manny Price had suddenly been replaced by an intense hatred of the man and an equally intense anger against prejudice, injustice and insufferable male arrogance; all condoned by the narrow obsessions of religious dogma.

Quite naturally, gossip reached the Reverend's ears, who, upon reflection, assumed that as God knew God would punish in his own time. He would perhaps speak privately with Manny Price, as this sort of thing could but should not happen within such a small community and in such a confined space. Furthermore he would use the underlying sin as a theme for his next major sermon.

A few more days of being ousted by some of the chapel women and Lisa's anger was rising. She was to blame. Price had already achieved a hero status with his cronies. He was a bit of a lad. So what was she – a slut?

'Do you think they believe that swine?' Lisa asked her friend.

'No, because he's always boasting about girls to the younger boys. Showing off, like. Nothing new there.'

At the Reverend's special Lord's Day service Lisa sat with her family, eyes lowered. The sermon was about carnal knowledge and desire.

'When Eve gave Adam the apple,' the Reverend thundered, 'Adam was helpless, a child in her hands. The power of women cannot be underestimated. They can induce in men desires – carnal desires! Devilish desires, from which there is no escape; desires that take over mind and body, and a man is rendered – helpless. Helpless!' He thumped the table for emphasis. The Reverend appeared to be enjoying himself.

'The Devil turns a man into an animal and he cannot help what he does. But a woman can; for it is she, and only she, who can control the Devil within her. The Devil will whisper in her ear, "Go on, woman – flaunt yourself. Toss your long hair, move in a provocative way, smile, speak in honeyed tones."'

No one in the congregation stirred.

The Reverend looked directly at Lisa. 'If you listen to him, you women – all of you – you will suffer!' And his voice rose in a passionate crescendo.

Lisa's cheeks blazed with anger, with humiliation, with impotence. She looked down at her hands knotted fiercely in her lap, while hot tears stung her cheeks.

She was being humiliated because she was a woman. Manny Price could get away with anything, it seemed, because he was a man.

She left the service trembling with rage.

'How can he blame us women for a swine like Manny Price, Dadda? Don't men have any self-control? Are some men really like children?' Lisa turned to her father. 'If men are so weak, then why do men govern us? Why do men make our laws?'

Dafydd put his arm about his daughter's shoulders. 'You are right, *cariad*. Society's structure is unfair to women, but our little community will try to put it right.'

'It's not society, Dadda. It's the chapel that tells us what to think.'

Dafydd knew she was right. He believed in God but not in the conventional accepted way, for he despised narrow chapel dogma, which was every bit as constricting as the Roman Church. The Reverend's sermon had demonstrated how unforgiving and judgemental it was.

He grinned. 'Lisa *fach*, if only God had had a daughter, it could have been the other way round.'

Lisa put her arms around her father's waist. 'Why can't all men be like you, Dadda?' she sighed.

★

The following day Lisa joined the women on cooking duty, and as they filed into the ship's kitchen Blod beckoned her over. 'I know what's going on with some of this lot, gel *fach*, – leave it to me, all right?' Half an hour into soup-making Blod said with a smile, 'Now, Lisa as we are all women together, something we'd all like to know – what made you go on deck that night?'

With all eyes upon her, some with open hostility, Lisa, though taken aback by the blunt question, answered simply. 'I went because I was feeling *hiraeth* for home, for Dadcu, the cottage where I was born, the mountain.' A tear trickled down her cheek. Several women nodded with understanding. 'And nobody except Bron knew I was there.'

'*Duw, Duw,*' said Blod, 'could have been any of us having a quiet stroll upon deck. But there we are – we get the blame, not the man. And a little thing like you could hardly have dragged him up there.' Blod smiled at the pairs of puzzled eyes staring at her. She broke into a hearty laugh. 'Now if it had been me, see, I could easily have dropped the little bugger overboard, and I'd have given him honeyed words all right – words he wouldn't have forgotten in a hurry neither.'

Blod had turned the tables. The ice was broken with everyone laughing at the very idea of Blod and Manny Price.

'Mind you, most men will brag about something, won't they? Manny Price is no different,' opined one woman in a group cleaning potatoes.

Another retorted, 'My old man, good as gold he is except for fishing. *Duwedd Mawr*, if you listened to him the Teifi's got fish the size of whales, which he says he's caught many times, but he then puts them back out of the kindness of his heart!'

'Believe him?' laughed Blod.

'Believe him? 'Course not, are you wise?'

With more laughter Lisa regained her old composure and, thanks to Blod, a new understanding from the women.

Giving Lisa a playful nudge Blod murmured, 'Don't you worry now, gel *fach*. No one believes his bragging, so he'll soon stop.'

Days later, the weather broke. Seas were high and treacherous, rain lashed the decks and gale force winds buffeted the small craft in all directions. It became increasingly difficult to keep her on course. Terrible seasickness struck.

Excrement and vomit began to soil the Captain's precious rails and decks. Passengers lay on bunks looking near to death. The crew were too busy controlling the ship to bother with the overflowing privy buckets. The stench was an added problem in the chaos. Dr Williams, on call day and night, was fortunate he was able to withstand the effect of tempestuous seas. His one fear was of epidemic.

The Reverend himself was laid low for a day and a night, but mind conquered matter and he visited the sick – even though the last requirement of a heaving body was a conversation with the Almighty.

Captain Willoughby, however, proved a popular visitor with his doses of medicinal grog and promises that the storms would abate as they approached the equator.

Bethan developed a cold and was beginning to vomit again. To avoid the possible spread of infection, the doctor had the child brought into an empty cabin next to his, where her parents took turns nursing her.

She complained of pains in her stomach.

'You don't think it's appendix, do you, Doctor?' Dafydd asked
'I do not think so.'

'But if it is, Dr Williams, could you do it – the operation?'

'Of course, but I'm sure that won't be necessary. She's gone through several days of severe vomiting, don't forget. The muscles are cramped. That's what is causing pain.'

Dafydd thought for a moment. 'Very hot she is, too, Doctor.'
'Intestinal problems.'

During the night the child began to shake and tremble, teeth chattering. Myfanwy and Dafydd called the doctor.

He leant over the little girl as she shivered, perspiring profusely.

'Does it hurt anywhere, Bethan?'

She pointed to her chest.

Dr Williams fancied the child's face had a blue hue but said nothing to her parents.

It was agony to see her face burning. They tried to bring the fever down, dousing her body with cloths soaked in cold water, but the high temperature remained and the rigors continued.

As Myfanwy stroked the hot little forehead Bethan seemed to drift off into semi-consciousness.

The next morning Dr Williams's worst fears were realized. 'I think – well, I'm pretty sure actually –Bethan has lobar pneumonia – double pneumonia.'

The colour drained from Dafydd's face. 'Oh dear God,' he whispered. 'And the cure, Dr Williams? There has to be one.'

'There will be a . . . a crisis Her fever will increase and her heart rate.'

'I know about this crisis. How long do we wait for it?'

'It is about to happen.'

Thankful this discussion was over and that Dafydd Rhys had been too distraught to challenge his unforgivable misdiagnosis, the doctor retreated to his cabin.

For the next few hours the Reverend Jenkins called prayer meetings. It was unthinkable that anything should happen to this child. Were the children not the symbols of their future as a colony?

At dawn, the doctor joined the family around the child's bed. He looked at her blue-tinged lips and listened to her rapidly increasing pulse.

'Is she fighting the crisis, Doctor?' Myfanwy asked fearfully.

'You must . . . er . . . you must – be prepared, Mrs Rhys. Be prepared.' This was the part of his profession the doctor hated above all.

After hours of silence Bethan opened her eyes wide and looked at Dafydd. 'I love you, Dadda,' she whispered. Her voice was barely audible. 'You'll make me better in Patagonia, won't you?'

She closed her eyes and fell into a deep coma, from which she was never to awaken.

The effect upon Dafydd, to whom she had spoken her last words, was shattering. Myfanwy lay beside her dead child moaning quietly in pain, unable to accept her death. Tomos and Lisa, with Bron and Huw, found a quiet corner where they could weep and comfort one another. The emigrants reacted, as any community would back home. The child was laid out in her best frock by Blod Trehearne who had experience of such things, and for two days they filed in to see her, one by one. Five days after her death a funeral service was held on deck. A warm sun shone from an azure sky. Myfanwy, white and listless, clung to Dafydd and her children and thought of Bethan's eyes, as blue as this sky. She had lost all interest in the child she was carrying.

After the mourners had disappeared below to eat as near a traditional meal as circumstances would allow, Captain Willoughby left the bridge to take a solitary stroll on deck. On the spot where the child's coffin had been lowered, he saw a little girl clinging to the rail, sobbing her heart away.

He approached quietly. 'What's the matter, child?'

She looked at him with brown saucer eyes. 'It's . . . it's my friend, my best friend Bethan, sir. She's gone in the sea – but she's my friend!'

Though unused to children, especially small girls, the Captain knelt down beside her and put a comforting arm round her shoulder.

'What is your name?' he asked.

'Elin Morgan, sir.'

'Well, Elin, Bethan's body has gone into the sea, but her soul, her spirit, is up there in the sky, with Jesus.'

Though Elin could not understand every word the Captain said she knew what he meant and looked up. 'Can she see me?'

The Captain, a man with a reputation for plain speaking, surprised himself as he said, 'Oh yes! She's probably looking at you this very minute, so let me dry your eyes.' He dabbed her wet cheeks with his handkerchief.

Carefully, the little girl pulled out of her pocket a bunch of dried flowers.

'I want to give her these – I want my friend to have them,' she whispered. 'Buttercups. Me and Bethan collected them before we left Merthyr – to remind us. I . . . I want her to have them.'

The Captain smiled. 'Well, why don't you give Bethan half and keep the other half, to remind you, when you are in Patagonia?'

Together they watched as half of the dried bouquet fell on the sea and disappeared into the foaming wake of the vessel.

In silence Captain Willoughby took Elin's hand and gently led her back to the 'tween decks staircase. The death of the child had touched everyone.

Late that night when the ship, save for the watch, was slumbering, Dafydd, whose heart was too full to rest, crept out on deck. He leant on the rail and looked up at the bright moonlit sky. Alone now, he gave full rein to his grief and sobbed until his chest ached and his heart was empty.

'Dear God,' he whispered, 'Why have you made us suffer so? My eldest put upon, my youngest dead?'

He looked up at the sky. 'Was it not freedom to worship Thee in our own language that first prompted us to make a new land?' He bowed his head. 'Take no more from me. No more.'

Raising his head, he stood for a moment longer, his hands gripping the rail and looked back at a point on the horizon to the watery grave of his dearest child, a grave he could never kneel beside, in quiet contemplation. He turned away and tried to think of the baby that would be born in August.

So much had happened since leaving Liverpool. So much had changed.

In his locker he took out the hard-covered copybooks given to him by his father. Since the first moment emigration to Patagonia looked like becoming a reality, he had kept a meticulous account of daily events. With a heavy heart he took out his pen and ink and recorded memories of his sweet child.

She would live on.

They were now entering the second week of July and sailing into winter along the coast of the Argentine. The weather was becoming cold and storms a regular occurrence. Captain Willoughby sent word that he wished to see members of the Senate.

'In about one week, gentlemen – one week if these weather conditions do not worsen – we should be landing here.' He indicated a map of Argentina and Patagonia on the wall behind his desk.

Taking a pencil, he pointed to a cove about halfway down the Patagonian coastline. 'It is called Porth Madryn, and, according to Charles Darwin's captain, it offers a fine anchorage and plenty of wood for fires.'

Glyn nodded. 'Yes, we were all aware of that, Captain, and is it the delta of the River Chubut where we are to find our green pastures?'

'No, Mr Morgan, it is several miles north of the delta across this promontory of land, here.' He indicated it with his pencil. 'One other thing: there is no fresh water, so it will be important that everyone knows what to expect.'

This was yet another blow. 'I don't think we were told that, sir,' said Trevor Trehearne.

'Then you must make it your priority to cross forty miles of terrain to get to the River Chubut as soon as possible.'

As they turned to leave the Captain added, 'Gentlemen, I would suggest you call a general meeting, so that everyone knows what to expect and, indeed, what will be expected of them upon disembarkation. Organization has to be tight – take my word for it.'

The unsmiling face of the Captain softened. 'Don't worry too much about the water. I'll leave you plenty of barrels, and you'll have rain – at the coast anyway.'

Everyone, young and old, assembled in the 'tween decks. There were dozens of questions, but generally it was concluded that there would be some sort of village-hall accommodation to start them off and livestock would be already there. Several were anxious to know where they proposed to establish their first settlement.

'We have been promised lush pastures just south of where we land, but I'm quite sure the advance party will have the answers to all our questions.'

Dafydd wrote in his diary, 'July 27. Tomorrow we sail into our Patagonian haven. The moment we have been waiting for. This is our promised land – our paradise.'

Excitement was intense, as emigrants, stumbling over trunks and boxes, made their way up to the deck. It was cold with a howling wind that whipped the waves into a frenzy, drenching the deck with spray. Rain lashed against the rocks of the cove as they approached.

Porth Madryn had been given its name by two Welshmen a few years before when a fearful storm had driven them into the wild harbour.

Bron and Lisa leant on the rail, determined to have the closest possible sighting of their new country. At the cove's entrance passengers on deck saw a rowing-boat coming toward them from the shore.

'It's the advance party!' someone shouted.

The small boat drew up alongside *The Mimosa* at the point where Bron and Lisa were standing.

Men and women as excited as children called out to the rowing-boat in which sat two young men. One of them, a dark, brown-eyed young man, shouted. 'Hello! Welcome! I'm Michael Edwards. This is Sion Williams.'

The second young man, as fair as the first was dark, grinned and waved.

'Advance party?' Dafydd called back.

'Aye, sir,' they replied.

Glyn leant over the side. 'How many are you?'

'Only us.'

Michael Edwards noticed a lovely girl with long dark hair leaning on the rail. Lisa noticed the dark boy in the rowing-boat and thought how handsome he was.

He called up to her. 'My name's Michael.'

She smiled. 'I know. You said.'

'What's yours then?' he called.

'Lisa.'

'What?' The wind was blowing strong now and the rain pounding the deck obliterated other sound.

'Lisa,' she shouted, 'and this is my friend, Bron.'

'Can't hear,' he shouted. 'But I'll see you.'

They turned and headed for the shore.

Bron put her arm about Lisa's shoulder and smiled. 'That boy, Lisa – good-looking, isn't he?'

Lisa looked at Bron nonplussed. 'Don't talk about boys to me, Bron Morgan. I hate them all.'

'Say you don't know, Lisa. You wait and see.'

Several hours later the beach was stacked with boxes, trunks, goods, chattels and a number of disembarked men. Walking down the slippery gangplank, Myfanwy tripped and fell forward with a scream. Those in front of her made way for Dafydd as he leapt up the swaying gangway from the beach to reach her. She had fallen face down on her arm. Fortunately one hand was still grasping the rail. Dafydd, with more help offered than he needed, lifted her up and carefully escorted his very pregnant wife down the slope to terra firma.

He hugged her. 'Come on, *cariad*, not the best time to be dancing a fandango, is it – so near your time?'

She was badly shaken and a little tearful. 'It must have been something slippery. Don't you worry, Dav, I'll be all right in a bit.'

He guided her to the nearest outcrop of flat rock offering some protection from the wind and rain lashing the grey shingle beach. Already Myfanwy hated the menacing rock-face bearing down on them. The Devil's castle, she thought. She looked at her husband and said not a word.

Dafydd met the advance party. Now came the truth. Not only were these two young men the only advance party, there was no communal accommodation prepared. In fact there was no shelter of any kind. However, the Argentinian government had provided some rifles and two-dozen horses, tethered securely lest they should wander into the dry scrub pampas that stretched endlessly into the distance.

The rocky escarpment surrounding the cove had weathered into stepped levels and small caves.

'So where are the lush pastures?' Glyn muttered.

The two young men looked at each other.

'About forty miles south, sir – to the valley of the River Chubut.'

'Forty miles? Good God! And when we go, what happens to our womenfolk?' shouted Trevor Trehearne.

Completely bewildered by the facts that so far contradicted all promises, Dafydd asked, 'And the promised livestock from the Argentine government? Where? Without that we might as well stay here on this beach and die!'

'It will be in the valley, sir, waiting for us,' said Sion Williams. 'By the time we get there, they told us. In a day or two. We arranged that in Buenos Aires.'

The rain was gathering momentum. Before casting off Captain Willoughby had given the emigrants bread, biscuits and candles on top of their own provisions.

Taking pity on the young children, the Captain also added the few tins he had of some new manufacture called condensed milk.

The first men to disembark used several very large tarpaulins to cover important equipment, both personal and general. Some were used as cover to protect the women and children, stranded like lemmings on the shingle beach.

Glyn pointed to the caves in the rock and suggested taking a few of the miners to search for shelter. These small caves, according to the men of experience, could be made much larger as the gypsum rock was soft.

By nightfall they and their pickaxes had provided enough temporary shelter for everyone.

Lisa and Tomos found a cave, easily accessible at the end of a shale path where they put down blankets and pillows for their mother. Tallow candles provided the light, but at least Myfanwy was warm.

After a supper of water and biscuits the Reverend held a prayer meeting to give thanks.

Looking down at the angry waves relentlessly pounding the shore, his clothes soaked by gale-whipped rain, Dafydd asked the question in many hearts. Give thanks for what? Broken promises?

Had they been through a tragic tortuous voyage for this? What in God's name had they come to? Could Merthyr have been worse than this?

Too late now. *The Mimosa* was already a speck on the horizon.

5

Throughout the night, wind and rain continued to pummel the escarpment of tosca rock, drenching entrances to caves over which sacks and pieces of tarpaulin had been hung. Only the children slept.

Dafydd, Glyn, Trevor Trehearne and some of the other men were up at dawn. An impromptu council meeting was called.

The Reverend interrupted. 'I hope it won't take too long. We need our morning prayer meeting.'

He was clearly peeved that he should be refused first call upon his flock.

'Reverend, we have women and children who have to be provided for – immediately. I'm sure the God of Love won't mind waiting a bit for prayers,' retorted Dafydd, irritated by the minister's insensitivity when their very survival was in question.

It was decided that half the men would go south with Sion Williams to the pasture land around the mouth of the River Chubut where the government had promised not only a delivery of livestock but also essential building material. Michael Edwards would stay with the rest.

The trekkers would take with them the two dozen horses, but Dafydd made it plain from the start: 'No riding – the horses will have to be loaded up with all our tools. When we've found a suitable spot we'll knock together some shelter for our families.'

In the semi-gloom of a cave he looked round the group of elected councillors huddled together. 'And don't forget the rifles.'

There was no joy to be seen, only faces creased with worry and fear of a bewildering unknown.

Glyn was in charge of drawing up the list of men to trail the forty miles south. They would take some of the younger men and those with any idea of carpentry. The rest would stay guarding the women and children. Trevor Trehearne, whom Dafydd had put in charge of food and rations, cleared his throat to speak.

'We can take biscuits and water and live off anything we can catch and cook on the way. Those left here have got plenty of flour for bread, fish p'raps and the food stocks. But we'll have to get used to rations now – every family.'

Food had been stored in holes in the rock surface and covered over with rushes. Now every family would have to queue to take their daily quota.

Dafydd nudged Glyn aside. 'Manny Price is coming with us, isn't he? Can't leave him here with our Lisa.'

'You bet he is. Don't worry.'

The rain had stopped and the wind was dry, so Blod Trehearne dragooned several men into making primitive ovens. Using crevices in the rock surface, they stuffed them with all the dry kindling they could find.

When lit, these ovens would provide enough heat for bread-making.

The men sorted out tools and equipment for departure while every family prepared itself for separation at the very time they needed the familiar comfort of each other. What would they find out there beyond those swaying miles of pampas? More lies?

Dafydd sought out Michael and Sion. 'This afternoon I'd like you two to address everybody. Tell them all you know, all the arrangements and what we can expect, if anything. It's truth we want now, all of it. No more shocks. We've got to be prepared for the worst. Understood?'

Sitting on boxes or tarpaulins on a sheltered patch of rocky out-crop, the settlers waited in dismal silence for the two young men to unravel more possible deceptions from the Welsh Emigration Society.

That they would have livestock, most of it obtained not through the Argentine government as promised but from traders, who would have to be paid, was the first shock. There was more to come.

'You know already that no accommodation has been prepared for you, but Sion will be taking a party to the area at the mouth of the Chubut, where the land is fertile and green . . . to . . . er . . . to . . .'

'Have you been there?' a middle-aged woman piped up.

'I have – once,' said Sion.

There was an embarrassed silence.

'Then how do we know what it's like for living in?' shouted an angry voice.

Dafydd stood up. 'We don't!' he replied. 'But, remember, these two boys are just as much victims in this ungodly mess as we are. We are all angry. We have all suffered. We've all got to make the best of it. Survival is our main priority.'

Murmurings of grumbling assent came from the squatting group.

As he sat down Dafydd thought ruefully about Captain Vaughan. His description 'God-forsaken continent' was proving to be close to the truth.

Standing on a large flat rock facing the group, Sion said, 'There is something else you should know.' There was a nervous edge to his voice. 'Indians.' He paused. 'There are tribes of Indians.'

There was a moment of shocked silence. Then murmurings became louder, voices shrill.

Even the Reverend paled. He raised his hands to quieten his flock. 'Others have taken the Lord's word to heathen lands before,' he intoned. 'And if God wishes, so shall we. Another challenge to our faith.'

'Oh yeah! And boiled alive for our trouble,' came an angry reply. A chorus of retorts followed. 'Didn't say a bloody word about Indians, they didn't.'

'They scalp you, mun!'

The Reverend's words had had little effect.

Men tried to calm their womenfolk, some of whom by now were almost hysterical.

'Take off women and children, they do,' shouted Will Davies from Pembroke.

His scowling wife hissed. 'Shut up, you damn fool! There are children by here!'

Myfanwy, one arm around her stomach, was feeling sick and gripped Lisa's hand.

The Reverend, continuing to mouth words of comfort and spiritual sustenance – as he thought – was ignored in the *mêlée*. Any practical help from the Lord in another possibly dangerous situation seemed to be very much in doubt.

It took several minutes before Michael Edwards could speak.

'Listen, what I'm going to tell you now is the truth. The Indians in the north, the Araucans, we don't want to know them. But they never come down this far. Never. All right? The others are the Tehuelches. No trouble. No trouble at all. Harmless. And that's the truth.'

'Have you met any?' someone shouted.

'No,' he replied, looking embarrassed.

'There we are then, boy. Say you don't know,' shouted an irate woman.

'How are we going to know which is which? Wait till they attack, is it?'

'Should have told us.'

'Bunch of crooks, that's what they are in Liverpool.'

A voice from the back of the restive group shouted, 'My father knew about the Tehuelches. If there was any danger he wouldn't have let me come, would he?' It was Edward Jones the Reverend Michael's son. 'We must respect the Indians, that's what my father said. They were here first – before the Spaniards.'

Though Dafydd generally had more effect on the immigrants than the Reverend, a prayer meeting later took the heat away. Singing together was a therapy, however short-lived.

The next morning at dawn, Sion, Dafydd, Glyn and the departing men gathered their tools and began loading up the horses. Will Fiddler, Michael, the Reverend and the doctor were to be left in charge at the beach.

Dafydd put his arms round his tearful wife. 'Come on,' he whispered. 'Don't look so downhearted, *cariad*. We'll be back for you soon enough. Take you home. D'you hear me? Home.'

Myfanwy dried her eyes. 'God, Dav, if anything happens to you.' She swallowed her sobs. 'We'd all die, wouldn't we, on this beach?'

Tears were welling up again in her eyes. He put a gentle restraining finger on her mouth. 'Hush now, my love. Nothing will happen. The Promised Land, isn't it? We'll find those lush pastures, we will, for our new one to grow up in. No more tin or coal for any of us. Remember that.'

Kissing her tenderly he added, 'You know I'd rather stay with you.' He patted her large stomach. 'I hope I'll be here. But who knows? Can't tell.'

Myfanwy turned away. She was frightened. She would give anything to have him by her side when the baby came. There were plenty of women to help. Blod had delivered dozens, and there was Dr Williams. But it wasn't the same. She knew he had to go. He was like their prime minister. Who else but Dafydd? He would have to oversee the fair division of the land.

Trying her best to smile, she said, 'Dav, nothing must stop you from going to Chubut. Anyway the baby's not due for another month.'

'That's the spirit,' he quipped. 'It won't be for long.'

She wished he had said more, tried to understand her fears about giving birth in a cave. But men were different. Sometimes she felt they had only about a quarter of the capacity for understanding feelings that women had, and that included her husband.

After a brief service – Dafydd had insisted upon its brevity – the immigrants climbed up to the flat expanses crowning the headland where the horses had been tethered. Sion, Glyn and Dafydd were already peering at a rudimentary map of tracks, which for the most part skirted the pampas finally opening up near the mouth of the River Chubut.

Not one soul in the orderly murmuring group that had now gathered around the forty men about to depart heard the rustling. Or if they did, thought it was the sea breeze. But gradually as the noise increased, heads began to turn to the tall grasses that formed a semi-circle around them. Something or someone was there.

Imperceptibly a tense silence descended, and blood froze with the realization they were trapped with nowhere to run but into the sea. Sitting targets.

Horses' heads gradually poked through the grass. Two dozen, three dozen.

It could be the end for them all.

Then slowly they appeared. A posse of fierce-looking mounted horsemen stared, a silent scrutiny. They had flat noses, swarthy skins and black hair tied at the neck. They were clad in leather and wore brightly coloured headbands. Murderous-looking knives swung from their waists. A few had rifles. As the riders moved slowly toward the frightened group, encircling them, the silence was palpable. Not even a skirt quivered.

Dafydd and Glyn exchanged looks. Both had their guns.

'Jesus,' whispered Sion. 'Indians!'

'Which sort?' Dafydd muttered to Michael Edwards who had joined them.

'Dunno. Not sure.'

'I reckon we're about to find out.'

'Speak any Spanish, Michael?' Glyn asked.

'A few words.'

'Better start remembering, boy.'

The Indian leader, wearing a brightly coloured poncho, dismounted and stood facing them. He stood at least six-and-a-half feet tall and was joined by four others, equally tall. The chief, with arms folded, scrutinized the group, his eyes darting from one to the other. Lisa and Tomos held their mother close. A few women stifled their whimpers lest they should draw attention to themselves. No one knew what these savages would do to women.

Dr Williams whispered to himself and anyone who cared to listen. 'My God, of course! Magellan's Patagons, the big-feet giants.'

The Reverend intoned the Lord's Prayer, his white knuckles grasping his wife's arm to steady himself, and wondered how he could stop these savages making off with her. In those minutes, all, except for the youngest children, imagined torture, scalping, rape and an agonizing death at the hands of heathens.

Dafydd slowly rose to his feet and, laying down his rifle, took a step toward the Indian leader. Suddenly Lisa, holding a freshly baked loaf of bread meant for her father's food rations and as terrified as the rest, astonished everyone by stepping forward, even closer to the chief than Dafydd. She broke off a piece of the bread, ate it and handed the loaf to the swarthy man. He broke off a piece as she had done and tasted it. They watched and waited.

He smiled and, nodding his head in confirmation of the verdict, passed the loaf back for his deputies to try. Elin crept up to stand beside Lisa, just as Bethan would have done, and clutched at her skirt. She could not understand why everybody seemed so scared.

All the same, she wished her friend had been with her. The chief gave a command to those behind him. A small boy of about five was lifted off a horse and walked out of the long grasses carrying a very large egg. A few words of instruction from the chief and the child walked to Elin and handed her the egg. Her saucer eyes were even bigger as she carefully put the giant's egg in her pinafore and, beaming, whispered quietly, 'Oooh! Thank you very much.'

The little boy ran back, pleased, to the chief's side, and tension began to subside. Dafydd stepped up to the tall chief, took his hand and shook it. That was what started the laughter. Obviously not an Indian tradition, they found it amusing, and several of them began laughing.

No sound was ever more welcome.

Within minutes everybody was joining in with relief that their new neighbours were in fact Tehuelche Indians.

Sion managed to explain in Spanish where they were going, and the chief looked carefully at their rudimentary map. A few words and gestures were exchanged.

'I think he wants to give us a better route, Dafydd.'

'Well, he should know, so long as you remember it.'

The immigrants' first confrontation with the Patagonian Indians had ended peaceably, particularly when the Indians knew the Welsh were not 'Cristianos', their name for the Argentinians.

Lisa puzzled over that. 'Funny they don't like Christians. That's what we are.'

Her brother thought for moment. 'P'raps it's those Roman Catholic Christians they don't like. Sure to be. We're chapel, aren't we? Different.'

Lisa shot her brother a look of total disdain. With her quick thinking and courage she had been the woman of the moment. The Reverend, during the short service held principally to ensure safe conduct for the men on their journey to Chubut, thanked God for rescuing them from 'the jaws of death'. He made no mention of Lisa.

This irked Dafydd. She had done well, fair play. He was proud of her. They all were.

In his heart the Reverend knew he was but a man as the rest of them, albeit a man of God. But how he wished it had been he, obeying God's command, who had diffused that moment of tension with the Indians! Why had God not commanded him to step forward instead of that scrap of a girl? Not for one moment did the Reverend consider that perhaps it was he himself who lacked the courage. Fortunately for him and his prestige, no one would have expected the man of God to risk his own life and limb. He was not like other men. Look at Manny Price – the courage of a lion and red hair to match. His misconduct on board ship was, if not forgotten by the rest of the men certainly forgiven. Was he not a man *in extremis* of male physical frustration? They all understood that. And as for that Jezebel of a girl, she was pretty enough to tempt Jesus Christ. You couldn't blame Manny.

It was true, Manny Price could be relied upon to throw himself fearlessly into any situation, and that was what counted. He could find solutions of the physical kind, where others could not. He was the instant tactician, hopeless with words and with few fine feelings, particularly towards women. Arrogant and lacking any socially endearing qualities, he was nevertheless a man you had to have on an expedition into the unknown.

Even Dafydd recognized that.

6

Following the roughly marked route given them by the Tehuelche
Indians, forty Welshmen and fully-laden horses trudged through a
morning of torrential downpours of rain and howling winds, skirting
the dry grassland; Dafydd, Glyn and Sion in the lead, Manny Price
and his adjutants bringing up the rear.

Glyn turned to Sion 'Did we fill up bottles of rainwater?'

'Don't think so – it was full pelt when we left, wasn't it. Why?
D'you think it's going to stop?'

'If it's like Wales, it'll rain every day near enough.'

They stopped only for nature and a handful of biscuit ration,
every man scanning the landscape despite Michael's assurances
about the Araucans. Thus far they'd had their share of disillusion;
therefore assurances could no longer be absolute.

By dusk, and several miles inland from the coast, the weather had
calmed, the rain stopped. Weeks of confinement on the ship had
stiffened leg muscles even among the younger men. There were sighs
of relief when Glyn found a clearing for the night's camp. The soil
here was sandy with dry hard tufts and bushes, dotted with stunted
trees.

'So where are the lush pastures? Not much green here, so
precious little rain, I reckon,' Glyn muttered.

Dafydd nodded. 'Looks pretty parched, doesn't it?' He turned to
Glyn. 'Something else we didn't know.'

Glyn shrugged. 'P'raps when we get more south?'

A fire was lit, every man finding the least spiky tuft of scrub on
which to place a blanket. They had each brought enough water to
make a brew of tea. Small quantities of rum brought from the ship
were passed around. Even the God-fearing teetotallers took it. Bread
soaked in rum-flavoured tea was not such a bad supper.

There was nothing else.

'God knows what'll come out of there tonight,' said Glyn indicating the dark clumps of grasses a few hundred yards away. 'Better keep this fire going.'

'A few rabbits, sure to be,' laughed Herbie ap Morris, a young man from Aberystwyth with a shock of auburn hair. 'Provided we get the water to cook them. Never thought I'd be praying for rain.'

Herbie had been put in charge of cooking and rations, for no particular reason other than his experience as a poacher. His sister Vanw, a pretty girl of twenty, was at the coast along with his younger eighteen-year-old brother Idwal. He could be a bit too adventurous at times, but Herbie was glad his brother had made friends with Dafydd's boy Tomos, younger but a much steadier lad, he thought.

'You know,' he said, addressing the group, 'when I was a kid I used to cry when rain spoilt an outing – it usually did. And my mam would always say, "The rain is good for you. Better for your complexion."' He made a comical girlish sweep of his hand, making everyone smile.

'In that case we must all be bloody beautiful in Wales then,' said Trevor Trehearne.

The laughter that followed was hearty and as needed as the rain.

They drew lots for look-out guard duty. Manny Price drew the shortest straw.

'Good boy! You'll fight them off, Manny!' someone shouted.

'Pity you can't roar as well,' yelled another.

Manny Price's green animal eyes glinted in the firelight. 'Want a bet?' he grinned.

As he settled into a patch of clearing, Dafydd asked, 'Sion, tell us again about this place we are heading for. Didn't you say something about Spanish?'

'Aye aye,' the young man replied. 'It was a Spanish fortress once. All in ruins, mind, but the old walls, parts of them anyway, are still there.'

A throaty laugh came from Trevor Trehearne.

'We got no worries then. Look what the Spaniards have conquered, and we only want a small patch! If it's good enough for them it's good enough for us!'

Throughout the night the red-haired North Walian dutifully toured the encampment, his foxy eyes darting across the terrain for signs of movement, human or animal. Rifle in hand he sat near the fire, rolled a cigarette and threw his blanket around his shoulders, for it was bitterly cold, stars bright in a velvet-blue sky. He didn't mind the cold. He was used to it. Hadn't he been with the sheep on barren mountains in North Wales all his life? He glanced at his sleeping companions. They'd be all right with him. He could smell a fox a mile away. Finishing his cigarette he strolled with a practised stealth around the sleeping, snoring bodies.

Dafydd was lying near a small scrub bush, warm in a sleeping bag Myfanwy had made out of an old feather eiderdown. After a few hours of deep sleep induced by sheer fatigue, he lay on his back, semi-conscious, his mind turning restlessly with worry and guilt; guilt that he had disclosed Captain Vaughan's searing condemnation of their promised land only to Glyn. Suddenly he sensed something close to his face, something warm and foul-smelling. Stabbing through layers of half-sleep, his heartbeat quickened, forcing him into abrupt consciousness. Opening his eyes, he met the green fox stare of Manny Price, barely six inches away.

'Good God, man! What the – ?'

He pulled down the sleeping bag and attempted to prop up on his elbows, his voice thick with sleep. Manny Price rose, his long legs astride Dafydd's body.

He grinned down at him 'Nothing's wrong,' he rasped. 'Just looking after you, I am. Like your mam!'

He walked away cackling quietly to himself, pleased he had given Dafydd Rhys a fright. If only he could have done more. It would have been so easy. A hand jammed against his mouth was all it would take. Pious goody-goody milksop, that's what Dafydd Rhys was, and always bloody right. Manny hadn't forgotten how Rhys had made him look a fool in front of everybody that day at Liverpool docks when he had all the men on his side. And as for that little bitch of a daughter, nobody believed her; a few women p'raps but nobody that counted. He snorted with contemptuous satisfaction. He'd get his own back, but for now there was only one objective: survival.

By the third day there was no water. The wind was bitter, the terrain hard. Many did not have the stamina to go on. It was only the thought of waiting families crouched in caves on the coast that propelled the next weary step.

Gwynfor Thomas from Cardigan, a man in his fifties, pleaded with Dafydd, 'Leave me by here, Dav. Can't go on without water, boy. You're all younger than me. You got your families waiting for you – relying on you. I got nobody. Go, you. Carry on. Only fair. I'll wait here.'

It was clear the man was weak. Another day's trek could kill him. A decision would have to be made. The men huddled together in painful debate. They could unload one of the horses, but it was doubtful he would have the stamina to sit upright.

'Gwynfor, we're not going to leave you. We're going to send some of the boys to find water,' Dafydd said finally.

Gwynfor, slumped against a rock, tried to raise his head in protest. 'No, no.'

'It's for all of us, Gwynfor, not just for you. God, man, we all need water!'

Winds were biting into cracked lips and skin was raw, compounding distress. There was no choice. Horses were tethered securely, yards away from the temporary encampment.

Despite Manny Price's personal problems with the Rhys family and his violent outbursts, he did not lack courage. Rising to his feet he surveyed the dispirited group. 'Who's coming then?'

Nine men, including Sion, volunteered. Despite his dislike of Manny Price, Dafydd knew he could be relied upon to use his native cunning to lead the group.

'Good luck, boys! Five hours – no more. Take rifles and enough ammo. We'll be all right by here. But we can't wait for you. We'll have to start on the trail again. Got to get to that valley.'

The remaining thirty men sat quietly saving their energy and waited. The only rations left were dry biscuits, so Herbie shot two kites and cooked them. The flesh was sour, what little there was of it between so many. He gave Gwynfor the kite's blood to drink.

Four hours passed and no sign of Manny Price's group.

Depression spread like a virus, affecting each one of them. Their comrades had to be either lost or dead. No one had the energy to even sing – nothing to sing about.

Dafydd rose to his feet. 'Better start packing up,' he mumbled.

Herbie gathered the bits of bones left scattered. Suddenly he stopped. 'Don't talk too soon,' he said. 'Listen! They've come back!'

No one quite saw what happened next, but in a breathless instant they were surrounded by Indians. Dafydd counted about twenty. They were not Tehuelches, though not dissimilar in dress; necklaces made from clumps of human hair hung around their necks, axes and knives from belts. Their faces were painted in dazzling stripes, and black hair sat lankly upon shoulders. Glyn and Dafydd were grabbed from behind, knives held to their throats, while they were bound by thick rope to wooden posts forced into the soil by mallets. Dazed and terrified, the rest were herded together and bound in a line across the centre of the clearing. Gwynfor, already slumped on the ground, was hauled up and bound to the others. Resistance was pointless and impossible. The few guns they had were surrendered and piled up beneath a tree stump.

They were going to die. Each and every man knew it.

The fire was relit. The chief, or so he appeared to be, shouted orders. Water bottles were brought out and the contents tipped into several pans suspended over the flames. In the face of death, the water for which their parched bodies yearned was suddenly insignificant. The devout muttered prayers, hoping for a miracle. But judging by the Almighty's record of intervention during past crises, even believers were beginning to doubt. Dafydd stood resigned, his arms and shoulders aching from the binding ropes that held him like an animal, trying to prepare himself for torture and death.

He thought of his lovely Myfanwy and the child he would never see; of Lisa and Tomos and the grandchildren he would never know; of their new lives here in Patagonia; and wished with all his heart he had listened to Captain Vaughan. As for his God, what more did the Omnipotent One wish to take? What great evil had he, Dafydd Rhys, committed for this supposed God of Love to wreak such vengeance? What would happen to all those women and children on that accursed beach? Did He not understand that one of the reasons for emigrating was to have the right to worship this God of Love in the mother tongue? Where was this love? Was it, too, as much a phantom as the Promised Land? Dafydd had always thought of himself as devout, in his own personal way, but his doubts were growing. Belief was reassuring, comforting. Uncertainty was its opposite, uncomfortable and lonely.

The chief issued more guttural commands. Immediately a few of his followers brandished knives menacingly close to the group roped across the centre. They laughed at the terror in the men's faces when knives were sliced close to the crotches of those tethered at the outer edge. Their blackened teeth were hardly discernible in dried leather faces. Dafydd wondered how many other poor devils had lost their body parts to those teeth, as surely they themselves would. He felt sick watching them sharpen their knives on stones, waiting for the water in the pans to heat.

Herbie at the end of the line gasped.

'They're going to cut our balls off! Christ Almighty! Why in God's name did I leave Aberystwyth?' His eyes were full and staring, his face white. He had remembered rumours about the Indians cooking prisoners' testicles and eating them in order to increase their maleness.

'For Christ's sake, shut up, will you!' It was more a scream than a shout.

Each man contemplated the unthinkable.

Glyn began the first line of a hymn – simply for the solace of familiarity.

The old melody brought back memories of the Wales they had left and of all their dreams for the new Wales they had hoped to create. Each breast was full to breaking with *hiraeth*. One by one they joined in. Gradually all thirty were singing. Their captors stood in amazement and listened. Perhaps it was the harmony, perhaps the melody. Whatever it was, it appeared to be one way of delaying murder or mutilation. Dafydd sensed this and began repeating verse after verse, hymn after hymn. They must not stop. They sang at the tops of their voices. They were singing for their lives, their captors bemused, mystified.

It would take only minutes now for the water in the pans to boil.

On and on they sang with what strength they had left. The chief, an evil-looking individual, sat down, arms folded, and muttered something to an acolyte who nodded in agreement. The water started to bubble. For how much longer could the singing of Welsh hymns hold the interest of hungry tribesmen?

The chief muttered more words of command to his men. A few gathered around him, squatting on the ground. He beckoned to the one standing over the bubbling pans and whispered in his ear. Immediately he took out a long curved knife from his belt. Every captive watched, rigid with fear. The singing became louder and more desperate. The chief muttered another command to his henchman with the long knife and pointed to the end of the line, to Herbie.

'Shut your eyes, boy!' Dafydd yelled over the singing.

The man with the long knife stood in front of Herbie and pulled at his shirt buttons to bare his chest. Herbie ap Morris crumpled to the ground, fainting. The man with the knife looked at his chief who shook his head. It was obvious that anything the fainting man could offer would not enhance their strength nor maleness. The singing once more gathered momentum.

The next in line was Trevor Trehearne. The knifeman approached with a sickly grin and sliced his victim's shirt open. Every muscle Trevor had was held taut in a state of readiness to withstand excruciating pain and certain death. A hand grabbed his testicles before thumping his victim's chest to feel his palpitating heart. He nodded to his chief. Trevor's face contorted, prepared for the unimaginable. This was it. The singing began to falter. There was no escape.

The Araucan, his long knife with a serrated edge held high in the air, prepared to gouge out the heart of the older man.. The chief and entourage now rose and began to move slowly in a circle, muttering ritualistic incantations.

The chief yelled a command. They stopped. But in the split second before the knife could sever the heart from its victim's body, a shot felled the knifeman. Manny and the nine men, each of them armed, had returned. With lightning speed, one of them unbound his captive comrades, while each released man grabbed a rifle from the pile. The Araucans, completely bewildered, had given the rescue team precious seconds to organize themselves. But the Indians were fierce in retaliation, and the settlers were no match for their dexterity with knives. They charged, savagely lunging and stabbing. Several of the settlers, more at home with boxing than shooting, threw mighty punches that left their attackers sprawling in the dry earth or running for cover.

'Shoot the buggers!' Glyn yelled. 'Come on! It's them or us!'

They had no alternative.

Within fifteen horrifying minutes fifteen Indians, including the chief, had been shot dead; the rest had run off into the undergrowth and four settlers were uncomfortably, but not seriously, wounded.

Who would have imagined they would come to Patagonia to kill? But had they not killed in self-defence? That was the rationale each one tried to hang on to. The reality of the scene they left was shocking. They had taken men's lives. That was the hardest truth to face. Death back home came either by natural causes or by accidents in the pit or the tin.

Surely the Almighty could see they did only what they had to do – especially as He had been proven fairly useless when they were inches away from mutilation and murder. So the problem lay with conscience and had nothing to do with the Almighty.

Forty weary men gathered their belongings and turned away from the spot where they would surely all have died had not Manny fired that first shot. It was not only the singing that had drawn the rescue team but the frenzied quality of those voices that suggested things were not as they should be.

A few hours later the profoundly shaken band found another clearing, lit a fire and sat silently. One or two sobbed with relief. Several could be heard retching in the undergrowth. They were white-faced, many still shaking with fear.

Trevor Trehearne was gripped with violent trembling. They gave him rum, but how he wished he was wrapped in the arms of his Blod and could sink into her big, warm, comforting bosom. 'I wish I was back home, boys – don't mind telling you,' he whispered.

'Why didn't the Reverend Jones know about this? Or at least find out before sending us here like lambs nearly to the slaughter.'

Dafydd was angry and frightened, and the guilty look he

exchanged with Glyn carried with it the memory of Captain Vaughan's words.

Rather shame-faced, Herbie muttered, 'Thought he was going to tear my balls off ,Trev, that's why I . . .'

Trevor Trehearne, still trembling, grunted shaking his head, dismissively.

'Don't worry about that, boy,' said Glyn. 'We aren't supposed to be magic men – just a bunch of poor buggers from Wales looking for somewhere to live in peace.'

'Aye, and what have they bloody sent us to?'

'Bunch of liars they are and that white beard worst of the lot.'

'If *The Mimosa* was still docked I'd be on her like a shot.'

'I keep thinking, what if Manny hadn't arrived when he did?'

Nodding heads and murmurs of agreement came from the still dazed group.

'Aye. Thank God for Manny.'

'*Iesu bach*, there's a death to have, aye.'

After such an experience it was difficult to think straight.

Manny Price's popularity had never been so high. He had saved all their lives.

They sat silently for half an hour.

A man from Treorchy, who had said nothing so far, uttered words that left them cold. '*Duwedd Mawr*, I keep thinking – our wives and kids on that beach – they could be dead in a month, either to the Araucans or starvation, all of them.'

After several minutes of contemplative silence in which each survivor digested this appalling possibility, Glyn added with a sigh, 'And nobody'd care, would they? A hundred and fifty-odd Welsh men women and children dead! So what? Those swine in government in London wouldn't give a damn.'

Eyes looked up and exchanged glances. It was a moment of touch-and-go, whether or not the group would turn around and return to the coast.

His voice quiet and subdued, lacking the conviction and power to which the group were accustomed, Dafydd said, 'What you have been saying is true, all of it. No one wants to go back to his wife and children more than I do. What Glyn says about nobody in the government giving a damn is also true. In their eyes we don't count. But look, boys, we've got to show them, make ourselves be counted, despite all those lying namby-pambies who would take our money and lead us into the jaws of disaster. We owe it to our families waiting on the beach in God-knows-what circumstances. So I think we have to work out the problem here and now. If we go back we could be going straight into another Araucan ambush. If we go on – '

'Who's to say we don't bump into another lot?' said Manny Price

'Fair enough,' said Glyn, 'but we can't stop here, that's for sure.'

It was Sion's turn now. 'Look,' he said, 'this has been totally unforeseen. I promise you, had there been bands of Araucans roaming the Chubut we'd have been told about it.'

An older man huffed. 'I wish I could believe that,' he said.

Dafydd had been idly drawing shapes in the earth with a twig. 'All right then, let's take the worst thing that could happen – another attack. The Araucans don't have firepower. That we know, so we must make sure every rifle is ready to be fired. Second, we shall have to stick to wide-open spaces from now on. No more bushes – too dangerous.'

There was general agreement that this was the only policy to be pursued, but it was half-hearted and lacking in any kind of enthusiasm. It was decided that ten men would form the night patrol, but no one had much sleep that night.

For the onward trek Gwynfor Thomas, his body now restored with water but still weak, was put on a horse.

Within a few hours there was a perceptible difference in vegetation. Sion took out the trekking route given them by the Tehuelches. He stopped and squinted into the distance.

'According to this, we're not far off.'

Herbie fell on his knees feeling the tufts. 'Well, no doubt, this grass is greener; healthier-looking.'

'First one to see the river, boys!' Glyn shouted.

Re-energized with their greener vistas, they trudged purposefully for several more hours through the ever thickening grassland.

Sion leading the party suddenly stopped. 'Look! There's the coast – over there on the left and on the right the estuary and the Chubut Valley. Only about a mile now to the old fortress. We're here, boys! We're here!' he yelled.

They stopped, unable to believe their eyes.

Before them was the valley of the Chubut river, wide and majestic, at this point flanked by pastures and woodland.

Dafydd did not suggest they should immediately praise the Lord. Neither did anyone else. They had arrived here despite His hindrances.

7

That first week for the coastal cave-dwellers without forty of their men was a nightmare.

Owing to a sudden change in tidal strength, twelve families were flooded out of their lower-lying caves. Removing their belongings to higher ground, Dr Williams and Michael Edwards organized the erection of rough wooden shelters from salvaged planks of wood higher up the sloping coastline to house the bereft families. In the absence of Glyn and Dafydd, these two had assumed the roles of proxy leadership.

When Michael had first spotted Lisa from his boat as she stood on the Mimosa's deck he had been immediately smitten. Now, seeing her every day, his continuing shy attentions were sometimes rebuffed and sometimes accepted solely as gestures of friendship. Ever since her Manny Price episode Lisa was understandably reluctant to engage on any deeper level with a man 'ever again', as she had expressed to Bron, who quite sensibly thought it best to wait and see.

To use this tense waiting time profitably, as well as giving distracted minds focus, Dr Williams held discussion classes each night for everyone; that is, anyone who did not object to shingle and rocks serving as cushions.

He read them extracts in English from Darwin's explorations around the coast and descriptions of Tehuelche Indians. He was teaching himself Spanish and, despite opposition, persuaded a few that it would be needed, especially with the Tehuelches who spoke not only their own tongue but Spanish and just a few words of English.

'So why should we bother with Spanish? We came here because we wanted to found our own Welsh colony,' someone opined.

'Let them learn Welsh. That's what I say.'

'This is our land now. They can keep out.'

Dr Williams was quite shocked to hear such reactionary views.

'Brothers and sisters, let me ask you – when the English came to Wales did they bother to learn our language?'

'No,' they chorused

'Did they bother to find out about our way of life, our customs?'

'Never,' came the sharp riposte.

'And I'm sure you will agree that we were in Wales before the English set foot on our soil?'

They agreed wholeheartedly.

'Question for you. Who were the first inhabitants of this country?'

'The Spaniards', 'The Indians', 'The Zulus like in Africa' came the assortment of answers.

'It was the Indian tribes like our friends the Tehuelches. So tell me, when the Spaniards came did the Indians fight them – tell them to go back home?'

'Yes. Yes!'

'Quite right, they did. Now then, are they fighting us? Telling us to go back home?'

'No.'

'Not so far.'

'Of course they haven't, and they won't. They are kind people, and I'm sure we'll get on very well. So that's why we should make an effort to learn some Spanish, so that we may understand each other.'

'Well I'm not going to learn bloody Spanish for anybody,' a man shouted from the back of the crowd. 'Anyway they are heathens.'

Dr Williams caught the smug look on the Reverend's face.

'Very well, I'm sure we can teach them some Welsh later on, but, brothers and sisters, surely we have not stooped so low as to tell people how to worship? That our God is the only one?'

'But, Dr Williams, he *is*,' the Reverend intoned.

Dr Williams's cheeks reddened, and he felt suddenly so nervous his slight stutter returned, 'Is it our b-b-b-business to tell the inhabitants of this land how they should worship? Many are of the Roman faith, which the Spaniards imposed upon the native population, often with cruelty. And the Tehuelches, a kind people who, I am sure, will become our much-needed friends have their own gods to worship. Are we so arrogant as to tell them that after perhaps a thousand or more years they should stop and change to our God?'

The group sat in what appeared to be a reflective momentary silence.

'Brothers and sisters, is this not precisely what the English said to us in Wales? "This is our country now, so speak English. No more Welsh in schools, nor in the law courts, and you will go to church not chapel where you will pray in English."' His voice rose. 'Think! Stop and think! Would we not be doing p-p-precisely the same thing as some of the English did to us? We are here for the sake of freedom to live as we wish for the greater good. What we wish for ourselves we surely have to give to others, and', he looked at the Reverend, 'if they are to be converted to our God, our religion, it must be b-by example not by force.'

Dr Williams had taken himself by surprise. Never before had he spoken in public with such passion. As he sat down someone started a round of applause that spread through the hundred or so who were sitting wrapped in blankets on the flat rocks.

In the discussion that followed the majority of opinions had softened as they realized the unhealthy parallels with those English attitudes they abhorred. But some of the older ones had made up their minds; it was going to be Welsh or nothing. Reactionaries they would remain.

As for the women, Myfanwy was too near her time for any active interest in group activity, but Blod Trehearne and of course Lisa, who had her father's nose for political organization, were in total agreement with the doctor. Besides which Lisa had earned the admiration of all, being the first to offer bread to the Indians.

Meeting and talking with Michael, was becoming a highlight of Lisa's day, despite her avowed intentions. 'I've seen him giving you the eye, Lisa Rhys,' Bron giggled.

'Think he likes me, then?'

'Crazy about you! Ask anybody.'

'Don't have to. He's told me.'

Bron's eyes opened like big brown saucers. 'Never! Hey!' She grasped her friend's face inching it nearer to hers and whispered, 'You haven't – you know?'

Lisa stared angrily at Bron. 'What d'you take me for, Bron? After all that's happened? No fear.' With a toss of her head she walked away.

Fresh water was running out. Dr Williams suggested a search party of three volunteers. From the top of the cliffs there appeared to be a vast expanse of flattish land before an arid sea of grass stretched into infinity.

'Now, for heaven's sake, be careful. Note your tracks, and stick together. Avoid the grass. Remember how high it can be.'

Eirwen Owen, her younger sister Mair, both kitchen maids from Abercynon, and Edwin, seventeen, the Trehearne's youngest, set off early with water containers for what they thought would be a couple of days' hike at the very most.

Myfanwy had already started labour during the night and continued with painful regularity throughout the day.

Finally, in the early hours of the following morning, with Blod Trehearne giving encouragement and comfort and Dr Williams attending with rolled-up sleeves and with instruments boiled in sea water, an exhausted Myfanwy gave a final push and another life came into their new world: a baby girl looking remarkably like the child she had lost. Myfanwy desperately wished to have Dafydd at her side because she knew how happy he would be having another Bethan, for that's what they would call her.

Dr Williams was also pleased the infant would be called Bethan for personal reasons. His wrong diagnosis on board ship had given him many pangs of troubled conscience. He felt he had been given a second chance.

This event, their first little Welsh Patagonian, was indeed something to celebrate for the new immigrants. What else was there? And how could they forget the death of the five-year-old on board ship? Women lined up to see the new baby and to take it in turns to hold her, their faces soft with caressing smiles as they gazed upon the warm bundle.

'Know what? They'll all want to be expecting now.'

Bron smirked, 'You are terrible, Lisa.'

'Fact of life, Bron. They get broody.'

'You, too?'

'I'll have to have the man first, won't I?'

'That one?' Bron slyly inclined her head in Michael's direction as they gathered round the Reverend Jenkins for the christening of the second Bethan Rhys.

It was now forty-eight hours since three of the group had left in search of water. Blod Trehearne tried not to show her anxiety, but, with her husband God-knew-where and now Edwin missing, when she was not involved in cooking and catering she shut herself away quietly in her cave, head in hands. The Reverend tried to give her strength, but in her heart she despised his platitudes. She believed in God, but she wanted something better than a milksop like the Reverend Jenkins with his lily-white rich woman's hands as His spokesman. Her strength and support would come from the band of women surrounding her, in their hearts as bewildered as she in foreseeing a future for any of them

On the fourth morning twenty men – led by Michael – spread across the plain and into the tall grasses, their hands held, in an attempt to find the missing youngsters. After hours of searching there was no sign. No one had realized how treacherous the uncharted acres could be, like a quicksand, engulfing in a silent suffocation.

It was nearly dusk when Edwin and the younger girl staggered into the camp with their water containers filled. They had found a good well but explained tearfully that Eirwen had wanted to go off on her own search. They tried to establish a meeting place, but it proved impossible. The tale was particularly poignant as Eirwen and Mair, orphaned from an early age, had no one, having been placed when children in the workhouse and thereafter taken into service. Blod took young Mair into her motherly arms, while the men continued searching for her missing sister.

It was Lisa this time who was first aware of the rustling. She and Michael had taken time out from their allocated jobs to stroll in an unusually calm dusk.

'Michael, look! There's something over there,' Lisa whispered, pointing in the direction of the noise.

As before, a band of Tehuelche Indians on horseback swished silently toward them.

Unafraid, Lisa and Michael went to meet the chief as he dismounted.

He bowed his head pointed to himself and in halting English said, 'Me Chief Kitchkum. I – sorry – sorry.'

He turned to face his men still mounted behind him, raised his hand and beckoned. From somewhere invisible another equally tall Indian appeared, carrying in his arms the fragile body of Eirwen Jenkins.

Lisa put her hand to her mouth and gasped.

Michael ran along the cliff shouting, 'Dr Williams – quick!'

The young woman's body was laid on the grass, and the doctor confirmed she was dead. With his rudimentary Spanish he understood from the chief they had found her half-conscious and had taken her back to their camp near by. They tried to revive her but with no success.

The urgency in Michael's voice had brought dozens of settlers running to the scene. Shock at seeing the wasted body of the young woman was too much for some. The chief turned to them.

'Sorry – sorry.' He shook his head and wagged his finger.

'Pampas – *nada*! Pampas – *nada*!'

A blanket was brought to cover Eirwen's body, and she was carried into one of the shelters. A distraught Edwin ran to tell his mother and Mair.

Meanwhile the Indian chief was continually turning towards the tall grasses looking at the small gathering, frowning and raising his hands.

Lisa grabbed Michael's arm. 'He's asking us why. I'm sure he is. What's the Spanish for water? Go on, tell him.'

'*Agua*,' he said without stopping to think if she was right.

'No *agua*,' and he mimed the action of drinking.

By now most of the settlers, having viewed the tragedy, returned solemnly to the caves below with the doctor and the body of young Eirwen, where Blod, of course, would be laying her out and comforting her younger sister.

A moment of silence was observed while the small cortege made its descent, followed by a stream of commands in Tehuelche from the chief summoning several more Indians carrying large water containers from somewhere unseen. Directed by their chief, they placed the precious liquid in front of the few dumbfounded and speechless settlers who had remained on the cliff top. The one who had been so against learning any Spanish mumbled, 'Michael boy, what's "thank you" in Spanish?'

In turn they each approached the chief uttering a hoarse *gracias* while he in response gave each right shoulder a strong protecting pat.

Water carried away, the chief beckoned to Michael, and with a stone he drew in the soil the position of the nearest fresh water sources. Fortunately someone had the foresight to copy down the simple diagram on a piece of paper before the wind destroyed it. They were learning.

Meanwhile Lisa had slipped away and returned with an apron full of fresh loaves. She held a loaf up for him as before.

He sniffed the crust. '*Muy bien.*'

'*Bara,*' said Lisa passing the loaves over to his deputies. Pointing to the bread she repeated, '*Bara.*'

The chief solemnly turned to his riding companions and held up a loaf of bread for all to see.

'*Bara bara,*' he intoned like a ceremonial mantra.

'*Bara bara,*' they repeated.

With a quick salute the chief mounted his horse, turned and led his men away. Michael and Lisa, alone now, watched them. He noticed tears trickling down her cheeks and squeezed her hand. 'What's the matter?'

She shook her head. 'Never thought I'd hear Patagonian Indians speak Welsh.'

Above the beach and caves that night the young woman was buried in Patagonian soil. The disconsolate group around the grave tried to stem the tears, not just for the lost girl but for all of them.

Were they also witnessing the burial of their dreams and the promises that had been made? In every female heart was the frightening possibility that they would never see their men again.

And then what would they do; repatriation, but to what?

Around the harmonium on a calm velvet night, melodious voices sang hymns of their motherland that soared across the infinite spaces of sea and sky.

Thoughts of loved ones left behind in Wales and loved ones facing unknown danger out there in this raw wilderness were in everyone's mind, and their impassioned voices became a plea to heaven.

Each soul longed to hold again the hands of the ones they loved on this bleak Patagonian beach.

8

Extreme thirst drove the men to the river before finding their way round the old fortress. Once inside, each man staked out a sleeping pitch against the crumbling walls that despite decay, offered a certain comforting protection.

'The first thing we need to think about is food,' said Dafydd. 'And as the Argentine government have sent nothing I hope somebody's got a couple of suggestions.'

'Fish,' said Herbie, 'plenty in that river. Who's coming then?'

A dozen went down to the riverbank, while others set about making a fire.

'Hope we've all brought a couple of saucepans.'

'Those Indians had some hefty ones, didn't they?'

'Aye, for cooking balls.'

'You can shurrup about that. When you lot arrived I was next in line to poor old Trevor. Bloody nightmare it was.'

'What about me, then? I fainted, didn't I? Be lucky you'd gone off for water.'

'Aye, OK, Herbie boy. We're here and alive. Close the book now – we'll have to, or we'll all go back home.'

The near-death encounter with Araucans had left its mark on these inexperienced innocents. While they would have to learn the ways of a savage world quickly in order to survive, it would take a long time for the book to close.

Dafydd, Glyn and Sion meanwhile looked carefully at the map of the region Sion had been given, showing the vast territory that would be available to the Welsh settlers. It looked as though each family would have several acres with river frontage. Glyn had brought with him a list of emigrants and households and, no matter the size, the division of land would be equal. Sion sectioned the land into numbers that would be placed in a hat.

'We'll draw lots when our families are here. Fairest way,' said Dafydd.

Glyn stroked his chin where a beard was sprouting. 'Sion, do you reckon they'll send us anything, the government?'

The young man shrugged. 'I can only tell you what I know. I met Señor Rawson – a government minister. Nice man. Wants us. He seemed keen to get us supplies. But I hope somebody has the sense to send livestock here and not to the landing point. At least we can corral them easily.'

'What d'you think, Dav? A few of us get on with fencing in a patch or two then, just in case? Don't want to waste time chasing cows when we've got shacks to build. Between us we've got tools – and plenty of trees over there.'

Dafydd, sitting on a piece of fortress masonry, scanned the terrain. 'We'll have to start doing something or we'll be wondering why we've come.' He sighed. 'We'll talk tonight. Fences and fish for now.'

'Weather changes like a baby's backside round here, honest to God.' Herbie ap Morris sat on the grass, chestnut hair tumbling over his forehead and perspiration running down his pink cheeks.

'What do you know about babies' backsides, Herbie?' asked Trevor with a suggestive nudge.

'Not so much yet, but I've got a plan or two up the sleeve, like.'

'Oh yes? Well, come on, which one of our beach beauties have you got your eye on then?'

Herbie wasn't going to be caught out. He grinned. 'All the single ones, OK?'

At last covered wagons pulled by oxen sent by the Argentine government arrived, piled high with supplies of corrugated tin for roofing, planks, boxes of tools, utensils, sand, cement and food. They had been delivered by boat to the natural harbour at the mouth of the Chubut's estuary. The wagons had but a short distance to cover from the coast to the green valley and the old fortress.

Fatigue forgotten, unloading began, each of them knowing he was building for their collective survival. It was to be timber for now with corrugated tin roofs; and later brick dwellings; the brickies among them would take over the role of foremen. Necessity would be a great teacher, and the learning of hitherto unknown skills would became commonplace. As the covered wagons offered protection, Dafydd persuaded the drivers to leave most of them behind ready for transporting families from the northern coast.

Later that evening when Herbie and Evan Davies from Llanelli, a lanky twenty-five-year-old, were upstream fishing, Evan asked, 'Do you fancy any of those girls, Herbie? Honest now.'

Herbie scratched his head, 'Well, there was one – had a bad time, poor dab – Eirwen; she and her sister, orphans, Abercynon way. Nice girl. Yeah, I liked her – probably found somebody else by now. Like Dafydd's girl Lisa – lovely little firebrand, that one. I reckon she'll get what's-his-name, Michael.'

Evan smiled a satisfied contented smile as he piled up their breakfast on the bank. 'Let's face it, Herbie. We haven't none of us got much choice, have we?'

'What about you then, Evan?'

The young man blushed. 'Tell you the truth I've always liked girls with chestnut hair.'

'Oh yes? Like our Vanw, you mean?'

'Uh – yes.'

Herbie laughed. 'Well, ye good God! OK, my boy, as I'm the head of the family you'll have to ask my permission, won't you, so you better get on with catching plenty of fish and I might put in a good word for you!'

Food was their main problem. Some of the men took time away from construction in order to search. They rode their horses sometimes miles down the valley and saw plenty of rheas, the Patagonian ostrich, and guanacos, the Patagonian llama.

Even one of these creatures could have fed them for days, but they seemed impossible to catch. Finally it was decided that time was better spent making simple dwellings rather than chasing after these incredibly fleet-of-foot animals.

Sitting one cold night shrouded in blankets just outside the ruins, Dafydd turned to Glyn. 'Three weeks we've been here. I – I can't think what's been happening back on those cliffs. Myfanwy must have had the baby by now.'

'Don't worry, boy. She'll be all right with the doctor and Blod – and there's Rhiannon, Lisa and Bron. She'll be well away.'

'I'd be happier if I thought the Tehuelches were keeping an eye on them.'

'Yeah! Me, too. Come to think of it, I'd like to see them here. A good fry-up of an ostrich egg suit me fine! '

As if on cue the following morning Chief Kitchkum and his band of Tehuelche Indians rode into the settlement.

The chief dismounted, and Dafydd and Glyn went to greet him.

The tall Indian smiled. '*Bara bara. Muy bien!*'

Everyone laughed.

The Indians walked admiringly round the half-finished timber shack community. Sion, who was trying to learn Spanish, explained they had no '*bara*' – in fact had nothing but fish.

Within half an hour the chief, in a mixture of Spanish and a few English words, was showing them the *bolas* – three long leather lassos each with a stone tied at one end. He first demonstrated how to throw it and made them practise on pieces of wood. He led Trevor and Herbie on horseback showing them how to throw the three cords in such a way that they wound themselves around the legs of even the fleetest creature. This was a life-changing skill they all had to learn. This was survival.

When construction was over for the day, the men saddled up horses and whooped like boys with a new game as they threw the *bolas* – sometimes well, sometimes badly. Within a few days they were good enough to go out rhea-hunting with the Indians.

Rhea steaks were good and nourishing. The Indians brought sacks of maize, an unknown vegetable to the Welsh, and all the herbs for making a tea drink they called *maté*. They were learning to hunt and eat the Patagonian way – and all within a few weeks.

However, there was the constant worry about their defenceless women and children, who could not be left on the coast for too long. They dared not contemplate what might happen if the Araucans found them.

The area around the old fortress was gradually becoming part-worksite and part-newly-erected timber shelters, some with two rooms, depending on the size of the family, and all with corrugated tin roofs.

Windows were going to be a problem with no glass – until Chief Kitchkum provided the solution with transparent sheets of rhea stomach lining. It was strong and fine, perfect for temporary windows.

As Trevor was fixing the skin carefully into the window frame of his shack, he declared loudly, 'Never thought I'd be looking at the world through animal gut.'

They felt safe with the Tehuelches making frequent visits, safe enough for Dafydd to call a meeting after work had finished for the day to decide if they were ready to go back to fetch their families.

'We've got horses for the covered wagons, but how many men can we spare to go and fetch the rest?'

They voted that twenty men, some with the wagons, some on horseback, would make the journey to the coast armed with rifles. Dafydd would go with them, and Glyn would stay behind with those left to finish the timber shacks that were now nearly ready for habitation.

'I suggest, brothers, that we travel through the night – shift work – we don't want another encounter like the last one. Volunteers, please.'

Manny Price, who had been keeping a low profile of late, put his hand up.

'Count me in. I'm used to keeping watch over my flocks by night.' His foxy eyes darted around the group.

'Thank you, Manny. We all know we could count on you in an – emergency,' said Dafydd, taking a leap into the realm of forgiveness. 'And, brothers, I think we can be pleased with what we have done. We have – some of us, me included – learnt to construct timber houses, and, thanks to our Tehuelche friends, hunt guanaco and rhea and make windows out of animal gut. There will be shelter for most of our people, maybe all of them by the time we return. We have fences for the horses and for the livestock if and when it arrives.'

'We'll have the chapel built by the time you come back, that's for sure,' said Glyn.

'Aye, and the minister's and the doctor's house,' added six-foot Evan Davies, known now as Lanky Evan.

There were loud murmurs of assent from the group. It would never be expected that a man of God and the man of medicine should soil their hands with physical labour. Dafydd kept his own counsel on this one.

Chief Kitchkum and his troupe arrived at the settlement as the wagons and men were about to leave. Sion explained they were going to bring back their families.

A broad smile wreathed the chief's face. '*Bara bara!*' he exclaimed, the chant taken up by his acolytes. After a short exchange with them in his new Spanish, Sion laughed. 'They'll be meeting up with you tomorrow, they say. I don't know whether it's to protect you or to collect some more bread!'

At the caves, young Tomos and Huw had been appointed the watchdogs for any activity on the horizon, particularly from the south, the direction their fathers and thirty-eight men had taken when they left. The boys had grown up quickly in this new environment, having to become the men of the family, Tomos especially, with his mother having the baby. He found that a bit embarrassing and ran out of the cave immediately the baby started yelling for a feed.

His sister was another source of embarrassment, because everybody knew that Manny Price had tried it on with her. He didn't mind her making cow eyes at Michael because he liked him and secretly hoped Michael would take Lisa off his hands – though he would have less to worry about when his dad and the others came back. Huw was also waiting for his dad to come back because, though his sister Bron wasn't as bold as Lisa, three women, especially his little sister Elin, were a handful for any growing lad.

After the regular morning service on the beach, with no rain, the boys would make their way to the top of the cliffs. Today Idwal ap Morris came with them. Always wanting to go off and challenge the terrain single-handed, Tomos had been the restraining force.

'You are a caution, you are, Idwal. You know what the Indians have said about the pampas. It's already killed one of us. You stay here, right? When your brother comes back you can explore the whole of Patagonia if he'll let you!'

Idwal laughed. 'Don't worry. I'm rooted to the spot till Herbie comes back.'

There was a cold wind blowing. Tomos took a stroll to stretch his legs while Huw and Idwal huddled under blankets to keep warm.

He peered into the distance. Rubbed his eyes to make sure. And there it was, first a shape, then a number of shapes, and movement on the horizon.

'Huw! Idwal! Come and look, quick! Covered wagons!'

Huw narrowed his eyes. 'We didn't have any covered wagons.'

Idwal, slightly taller than the other two, exclaimed, 'There's men on horseback, too. I reckon it's those Indians.'

'No – it's our men – it's them! Look! They're galloping ahead of the wagons! They've come back!' Tomos shouted 'You two stay here. I'll go and tell everybody!'

He ran, yelling, 'They're back! They're back!' Never had he run so fast.

Within minutes most of the immigrants, led by the doctor, the minister, Michael and Lisa, had formed a welcome party on the clifftop.

Myfanwy had remained in their cave. She wanted her own private reunion with her husband and the baby.

Lisa ran to her father and grabbed his hand. 'Come on, Dadda. Something to show you.'

'Where is your mother? Is she well?'

'She's fine. Come on.'

'Baby? Boy, girl?'

'Mam wants to show you herself.'

She pushed him into the cave and left. Myfanwy ran to her husband's open arms, hugging and embracing. 'You're back! You're back! Thank God! How I've missed you!'

He touched her face tenderly. 'I couldn't live without you, Myfanwy. Wouldn't want to.'

'There's something else to show you.'

He grinned. 'So come on, tell me.'

She stooped down to pick up the sleeping bundle from the box serving as cradle, 'Your new daughter, Dafydd. She is called Bethan.'

Dafydd held out his arms for his new child. Mute, lost for words, he nuzzled the baby close to his face. 'Bethan, Bethan,' he whispered, 'my new little Bethan.'

Putting his arm around Myfanwy, they stood quite still, arms entwined, holding their new baby, tears of joy and remembered sorrow falling from their eyes.

9

Now that every family was sheltered with tin roofs over their heads, Dafydd called a general meeting in the chapel, their community meeting point. Supplies had arrived by the shipload from Buenos Aires. They had grain, flour, sugar, seeds to plant, livestock and poultry. But this first meeting was important, as they would be drawing lots for allocated land.

Will Fiddler, who had always been good at art and Euclid, had drawn a large plan of the terrain available and numbered the equal blocks of land for each household with the exact measurement. Winifred Howells had cut neat squares of paper. On each one was written the name of a family. They were then put into a hat.

Lisa cut up more paper squares and on each one wrote a numbered plot, placing them in another hat. Each member of the elected Senate would in turn draw a name and a plot from the two hats.

Dafydd had taken some time off to work on the outline of his speech and had made lists of what in his opinion the most egalitarian community in the world was going to do. The night before in their cabin lit by candles Myfanwy looked it over.

'It's great, Dav, but don't be disappointed if they don't all feel like you.'

He smiled. 'Got used to that.' He walked over to the crib he had made for Bethan, where she lay soundly asleep, and kissed the small chubby hand. 'But we've been given a chance. Can't throw it away – especially when we've got Welsh Patagonians to think about now.'

At six o'clock on the dot the community trooped into the chapel.

Dafydd, as president, sat with the other members who included the doctor, the minister and Manny Price, all elected on board ship. He proposed they would now officially be called a Senate with ten more members to be voted in, plus their own policeman.

Blod Trehearne put up her hand. 'Are we women still going to have a vote, like you promised? Because if we're not, it's down tools for me.'

'And me.'

'And me,' rose a dozen voices.

Amid laughter they were told, 'Of course – egalitarian society, votes for all over eighteen, elections every three years, and don't forget we would like some women senators, too.'

This caused a disapproving ripple among the chapel die-hards. Government was surely for men.

'Now, questions, please. We have to know your worries before we can work out our community charter.'

The doctor was concerned with health and sanitary arrangements and asked Evan Davies, who was a plumber by trade, 'What do you think, Evan? We need about twenty latrines and a dozen taps for water. With this cold weather we can't be carrying buckets of river water.'

'No indeed, Doctor, so me and a couple of others – we've had a chat and we can put up about twenty latrines covered in the tarpaulins we've got. Each one separated by wooden walls and doors. Taps – no problem. Government supplies have sent enough and a few pipes.'

'Excellent, so you'll start tomorrow morning.'

'Yes, Doctor, but we do have some problems. They haven't sent us any pans, water tanks nor pipes, only one big sewage pipe – so we can't have flushing toilets.' Lanky Evan looked round nervously 'But we can make you beautiful seats.'

'Comfortable, I hope,' came a shout from the hall.

Evan grinned. 'Like velvet, boy. You won't want to get up!'

Fortunately the doctor was an avid historian, so he proposed using the old Roman method for flushing latrines with a constant flow of water from the river along a cement trough running into the latrine block and continuing underneath the toilets, with all waste delivered at the other end into the one large pipe and out into the estuary. No need for pans, cement sides would do, but seats would be advisable. It would have to do for now at any rate.

The plan was accepted, much to the doctor's relief that at least conditions were going to be hygienic. He had heard that Señor Rawson, the settlement's champion, was also a doctor, a possible ally in getting more supplies. Outside taps laid in the centre of the settlement would all have waste conducted into the same main drainage system. They could now keep clean, wash themselves and their clothes. He dreaded the repetition of conditions onboard ship and the possibility of easily carried contagious diseases.

Next came education. Winifred Howells, the mild but strict schoolteacher, had already started writing textbooks in Welsh by hand. School would run every day, Monday to Friday, on one side of the chapel from nine o'clock until four for all children aged three to twelve. The minister's wife, Mrs Jenkins, and two other unmarried women, as before, would help. A blackboard and a supply of chalks had been sent by the government along with Spanish textbooks, which were ignored. The other side of the chapel was their prison with a couple of cells and rifles just in case.

That evening each household left the meeting clutching in their hands their numbered personal allocation of land, vastly more than they could ever have foreseen in their wildest Welsh dreams. Though there was minor quibbling later, this was the fairest way, so no one had real cause for complaint.

So their new lives in Patagonia began. In spring they worked all daylight hours, men and women side by side, digging, planting. There was much to learn, for only a few had any experience of the soil and certainly not such dry, brittle soil. Beyond the wide Chubut was the unending parched pampas standing like the serried ranks of any army waiting to invade.

Despite their hard work, the first summer was so hot that only wheat planted near the river seemed to be growing. And though every plantation was close to the natural water supply, half the wheat shrivelled in the heat.

Nevertheless the community bustled with the positive accessible elements of their lives, like the sounds of livestock, sheep, cows, chickens, dogs, cats, children and song.

Midweek they held a prayer meeting, with melodious hymns from the homeland to give thanks to the Almighty for allowing them to survive, though Dafydd felt more and more uneasy. Something was happening to his hitherto blind faith. It was now tinged with scepticism. In his heart he challenged accepted religious practice and faith and regarded the Nonconformist movement more as a national search for identity. Dafydd was turning the chapel-based dogma he disliked so intensely into his personal political quarry. He dared not disclose this to anyone else, not even to his beloved Myfanwy, not yet anyway.

The problem with the wheat was perplexing, but they had meat, potatoes, maize and *maté*. They could worship every Sunday in their own chapel and in their own language. Life was beginning to be good.

Chief Kitchkum and his braves were now regular visitors. It was clear they wanted bread, so with great sensitivity they brought gifts of rhea feathers and warm capes made from guanaco hide.

'Keep you as warm as toast,' declared Blod to the other women as she paraded in chapel with her new outfit.

The younger ones adorned their plain felt hats with fulsome displays of beautiful feathers arranged rather too coquettishly for some of the 'old chapel hags', as Lisa termed them.

Young Elin and the chief's son, Francisco, were becoming firm playmates. He spoke Spanish to her, and she spoke Welsh to him. Myfanwy loved seeing them laugh and play together, but tears filled her eyes with thoughts of her lost child who should have been there with them.

That the Tehuelches tolerated, even liked, these quiet non-aggressive settlers was a fact, and, though completely bemused by their singing and their folk-dancing, they were sometimes persuaded to join in.

Official communications from Buenos Aires were sent to Sion, since he was the one immigrant who had met government ministers and, more to the point, one of the few who showed some command of Spanish. One morning he ran with speed to Dafydd's shack. He had received a letter from the Minister of the Interior, Señor Guillermo Rawson. He would be coming to meet the new community in two weeks. Reading his credentials, Sion whistled through his teeth.

'He's not only a doctor, Dav, he's a doctor of hygiene.'

This visit was going to be important. Without Señor Rawson's understanding up to this point, and his compliance with their demands, survival on any level would have been doubtful. He would be sailing into the estuary and then riding with a number of government officials into the settlement. A community meeting was called in the chapel.

'It will be an important day for us, brothers and sisters, when Señor Rawson visits us for the first time. Our little community is swelling in number,' Dafydd announced as his eyes swept across the benches, causing the few pregnant married women to lower their eyes modestly. 'You may not know that Señor Rawson is a medical doctor, like our Dr Williams, and his speciality is hygiene, and I know he won't be disappointed. This visit means we are being recognized as a separate state within the Argentine. Could we have imagined that, even a year ago? There is no need for us to be reminded that we all have to make his visit memorable, so that Señor Rawson returns to Buenos Aires with nothing but praise for us, the new colonists. Now then – ideas and suggestions, please.'

Blod Trehearne put up her hand. 'We'll all pitch in with Welsh cakes, *teisen lap* and bread for him.'

'What about *cawl*? He's bound to like that.'

There was a chorus from the women.

Glyn, who had now been voted in as community policeman, rose to his feet. 'We're talking about what we are going to give him to eat. Fine. Dafydd has been talking about us as a recognized community, but, I ask you, who are we, where are we? Yes, I know we are in Patagonia, but where is this settlement? I think it's about time we gave it a name.'

This suggestion met with obvious approval, for the names came in thick and fast.

'Mountain Ash.'

'Aberystwyth.'

'Gowerton.'

'Machynlleth.'

'Rhondda Fach.'

Glyn held up his hand to subdue the enthusiasm and laughed. 'You see we'll never agree if we look for a name from the old country, because we all come from different parts of it. I have a suggestion. There will be other settlements by and by, but why don't we call this one, our very first, after the man who made it possible for us to survive: Rawson?'

There was a moment's pause for reflection. Then hands shot up in approval. Rawson it would be.

'Any other ideas for the visit?'

Will Fiddler proposed a concert with a children's choir, which he would rehearse and conduct. The Reverend Jenkins, on the podium, rose and suggested a service in chapel for the visiting Señor Rawson, never dreaming his wishes were about to be questioned.

Lisa, sitting at the back with Bron, Michael and Sion, had been waiting for an opportunity to challenge this man for months. She stood up. There was a distinct shuffling of feet as heads turned in anticipation. Myfanwy shut her eyes and prayed. Dafydd looked at his notes.

'No, I don't think you can do that, minister.' She spoke loudly and clearly.

A perceptible gasp arose from the audience. What would this girl say next?

'After all,' she continued,' this man is not chapel like us, is he? He is a Roman Catholic. We wouldn't want him to shove his religion down our throats, would we? I'm sure you wouldn't, Reverend. So why should we do it to him? Why don't we just have a *cymanfa ganu* for him?'

As she sat down there was a little round of applause led by Blod Trehearne. Myfanwy sighed with relief. Dafydd smiled to himself. The Reverend was being kept firmly out of politics. The idea was carried unanimously.

The last one to make a suggestion was Lanky Evan. 'I'm speaking as a plumber now. This man is important in the government and important to us, right? And because he's a doctor and a hygiene expert he's got to have proper toilet facilities.'

'He'll have a proper one on his boat, Evan,' muttered Herbie.

'I know, but he's bound to be taken short if he's here for the day. Anyway he'll want to see how we're managing. So now, what I suggest is we give him the first latrine and mark it "Señor Rawson".'

'Why not the last one?' shouted Trevor Trehearne from the back.

Evan had already thought this out. 'Because – because, unless you close off all the latrines while he's using his, he'll have to watch the whole . . . er . . . what-d'you-call . . . run past below him, and he is hygiene, isn't he? So giving him the first one means we can keep them open for everybody and he only sees his own – um – um what-d'you-call, isn't it?'

Despite the smiles and sniggers, there was no challenging Lanky Evan's logic.

'The other thing is paper. No good using our weekly news-sheet, because his hands, poor dab, will be black as coal. Anybody got any ideas?'

'Calico,' someone shouted.

It was agreed that small squares of calico, washed and ironed, would be secured to a nail on the back of the Rawson latrine.

Within a few days a shortlist of possible senators had been posted up on the noticeboard outside the chapel. It included several women. The results of the voting made Will Fiddler, Evan Davies, Herbie ap Morris, Winifred Howells, Blod Trehearne, Michael Edwards and Sion Williams new members of the Senate.

The day arrived. At about eleven o'clock word came that three ships were pulling into harbour.

Lisa was curious. 'Why three, Dadda? Only him and a few officials, isn't it?'

'They'll have their horses won't they?'

By twelve o'clock the community, dressed in their Sunday best, gathered in the open space outside the all-purpose chapel centre on the other side of the water taps and latrines. Facing the small crowd, the carpenters had erected a podium on which had been placed twenty-one chairs. The children's choir stood fidgeting near Mrs Jenkins at the harmonium waiting for Will Fiddler to raise his hand.

They would welcome the Señor first with song, followed by an opening address given by Dafydd in the chapel in which he would announce the new name of their settlement. There would be time for a reply from Dr Rawson – he spoke good English, they said – before the women served up the *cawl* on rather crude-looking long tables lined up outside the chapel. In the afternoon he would meet people and then, to crown it all, a *cymanfa ganu* followed by tea and Welsh cakes. There remained only the inauguration ceremony where the village would officially be born; and they wanted the Señor to perform the honours.

Members of the Senate made their way to the podium in readiness for the great man's arrival, while Dafydd, Glyn and Sion waited just outside the compound to escort Señor Guillermo Rawson into the new settlement.

Glyn turned to Dafydd, 'Pity we haven't got the flagpole up.'

'No matter. We can do it after the ceremony. Better.'

Señor Dr Guillermo Rawson was of medium height with a moustache and a short beard that cushioned his chubby jaw. He greeted the assembly with smiles and courtesy. It was plain to see he was delighted with the results of his endeavours. He applauded the children's choir with great enthusiasm and responded to Dafydd's welcome speech in an English that most of the settlers understood. He was honoured that the settlement should carry his name and looked forward to an excellent Welsh meal.

There was one puzzling feature of his visit that no one had envisaged. Fifty fully equipped Argentinian soldiers arrived with Señor Rawson and formed a semi-circle behind the podium.

Lisa looked at Michael. 'So that's why there were three ships. Did you know they were sending troops in?'

'No.'

'What are they doing here?'

'Just an escort for a government minister. Normal.'

Señor Rawson spoke at length in private to Dr Williams about hygiene and public health.

'Don't worry, Dr Williams, I shall make sure you will have the equipment you require. With the usual government protocol, delivery will take a few weeks. Meanwhile I congratulate you upon your Roman sanitation – admirable improvisation.' He smiled. 'Quite ingenious.'

After the singing, and copious tea, came the moment they had been waiting for, the inauguration of the community. A flagpole appeared from somewhere in the ranks and was taken in military style to a spot near the chapel where it was firmly fixed into the ground.

Señor Rawson made his formal speech naming the town Rawson. There was so much cheering and clapping it was several moments before the excited settlers realized it was the Argentinian flag that was being hoisted aloft by a couple of soldiers, followed by a drum roll. A gradual mesmerized silence fell over the hitherto excited crowd.

The officer-in-charge barked a command. Troops stood to attention clicked their heels, presented arms and saluted the flag. Another drum roll, then the Argentinian National Anthem was sung by the military and Señor Rawson's group. There followed a deathly silence.

Something had gone terribly wrong. Where was their new Wales? Suddenly from the back of the crowd Will Fiddler played the opening bars of 'Mae hen wlad fy nhadau'. Together their voices rang out with defiance, pride and passion, after which there was total silence.

Señor Rawson left with half the soldiers unaware of the animosity this unnecessary manifestation of Argentine nationalism had created. As for the remaining troops, they had no intention of going anywhere in the immediate future, for their tents were pitched just outside the community's compound.

That night Dafydd sat at the table writing in his diary. 'Our small community now has a name: Rawson. But are we still counted as Welsh? Do we have our little Wales? Or are we now a part of the Argentine as we were part of England? Time will tell.'

10

The immigrants were angry, particularly the younger ones. Why should they have to accept this blatant disregard of the promises that brought them here in the first place? The elected Senate met to discuss the situation. A general meeting followed.

Every adult had something to say, and it was some time before Dafydd could calm tempers for a sensible discussion to take place.

'Are we sure the Argentinian government remembers their promises?' asked a frowning Trevor Trehearne.

'We'll have to remind them, won't we?' replied his wife from the podium.

'Aye, in Welsh!' shouted an angry voice.

'And why have we got troops here?'

Dafydd stood up. 'Look, no one feels more insulted than I do after the snub to our national identity, and something has to be done about it. But we have come to the conclusion that it was unintentional.'

'The flag's not unintentional, is it?' shouted someone at the back of the hall.

Voices raised in anger now threw questions at the bewildered senators sitting on the podium like coconuts at a fairground. The situation was getting out of hand, but Dafydd insisted, 'I think we must all try to remember that we are in fact in the Argentine, and they have a right to fly their flag.'

'No they damn well haven't.'

'We're supposed to be in Patagonia, aren't we?'

'Aye, Welsh Patagonia.'

'What's behind all this?'

'They are not giving us these goods for the sake of their health, are they?'

'And why did they want us here in the first place?'

'There's something going on, there is.'

'Ask them soldiers. Why are they here?'

Glyn conferred with Dafydd, who this time attempted to calm the assembly by shouting above the cacophony of voices.

'As your senators – as your senators – we intend to find out the reasons why Rawson has an unexpected military presence. At our next meeting we hope to have all our questions answered.'

Will Fiddler remembered something from his schooldays; Shakespeare it was – something about music soothing the troubled breast. He grabbed his violin and beckoned to Mrs Jenkins, who quickly sat at the harmonium. They launched into a well-loved traditional folk song.

It was irresistible. The effect was like a drug, the timing perfect. Voices soared, and anger had been successfully diffused. But Dafydd knew it was only for now. They could have a serious problem on their hands. Argentinian law had to be upheld if they were going to survive.

As they left the chapel Lisa beckoned to Bron. 'I've got an idea,' she whispered. 'Get Huw and Tomos. I'll wait here for Sion and Michael. Five minutes.'

Just before midnight the six young people crept quietly out of their shacks and met up behind the chapel. There had been no soldier in sight since the meeting dispersed but now four appeared, patrolling aimlessly around the settlement.

'Listen,' whispered Lisa. 'Michael and me, Sion and Bron will go and chat to those soldiers. Got the flag, Huw?'

'Oh, aye, don't you worry. Me and Tomos will be up that pole like greased lightning.'

Tomos grinned 'We know exactly what to do.'

'But you've got to keep them talking and over the other side if you can.'

Bron patted her brother on the back. 'Don't worry, our Huw. Sion'll be talking Spanish to them.'

'Right then,' said Lisa. 'Let's go.'

No sooner had the two couples distracted the soldiers in conversation, mostly about their lives in Buenos Aires, than the two boys were shinning up the flagpole. They tore down the Argentinian flag and quickly substituted the Red Dragon.

It was done quietly and efficiently. The four soldiers on patrol, completely engrossed in conversation, with Sion translating as best he could, had no idea of what was taking place under their noses.

Unfortunately two more soldiers had just come on duty. Seeing their national flag thrown to the ground, they watched in horror from the cover of a thicket. The two boys, delighted with their daring escapade, ran straight into the waiting arms of the military. Getting caught had not been on the agenda.

Glyn, as law enforcer, was summoned immediately, as was Dafydd, and by now half the settlement had left their beds to see what the noise was about. Arresting his own son and the chairman's son in front of the startled crowd with the other three young men, two of whom were members of the Senate, was mortifying. As no prison provision had ever been made for women, Lisa and Bron were ignored, though Dafydd was quite sure his daughter had been an inspirational voice in all of this.

They were sentenced to three days in prison, the small wooden sheds erected at the side of the chapel. Each prisoner would be given different passages from the Bible to learn by heart, to be selected by the Reverend Jenkins and chosen carefully to put the fear of God into transgressors.

Heads lowered, they were marched away into incarceration by an armed guard, with not a word exchanged. From somewhere came the sound of clapping.

It grew quietly at first then rose to a wild crescendo and shouts of:

'We are on your side, boys.'

'You did it for all of us.'

'Well done, lads.'

The soldiers could take no more. After all, their nation's flag had been insulted.

They began to disperse the crowd using elbows and shoulders.

'It'll be rifle butts soon! I'm going to talk to that major – he speaks English.'

As Dafydd walked towards the officer, Glyn called, 'Careful what you say.'

Major Gonzales was a stocky, well-built man with a pugnacious jaw, but Dafydd was in no mood to pussyfoot around this representative of Argentinian authority.

'I would like a word with you, Major, if you please.'

The Major appeared somewhat displeased at this further interruption to his night's sleep. He huffed, 'Very well, Señor – uh Señor – ?'

'Rhys. I am the community's chairman, and first of all I would like to apologize on behalf of the culprits. They meant no offence, no disrespect, Major. It remains simply a question of establishing our own identity in addition to yours, not instead of it.'

The officer clearly did not like civilian interference, but before he could reply Dafydd continued, 'In order to avoid any unpleasantness and to live harmoniously, as indeed we have shown with Señor Rawson's visit, may I suggest our Welsh Dragon flies from the chapel?'

It seemed to Dafydd the Major was searching for a reason to disagree, to establish military law without question or compromise.

'After all, Major, you are surely not an army of occupation. Or are you?'

Though the officer looked momentarily shocked at this suggestion, he was also aware that there were limits as to what he could and should impose upon invited immigrants like these Welsh. He knew that in the event of invasion or skirmishes with neighbouring Chile he would need their manpower and cooperation. Mustering a smile, he replied, 'Señor Rhys, I know what young people do without thinking of the consequences and that their intention was to fly your flag rather than insult ours. Of course we must live together in harmony, so,' he paused, searching for a reply that was not capitulation, 'unless I receive orders to the contrary, for the moment you may fly your wild dragon from your chapel.'

The following morning the prisoners were brought outside, before the settlement and by all fifty soldiers. Tension was high.

Not a word was uttered as the four young people took down their beloved dragon and replaced the Argentinian flag. The settlers glared, sullen, resentful. Surely a crime had not been committed? Flying their own flag was something they all wanted, all shared. Where was the harm?

An Argentinian soldier marched smartly up to the four culprits, snatched the Welsh flag ungraciously from their hands and presented it to the Major who in turn handed it to Dafydd and Glyn standing close by. Herbie Morris then appeared from nowhere carrying a flagpole, followed by Lanky Evan.

The crowd watched anxiously as the two men dug the pole into position next to the chapel. Taking the flag, they hoisted it high amid loud cheers and applause. Will Fiddler struck up the National Anthem. The soldiers stood to attention. The Major saluted. The immigrants sang, some had tears in their eyes. Dafydd had stood firm and identity had been restored. But there were no extenuating circumstances for the four prisoners; three days on meagre rations it would remain, the Major had insisted.

Later that evening Lisa and Bron collected bread and meat for the hungry captives, and, after ensuring the soldiers on guard duty were occupied chatting to a few unmarried girls, they stood on tiptoe outside each of the prison shacks and pushed food through the small open windows.

But tonight Lisa had other thoughts.

Ever since the days on the beach, she and Michael had been developing their obvious mutual attraction and were growing closer. It was clear to see Michael was in love with her, but each time they found themselves alone Lisa would respond only to his kisses. She rejected anything more.

'But I love you, Lisa,' he would say. 'I want to marry you.'

She would sigh and kiss him tenderly. 'I know – I know, and I love you, too, and I want to marry you – but no more – not yet.'

It was only Bron who knew why.

'How can I tell him, Bron, about Manny Price?'

'P'raps he knows already?'

'If he does, he thinks I'm easy then, doesn't he? That's why I can't – can't . . .'

'Go any further than spooning, you mean?'

'Yes! Oh, Bron, I'm afraid.'

'Just because you were attacked by that animal – what difference will that make? Michael loves you. Nothing to be afraid of.'

'Bron *fach*, don't you see? I'm not what he'll expect, am I? Not now. And I'm afraid to tell him in case he changes his mind – that's why. And after that pig – well, I'm scared, too. Don't know if I want to be touched at all – know what I mean?'

'Now you listen to me, Lisa Rhys. The fact that you are not a virgin any more, through no fault of your own, shouldn't make a scrap of difference to Michael if he really loves you. So you have got to tell him exactly what happened. If he goes, then you are well rid of him, that's what I say. And, as for you – tell him how you feel about being touched – stands to reason you do, and if Michael's got any sense he'll understand that, too. And, look, there's no hurry is there? Take your time. Mother Nature will let you know when you are ready. See?'

Lisa smiled, 'Didn't know you had so much common sense, our Bron!'

Bron chuckled. 'Now – promise me you'll tell him. All right?'

Though Lisa had agreed, no firm date for this important disclosure had been mentioned. But tonight seemed the perfect opportunity.

With her chin on the window ledge of Michael's prison shed, their mouths met, their hearts raced.

'Come on out,' she whispered.

'Where are the guards?'

'Miles away – jawing to some girls. Don't worry.'

'Keep a look-out while I squeeze through.'

Within a few minutes they were hand in hand, stealing stealthily into the short grassy fringes of the pampas surrounding the settlement, well out of sight of prying eyes.

It was a beautiful night, the moon large and clear. Lisa put her shawl on the grass. One passionate embrace after another, and eventually they were lying side by side under an ultramarine sky. It jolted Lisa's memory of that terrible night on deck. Heart thumping with fear of what could happen, she broke away from Michael and sat up.

'What's the matter, *cariad*?'

'Something – something I have to tell you, Michael.'

He smiled. 'Don't look so frightened. It can't be that bad', and he tried to pull her back down to him.

Shrugging him off she said, 'No, Michael, no. Listen to me. I'm not what you think. I'm not – a virgin. Manny Price attacked me on board ship – and – and he . . .' She began to weep. 'He was horrible, horrible!'

Michael quickly gathered her in his arms. 'It's all right, *cariad* – it's all right. Hush now. Hush! I know, well, I guessed – something – I'd heard rumours – from the start.'

'They are true. He did attack me – not just try it on. Nobody knows except Bron – and now you.'

'The bastard. I'd like to kill him.'

Stifling her sobs, she looked at him in bewilderment. 'If you knew, then why didn't you say something to me?'

He took out his handkerchief and carefully dried her eyes. 'Why? Well, Lisa, my lovely girl, I thought it would upset you – bringing back bad memories. Besides, it was in the past. I could kill him for what he did to you, but it's not important to us, is it?'

'But I can't marry you now – don't you see?'

'Lisa Rhys, it's the first time I've heard you talk such rubbish! Now you listen to me. You are important. We are important. And if you let this bloody man come between us then he will have won. An animal like that, he mustn't destroy us. Don't let him, Lisa. Please!'

She felt a weight lifting from her heart. Touching his cheek, she whispered, 'Michael, I won't let anything or anybody destroy us – ever. I love you so much.'

'That's better. So will you marry me?'

'Tomorrow! But you'd better ask my father.'

Their embraces became more and more passionate and all memories of Manny Price, of physical pain, of disgust with his odorous body, of self-disgust, slowly began to dissolve in overwhelming and unstoppable waves of desire for Michael.

He was tender, gentle and patient – aware of how much she had suffered. And of how difficult any physicality was going to be. But slowly she surrendered her trusting body to him, unafraid, and found out how easy and pleasurable real love could be.

Miraculously they each returned without being seen, he to prison through the small aperture, she to the family shack, both floating on a warm cloud of requited love.

11

Michael and Lisa sat waiting anxiously for her father's verdict on their marriage plans, watching every movement of his face as he frowned and stood quite still pondering for several minutes.

'Very well,' he said at last. 'But when she's eighteen.'

Lisa leapt to her feet and hugged her father. 'Thank you, Dadda! Thank you! And I can vote at the same time,' she laughed.

Myfanwy looked both happy and relieved, for she knew things must be going on between her daughter and Michael – all those evening strolls along the river. Privately she was keeping her fingers crossed that Lisa wouldn't suddenly stop 'seeing' and that Michael used common sense and restraint, like his future father-in-law.

The young lovers beamed with joy. Embraces and enthusiastic handshakes followed.

Tomos, who had been waiting outside with his toddling sister, was summoned, and they all sat together over a pot of tea and Welsh cakes to make plans for Rawson's first wedding eight months hence. Just time enough for Michael to build a house, of bricks this time. He had his sights set on a higher piece of his own grazing land overlooking the settlement. News of the first wedding spread quickly and brought in offers of help and contributions along with the congratulations.

'Myfanwy *fach*, there's happy I am for you and especially for your Lisa. I can still see her little face after that swine Price. *Ychafi*, there's no way I could ever like that man.' She paused. 'Scraggy and ugly he is, but I'll say this, fair play – if it hadn't been for Manny Price p'raps we wouldn't have our husbands here now.'

Blod Trehearne sat heavily on one of the Rhys family's wooden chairs.

Myfanwy smiled. 'Exactly what Dav says. Manny Price – not short on courage, that one.'

'Must be hard on Dafydd. There's a man who tries it on with his daughter then saves his life. Takes some working out that does.'

Myfanwy nodded. 'I think he's done that.'

'Hope it's not through Redemption and God's will again – all you get with some of them.'

Though Blod could be trusted beyond doubt, Myfanwy was anxious to leave the diminishing degree of her husband's religious fervour to Dafydd himself. She kept her own counsel but knew that being seen to toe the Reverend Jenkins line in so young a community was obligatory, for the moment.

'But whatever, Lisa's lucky she's found Michael. We've been worried about her – being so young and how she would feel about – well, men.'

'Good God, yes – enough to turn any young woman! Never mind – be all right now. Michael's a good boy he is.' Blod rose from the chair and made her way to the door. 'I'll be getting her some Indian petticoats – beautiful they are. What about her frock?'

Putting her fingers to her lips Myfanwy whispered. 'I've got a lovely cream linen sheet of my mam's – never used – huge. It'll work a treat and one of the Griffiths sisters has promised a few yards of lace – she's started on it already.'

Blod smiled warmly. 'There we are then, Myfanwy *fach* – all work out lovely it will. *Duwedd Mawr*, it's going to do us the world of good this wedding.'

The following day, Maisie Jones, the best pastry cook in the community – she had worked in an English mansion – started on the wedding cake. 'The mix should be left for a year, mind, but eight months will have to do,' she chirped.

Adhering to the cooperative spirit in all things, Michael not only enlisted help for his house building but others began making plans to do likewise. This was largely due to Señor Rawson's promised delivery of building materials and sanitary equipment which would be sufficient for all members of the community to be housed securely in brick houses with outside privies.

Already, clustering piles of bricks were gathering, a distance away from the first shacks but near enough to be counted as part of Rawson.

Though the building of a new community with solid foundations could be started, they were being kept alive for the moment by the Argentinian government. The harvest had been bad, crops shrivelled in the searing dryness that no one had warned them about. What use was land when it produced stubble? Of what use were heads of cattle and flocks of sheep without sufficient good pasture? These were the questions everyone was asking.

'Know what I think? Them – those in Buenos Aires wouldn't have any more idea than us poor buggers how to make this soil produce.'

Glyn and Dafydd were strolling together along the pampas edge watching the youngsters ride their horses, some bareback and with such confidence as they galloped and cantered. Young Elin and Francisco, Chief Kitchkum's son, were even tossing balls to each other.

Dafydd nodded. 'Too true.'

'Maybe that's why they sent us here, Dav, guinea-pigs to tame the desert.'

'A buffer against Chile, I'd say. They haven't long had their independence from Spain, have they? So stands to reason they've got to seal the frontiers.'

Dafydd paused for a moment, 'Would you go back, Glyn?'

The two men stopped in their tracks and looked at each other. This was a question that could be asked only of those who could bear to acknowledge the reality of their plight. For Dafydd, the memory of Captain Vaughan's descriptions and warnings about the terrain were undermining and uncomfortable. Thoughts like this were tantamount to treason.

'Well, straight now, would you?' he repeated.

'For me,' said Glyn, after moments of thoughtful silence, 'p'raps I would. But, see, when I look at those youngsters over there, healthy, playing as they never could have played in Merthyr, I wouldn't. For them, isn't it?'

Dafydd threw an arm over his old friend's shoulders.

'Aye aye. Their future it is, and whatever happens we have to keep remembering that. There's many a night I can't sleep, thinking I should have told everybody what Captain Vaughan said, not only you.'

Glyn huffed. 'Come on, Dav – where's your sense gone, boy? We'd given up everything, sold all we had, hadn't we? What could we go back to? Nothing!' He sighed. 'No! It came all too late, but we'll make it work, Dav – we will.'

Despite the privations, local husbandry was constantly making efforts to be as self-sufficient as possible. A couple of the women started their own dairy, making cheese and butter. Herbie's younger brother Idwal had worked for a time with a blacksmith in Carmarthen. With so many horses to shoe, he was becoming the source of supply for both Welsh and Indians, who were very taken with his forged iron *bolas* that proved more effective than stones when hunting. But yet another crisis seemed to be looming.

There was such dissatisfaction some had even talked about getting the next ship back to Liverpool, but for the moment the community's first wedding was a welcomed diversion.

One dusky evening as Michael made his way back to his shack from the building site, he was aware of movement in the bushes lining his path. Suddenly Manny Price materialized out of nowhere and began walking with him. As these two had exchanged barely a word since *The Mimosa* landed, especially after Michael learnt what had happened on board ship to his Lisa, he was somewhat surprised at this sudden appearance.

'Good evening, Mr Edwards.'

'Oh? Manny Price, is it?'

'The very same. House getting on all right then?'

'Yes, good, thanks – windows in tomorrow.'

'So you'll have it finished – for the princess?'

Michael could feel his muscles tautening. How dare this scoundrel mention Lisa. He tried to quicken his pace to avoid any confrontation.

Price quickened his.

'Er – princess, who do you mean?'

'Don't you try and come the lah-de-dah with me, boyo. I've fucked your girl before you – good and hard – know that? I was the first. Loved every minute of it, she did. Beggin' for more. So I hope you've got enough for her. Look a bit short on length to me.' He cackled. '*Duw*, man, those tits she got . . .'

He didn't finish the sentence. In a blind rage Michael stopped and swung him a thumping right hook. Manny Price fell, reeling. Glowering, he got up and rubbed his jaw.

'I'll bloody get you for this, Michael Edwards. You wait!'

Michael, who stood an inch taller than Price, grabbed him by his shirt collar. He could barely speak with rage. 'You just keep your filthy mouth shut about my future wife then. Understand?' he hissed. 'Or you'll cop another one on the other side. And you won't get up so quick next time either.'

Manny Price jerked himself free and turned away. 'Oh yeah? We'll see about that,' he shouted. 'Indeed we will!'

Michael was trembling. It had been a long time since he had practised the boxing skills taught him by his uncle in the Rhondda. That night he made sure the doors and windows of his timber hut were fully secured. He mentioned nothing about the incident to anyone.

During the following weeks, tools and supplies began to disappear from the house site.

Sion, helping his friend, scratched his head. 'That's the second hammer I've lost this week. You haven't seen one, have you, Mike?'

'You seen a bag of sand?'

Together they made a list of missing items. Sion wanted Michael to have a word with Glyn.

'No, mun, not worth it. Not yet anyway. Only bits we've lost. Sure to be somebody taken short of building stuff.'

'Indians, p'raps?'

'I doubt it – they wouldn't steal. Don't need sand to build tents, do they?'

Walking to his building site that morning, having put the windows in the day before, Michael felt happy and proud that he was a making a home for the girl he loved. Up to now she had been forbidden to visit because he wanted to keep progress a big surprise. But tonight – yes, he would bring her up to see it. As he approached, he noticed mounds of glass and wood scattering the pathway. Something was wrong. He and Sion and any of the others who dropped in to help were tidy workers who always cleared up. They never left a mess.

He rushed through the door space and stood rooted, motionless, aghast at what he saw. Every window that had been so painstakingly put in had been smashed – even the frames were crudely torn away. Over the two floors of the small house, glass had been strewn everywhere. A sledgehammer had been used to severely gash new brick walls. It was unbelievable; impossible that this could happen within their new community.

The young man sat down with his head in his trembling hands. Tears trailed down his cheeks, until his initial despair gave way to a savage rage. He knew who was responsible for this. It had to be Manny Price and his cohorts, and he had a fair number of them. No doubt now it was they who had been responsible for the petty pilfering that had been systematically carried out.

With two months to the wedding, the house was becoming the community's showpiece, so it was inevitable that news of the catastrophe spread. There were plenty of explanations, and privately gossip flourished. The finger generally pointed to Manny Price, but to talk about what happened on board ship between him and Lisa Rhys would have been a little insensitive at this particular time. Some even thought the event on board was the result of a lovers' quarrel between Lisa Rhys and Manny Price and he was so jealous of her intended that he roughed up her new house. As there were only two people in the community privy to the facts, conjecture gave rise to the most colourful interpretations.

That evening Michael was obliged to inform the community's policeman. There were difficulties in questioning everybody, but Glyn immediately proposed a few night watchmen to patrol around the house to protect the repairs that were to start the following day. They decided, along with Dafydd, that the Argentinian soldiers still camped outside Rawson performing their nightly routine watch should on no account be involved. It would reflect badly on the immigrants and perhaps affect the government's attitude toward them.

To Manny Price, Lisa Rhys was the bitch who had told on him, the bitch who had tried to shame him. He vowed then he would never forget nor would he ever forgive. And the same went for that goody-goody father of hers.

Michael was relieved that the house would now be protected at night. He had no intention of telling anyone, not even Sion, much less Glyn, about the right hook to Manny Price's jaw weeks before. Protecting Lisa was paramount. He had persuaded her and the family that damage to the house had been caused by vandals, probably a roaming Andean Indian tribe. Lisa kept her own counsel.

Though the community's women bustled with wedding activity there was a palpable unease among the men. Manny Price and his gang had taken to swaggering past the Argentinian guards joking and swearing, unless of course the Reverend Jenkins happened to be within earshot.

Myfanwy was worried for the young couple but said nothing, and Dafydd refused to be drawn into any sort of discussion, so she busied herself with dressmaking, for the bride, for herself and for the little one.

As she sewed, her head bent over Lisa's dress, she had time to think, time to remember. The more she remembered, the tighter the coils in her stomach wound; so tight she wanted to scream. But she didn't.

She couldn't. She remembered the morning her other Bethan clattered down the stairs of the old house in her new smock. She could see her face, hear her voice and her laughter as she played in the field with old Gors or sat on Dadcu's lap. And her father; how she wished she could see him, catch the comforting smell of his tobacco wafting in from the garden. So often tears dropped silently on to her nimble fingers as she stitched. She knew these memories had to be shut away; they were no good to anyone.

This was Lisa's wedding, her future with Michael, and that was just it.

The future was what counted now, not the past. The past was over.

With only three weeks to go, all arrangements for the music and the food had been organized. Lisa's dress was all but finished, just some last-minute fittings for the hem. Lisa herself was in a dizzy delirium of happiness. She could barely wait.

Dafydd laughed. 'That girl doesn't know which day it is!'

Myfanwy playfully put an arm round his waist. 'She's in love, Dav – don't you remember?'

''Course I do,' he grinned.

Michael had promised her their house would be completely ready – furniture, everything. In fact being the first to get married they were not only given all the surplus from community households but some of the carpenters had helped Michael make tables, chairs and a sideboard.

'My little palace it'll be, Michael,' sighed Lisa.

'And I'm going to carry you over the front step, so I'm glad you're not fat!'

'Not yet, Michael Edwards,' she replied slyly. 'Give me a few months!'

Meanwhile others were also starting to build, now the prospective newlyweds' home was pretty well finished. Painting the interior of the little house was all that was left, something Michael had not done before, and Lisa wanted pink and green. He need not have worried, Herbie ap Morris, who knew how to mix distemper and had done a fair amount of decorating, offered it as a wedding present.

'The Chief will give me Lisa's colours, don't you worry, boy – knows where to find the leaves and berries. Look at his ponchos!' he laughed.

In the last two weeks Michael began clearing the land around the house. The soil was dry, not as bad as lower down, but he wanted to make a small kitchen garden for Lisa to manage when he was out tending the animals and the crops. He worked until Glyn's night watchmen appeared – no one was taking any chances.

Rawson was a fifteen-minute trek away down into the valley, and tonight he wished he could have stayed in his new house. Despite being young and strong, Michael was beginning to feel the strain of unremitting labour and so little in the way of crop production to show for it.

It was a balmy evening. Below him the powerful river nosed its way to the sea, and, in the very far distance behind him, the foothills of the magnificent snow-capped Andes were just visible He smiled to himself at the thought of the wedding and Lisa. If only they could collectively solve the problem of the land, their only future, how good life would be.

Lost in his thoughts, he heard nothing but suddenly felt a sharp stinging blow to his right shoulder that felled him. Three men dressed in black converged upon him. Two had black scarves tied across their faces, the other one, wearing a red scarf and a black sombrero, delivered blows to his stomach and face. Punched repeatedly in the back and aching from his stomach blows, Michael valiantly tried to stand, but his shoulder was wrenched back so fiercely it forced him down again.

He shouted at them, but no sound escaped their lips save grunting noises delivered with each blow to their defenceless victim. Who were they these mute assailants? He could feel his eyes swelling up and the taste of blood in his mouth. He tried once more to stand. There was no power left in his right arm, only a sharp sickening pain. He tried to fend off more blows with his left arm, but the pain in his rib cage was too much. Finally he fell again, his body throbbing, his head swimming, his eyes seeing nothing but an enveloping cavernous black.

12

Lisa was inconsolable; the community severely shaken. 'Why?' was the word on everyone's lips. As to who had perpetrated this outrage nothing was said, though it was guessed that Manny Price was implicated.

Michael would survive, but it could take months. For the moment he had been moved to the safety of Dr Williams's house, where Blod Trehearne took over the duties of nurse.

He had been found at dawn, hours after the attack, semi-conscious, having lost a quantity of blood. Dr Williams immediately made contact with the army. He needed the urgent help of an orthopaedic man, supplies of bandage and plaster of Paris. Meanwhile, two broken ribs, a fractured collarbone and a broken leg were diagnosed. Michael's stomach, having been used as a punchbag for fists and boots, was severely bruised, though at this stage the doctor could not tell whether his spleen had been damaged. Speed was of the essence. Thankfully a suitable doctor was contacted at an army post far nearer Rawson than the capital.

Dr Williams had done what was immediately possible with the broken limbs. Attempting to realign cracked bones was excruciatingly painful for the young man and a testing time for the doctor, for he knew that the merest fraction of misalignment could result in a permanent handicap. He had bathed and sutured Michael's ear and around his eyes. Despite extreme care it had still meant unavoidable pain for the patient. Blod had thoughtfully placed large pieces of steak over the bruises. She also made sure there was plenty of liver in his daily diet 'to make up for the loss of blood. So don't you worry, my boy. We'll get those wicked devils, we will.' Though Lisa and Myfanwy principally saw to his food, the support with donations of food from the community was overwhelming. The young bride-to-be sat at her beloved's bedside all day. She would like to have remained with him every night watching over his broken body, but the Reverend declared it would not have been seemly. Myfanwy thought this quite ridiculous.

'Honestly, Dav, in his state what on earth can they get up to? I ask you.'

Dafydd scowled. 'Men of God have very suspicious minds, Myvi *fach*, probably reflecting their own weaknesses. They like their flock to obey. Gives them power.'

Though in pain Michael was able to describe to Glyn and Dafydd the few images he could remember. Dr Williams would not let them talk to the boy for too long, so details were obviously going to take time to put together.

Within a couple of days Dr Williams had the assistance he needed in the person of Dr Juan Castro, who had brought what was required. The Argentine doctor rubbed the plaster of Paris into yards of bandage, soaked it in water, then both doctors carefully set the broken bones but bound Michael's rib cage with calico. When the plaster casts dried off they were heavy, cumbersome and restricting, but at this moment Michael was barely fit to move from his bed.

The common bond of medicine between the two doctors, rather than language, gave them an amicable understanding. It had to be said the handsome, raven-haired Dr Castro caused ripples of excitement whenever he walked abroad – and not only with the young unmarried women.

This unprovoked attack raised serious concerns, and it was only after two weeks of gentle questioning that Glyn and Dafydd were able to glean from Michael some information about the masked men. It was agreed that in this sort of attack the assailants would generally speak in order to intimidate or to goad. Why had they been silent?

'Has to mean they were our own people and Michael would have recognized their voices.'

Dafydd thought for a moment. 'They were dressed as bandits, and they could have been. A black hat; scarves over their faces; not wanting to attract attention.'

Glyn shook his head. 'No, I'm sure they were our people. Bandits would have robbed him, but he lost nothing; and one of them with a hat to cover his hair? There's only one person who would need to do that, and I don't have to tell you who.'

Dafydd sighed 'Aye aye, I know – but we have no proof. None.'

In fact Manny Price had been most sympathetic about Michael's injuries, and though he had not visited the sick man in person he had added his signature to a letter from the community to the Rhys family expressing their best wishes for a speedy recovery and welcoming a new date for the wedding.

The next time the Senate met, Dafydd and Blod raised the subject of another doctor in the community and the real need now for their own hospital, however small. It would cost money, and as Dafydd pointed out that while their crop productivity left no surplus for export they were still a liability to the Argentine government, therefore they should wait. Not all agreed with him. Many thought he was too soft.

Glyn combed the area and the community for clues about the attack and attempted to gather information from a list of the wildest young men, particularly Manny Price and his cronies. It was total stalemate. Everyone had alibis for that night.

Chief Kitchkum's assistance, however, was invaluable. He and a couple of his men traced the tracks of the assailants to somewhere in the village. There was no question now; his findings supported Glyn's theory that no bandits and no Indians were involved but that three people in the community were.

Dafydd remained confident. 'Don't worry, Glyn, Michael told us the one wearing the hat was the one wearing a red-striped scarf over his face, and, remember, only we know that; nobody else. A chap who's committed a crime and thinks he got away with it can be very stupid and very careless. So be patient.'

A month later Michael was well enough for the wedding to be rescheduled for two months hence, but he had a long way to go before complete recovery. Understanding the impatience of the young lovers, Dr Castro arranged the delivery of crutches and a wheelchair.

Since the incident, the presence of Argentine soldiers had become more apparent. They behaved rather like guardians of the law, patrolling more frequently and, according to Glyn, who in his capacity as community policeman had more to do with them than anyone else, the numbers were to be doubled.

It was true that since that night many people were now ill at ease walking out alone after dusk, and the news that more troops were arriving at the camp was greeted generally by sighs of relief.

'I can understand why they want them in the community, but, believe me, more troops mean more meddling in our affairs.' Dafydd drew a chair up to the table as Myfanwy ladled out beef stew on to his plate.

'How? They can't come into the Senate meetings, and they don't speak Welsh, do they?'

Dafydd huffed. 'They've been hanging round the school giving Spanish books to the youngsters as they leave.'

'So? No harm in that.'

'But, Myvi, it won't stop there. What did Rhiannon tell you about young Elin?'

Myfanwy laughed. '*Duwedd Mawr*, that was nothing; a nice young soldier who's been giving a few of the children Spanish lessons? Elin took him back to meet her mother and give him a Welsh cake, that's all – he'd never tasted one.'

'Yes! Spanish lessons!' Dafydd put down his spoon. 'That's my point. We are Welsh, aren't we? What the devil next?'

Myfanwy pulled her chair up to the table, folded her arms and looked her husband straight in the eye. 'Now you listen to me, Dafydd Rhys. We came here of our own free will because we believed in a better life for ourselves and our children; where we could use our native tongue without punishment. What happened to us personally – our family tragedy – was nothing to do with the Argentinian government. They have given us what they promised a bit late maybe, but we have livestock and crops to plant, and they are supporting us until we can support ourselves and make a bit of money, too!'

Myfanwy curled her small hand into a neat fist, something Dafydd had never seen her do before. 'If the Argentinians want us to learn their language, so what?' The fist came down on the table.

'We've got to be able to speak to them. Good God, Dav, we're not a separate country with our own prime minister. Where's your sense?'

Pushing his food aside Dafydd folded his arms likewise and faced his wife. 'I understand all that, but what I don't want is integration to the point that we lose our own identity. Our community is growing. Don't you see, our children and grandchildren could get lost in the culture and language of Argentina?'

Myfanwy rose from the table to fetch her own plate of stew. 'That will be up to us, won't it?' she said quietly. 'Anyway think what it would have been like if we'd stayed in Merthyr. We would have been forced to integrate with the English.'

She sat at the table and gave a little smile. 'So be thankful, Dafydd Rhys.'

At midday on the following Sunday just as the last hymn was rolling to its finale, the doors of the wooden chapel were noisily pushed open and the army lieutenant in charge stood in the open doorway, behind him a phalanx of troops. Heads turned, the hymn tailed away, and the Reverend, for once, was speechless. Dafydd stepped out of his pew and looked enquiringly at the intruder at the door. There was total silence.

'May we help you, Lieutenant?' In those split seconds Dafydd's thoughts ran riot. Had they found Michael's attacker?

In broken English the officer replied, 'We have orders from the government in Buenos Aires that all young men of eighteen until twenty-five must come to training every Sunday. So, you will please stand outside where we wait to start first session. It will be three hours. Thank you!' He clicked his heels and marched out.

A bigger bombshell could not have been imagined. He wanted the young men to do army-training sessions – on a Sunday? The Welsh community never washed clothes, nor sewed nor knit nor crocheted nor did any work in the house on a Sunday. The only book they read on a Sunday was the Bible. Some people didn't cut their toenails on a Sunday; some didn't even spit, for fear of offending God. You certainly didn't laugh much on a Sunday. It was the way they had been brought up. Observance of the Lord's Day was paramount. And now this Argentinian wanted the boys in uniform playing with guns?

The first whispers from inside the chapel rose into voiced antagonism. Members of the Senate put their heads together in the front pew. It took a couple of minutes for Dafydd to calm the unrest.

'This has come as a shock to us all. But we will be having words with Señor Rawson. I don't think he realizes that we are different from the Roman Catholic religion that treats the Sabbath almost like an ordinary day.'

Sion whispered in his ear.

'Sorry – no. Only after the morning service, then I'm told can they do pretty well anything.'

The first semi-conscripts had no choice but to drill with the Argentine army. Some of them in fact quite enjoyed it. They found it more entertaining than sitting with family in a stuffy Sunday atmosphere, depending of course on the degree of devotion. But everyone feared that for every boy of eighteen, conscription service, not just drill, could be introduced in a year or two.

A general meeting was called. There were a few other problems looming. The agenda was long: promised freeholds in two years when the new brick houses were built; army drill; and now the government was insisting that afternoon school was to be in Spanish. When they had dispensed with the community's medical necessities, an anxious-looking Herbie ap Morris stood up to put his question.

'Is it true, Dafydd, that we can only have freeholds in two years if we take out Argentinian citizenship?'

'That's not what I was told, but as we have only one brick house completely finished we can't confirm anything until we are all housed and the two years is up.'

Lanky Evan stood up. 'If we have to be citizens, those of us the right age will have to do military service, same as everybody else, won't we? Stands to reason.'

The temperature was rising.

'Look, if we refuse a freehold because we don't want to be citizens, could they chuck us out?'

'Well, I don't want to be a citizen!' someone shouted.

'Neither do I. I'm staying Welsh, I am.'

A chorus of agreement followed and Glyn had to call the meeting to order. Calmer now, it was voted that they should be civil to the soldiers and the question of freehold could wait. But the new government demand for Spanish in the school had to be put to the assembly.

Glyn took the chair. He knew Dafydd would find it impossible to sound convincing on this topic.

'We all remember the chants of "Welsh Not", don't we? Our children with slates around their necks and made to stand outside even in the rain? And we were in our own country then. So is it as bad as some of you think that our children have school in Welsh in the morning and Spanish in the afternoon?' He paused for a brief moment waiting for this simple truth to dawn.

'Are they punished for speaking Welsh here? Do they have heavy objects tied around their necks? No indeed! They can canter and gallop on their horses shouting and yelling in Welsh to each other with complete freedom and no punishment.' He emphasized the last two words.

'So then what is the harm if the country that has given us the freedoms we would never have had back in Wales would like our children to learn their language in the afternoons?' He paused. 'A bit of give and take; *chwarae teg*, isn't it?'

His argument was sound. Glyn was developing into quite an orator, and for the moment he had quelled the anger. But an anger that arose quite apart from these political issues was with the dry unyielding soil. Some felt they had sold themselves for one measly bag of corn.

There was no doubt that the attack on Michael had fanned the flames of dissatisfaction with their leaders, particularly as the criminals were still at large.

Aneurin Jones from Tredegar, an older member of the community, rose. 'Now it's all very well for Dafydd Rhys and Glyn Morgan to tell us to wait, be patient, *chwarae teg*. Is it *chwarae teg* for our boys to do army drill on a Sunday? Is it right that our children have to have half the day's school in Spanish? When that's not what we were promised.'

He turned around surveying the crowded assembly. 'If you ask me, I'd like to see our leaders with a few more teeth when they speak to the men in power.'

'Hear, hear!' was shouted from all corners of the building.

Dafydd rose to his feet quickly. 'Look, Aneurin, there is no one who feels more strongly about this than I do!'

Protocol was swept aside as angry voices came from the floor.

'Then do something about it.'

'Aye, don't just talk!'

'Only hot air, that's what it is.'

Aneurin, still on his feet, shouted to make himself heard. 'Those people – those ministers in Buenos Aires – wanted us to come here. We didn't ask! They offered. A new Wales, they said. And what are we? A colony of Argentina, same as we were, always, a colony of England!'

There was an uproar of agreement. Aneurin sat down mopping his brow to the plaudits of the crowd. He had struck a chord with his community. Half the men in the audience seemed to be standing, throwing questions at the startled Senate on the podium; startled that is, all except Manny Price who sat silently with a knowing smile on his face. The meeting closed in uproar.

Community problems were not affecting youngsters in the rosy glow of first love, particularly Sion and Bron who had been 'walking out' quite regularly for months.

'Have you, you know – done it yet?' Lisa had to know if she was still in the lead so far as sexual matters were concerned.

Bron blushed and grinned. 'Yes – but, shush, don't say anything, will you? My mam would kill me.'

''Course not silly – so where?'

Bron's saucer eyes opened wide. 'The night of the last general meeting – my dad was on the platform, so was Sion. My mam was sitting in front. I was at the back. I crept out at the end, and Sion slipped through as they were all coming out jawing ninety to the dozen.

Lisa looked surprised. 'I wondered where you'd gone so quickly. So where did you go?'

Bron started to giggle. 'Back to Sion's hut!'

Lisa laughed. 'Never! Ooh, you fit thing. Somebody could have dropped in to have a chat after the meeting.'

'We locked the door.'

'Like it?'

A broad smile spread across Bron's round face. 'Great, really great.'

'Well, don't get – what-dy-call – that's all.'

'It's all right. He wants to marry me.'

The two friends whooped around each other hugging and giggling.

A few days later Bron told Sion that Lisa knew. 'You don't mind, do you?'

'No, no, but we can't get married yet. We'll have to wait for them first; only fair. Besides Mike's going to be our best man, isn't he? He'll have to be well, poor old bugger.'

When Michael decided he wanted to walk down the aisle with his bride using neither crutches nor a wheelchair, Rawson had to wait another two months for their wedding.

Discord in the community now took a turn for the worse. Manny Price resigned from the Senate, much to the relief of Dafydd and Glyn.

'Wonder why he's done that, Dav.' Myfanwy was combing little Bethan's golden hair, as beautiful as her dead sister's had been.

'Hm – there's only thing I can think of, he wants the freedom to say what he likes from the floor.'

'Has he disagreed much at the Senate meetings?'

'Always. He seems to hate Patagonia, me in particular. Wants to make money, says his acres are useless, so he wants to take more land, but we won't let him.'

'We?'

'Well – me, I suppose. We have to take what we're given. Complains about his livestock, too. Not good quality, he says.'

'Isn't it?'

'Same as everybody else, and I've told him till I'm blue in the face.'

As predicted, at the next general meeting Manny Price was the first on his feet when the meeting was thrown open to the floor. He had positioned himself well, about halfway up on the aisle. He rose with a look of smug self-importance. Dafydd sensed unease in the pit of his stomach. Like a seasoned orator Price waited for the last cough and shoe shuffle to fade away.

'I would like to ask our respected chairman a few questions, if you please, about Liverpool.'

Seated on the podium Dafydd nodded acquiescence and exchanged a look with Glyn.

'Mr Rhys, did you have a meeting in Liverpool docks with Captain Vaughan?'

Dafydd rose slowly from his seat, all eyes upon him.

'Yes,' he said quietly. 'I did.'

'Why then did you not tell us of Captain Vaughan's warnings about Patagonia? The land where, according to the Captain, the Devil himself wouldn't care to loiter? That it was the last place on earth he would want his compatriots to go? That in fact he had refused to bring us here? That in two years we would be a colony of Argentina, all promises forgotten?' He paused turning to sweep his eyes over the astounded assembly. 'Didn't we deserve to know that?'

There was a shocked silence. Some lowered their eyes others cradled their heads in their hands, dumbfounded and fearful.

'May I ask how you were privy to this information?' Dafydd asked, wildly searching his brain for an honest, reasoned reply.

Price smirked. 'Went to see him, same as you, didn't I? And I know what he told you.'

'Yes, Mr Price, you are correct. He did tell me. I spoke at length with him, but it was just one man's opinion against the Welsh Emigration Society, and we were being sponsored by them. Captain

Vaughan was an experienced mariner and knowledgeable about many things, but, as he had had angry words with the Reverend Michael Jones, could his opinion not have been biased?'

'Biased or not, it's we who were coming here and not the Reverend Jones. And we deserved to know.'

Again Price turned, taking in his captive audience. 'But we were sold down the river, my friends, by the Reverend Michael Jones, his cronies and this man,' he shouted, pointing at Dafydd, 'our chairman. The Welsh Emigration Society needs its head read! A bunch of evil fools, that's what they are – you, too, Dafydd Rhys!'

Glyn stood up. 'I knew what Captain Vaughan said, too, Manny Price, so a question for you. Why didn't you tell us when you knew?'

'Too late by then. We were sailing next day. But I told my friends. More than you did.'

With arm raised and finger outstretched, Price again pointed to Dafydd. 'Playing dictator even then, he was! That's what they do, don't they? Conceal the truth from their subjects; decide what information they can have and what they can't have?' His shrill voice cut through the hall like a knife.

There were cries of 'Sit down' and 'Be quiet' over the growing cacophony of voices. Blod was the next member of the Senate to rise majestically from her chair on the podium to face the noisy meeting. With arms folded, she glared at them as if to reprimand a pack of children.

'Be quiet!' she commanded. 'Now, all of you, listen to me. Come on!' There was something about Blod that commanded attention.

'Now then, Manny Price, another question for you, if you please. Why didn't you go back up your bloomin' mountain to your old sheep after you'd talked to Captain Vaughan, eh? I'll tell you why. Like Dafydd, Glyn, Will Fiddler, me, Trev, Herbie, Lanky Evan, the lot of us, what did we have to go back to? We had left our homes, left what work we were in, used all our savings. We had nothing,' she spat out the word. 'Nothing, do you hear? We were committed, no option. So remember that. And tell me what good would it have done if we'd known what the Captain said? What would we have done? Sat in the corner and cried our eyes out? Nobody here has the right to blame Dafydd and Glyn for keeping their mouths shut, and, don't forget, they were in it as well with the same problems as anybody else.'

Her voice softened. 'Hasn't been easy for any of us. Dafydd's family alone has seen plenty of personal tragedy since leaving Wales.'

Price jumped to his feet again. 'Every one of us here has had problems. I want better land, but I can't have it because our dictator says I can't. Life in this God-forsaken part of the world is one big problem, and it will continue to be so while our esteemed chairman kowtows to the papists in Buenos Aries!'

He put his hand in his pocket and pulled out a collection of pamphlets, which he held up like a fan. 'See these? All from emigration companies back home, for Canada, the American Middle West, South Africa, and they'd pay for us, too. Countries where we would be welcomed, where the soil is rich and fertile; where we can make a living without breaking our backs for nothing; where we don't have to serve in the Pope's army and we don't have to learn another bloody language either!'

He turned sharply and strode to the door where, before leaving, he threw the pamphlets with such force they slid down the aisle.

Later Dafydd opined to Glyn that it was a pity young Edward Jones had to hear all that criticism about his father.

Glyn smiled. 'I wouldn't worry about that. Why do you think he came here? 'Bout as far as you can get from Wales, isn't it?' Laughing, he gave his old friend a playful poke in the ribs.

There was more depressing news for the Rhys household. A letter from Merthyr informed them that Dadcu had died suddenly of a heart attack. Myfanwy was distraught. The old saying was so true – one death brings back all the others. They had wanted Dadcu to come out to join them next year and stay for ever.

In bed that night she sobbed with the pain of not bidding her own farewell to her adored father, of not being able to hear his voice. She remembered familiar sounds – how he would tap his pipe against the grate and puff contentedly until the new baccy was lit and smouldering. She remembered the smell of tobacco on his waistcoat and those tobacco-tasting toffees he managed to find for the children buried deep in his pockets.

'I'd dreamt so often – so often, Dav, of Dadda with our Bethan –

I can't bear he never even saw her – we were always so close,' she sobbed. 'I should never have left him. Never.'

Dafydd put his arms around his wife, resonating with her desperate sadness and indeed helplessness in the face of tragedy so far away. The loss was more poignant to the family because they could do nothing.

'If only I could kiss him goodbye, touch his hand, tell him how much I loved him – anything.'

When Tomos heard the news about Dadcu, remembering particularly the night of the pit accident, he buried his tears in old Gors's coat, the only link left now with the old life and his beloved grandfather.

A week later a ship bound for the Falklands docked in Rawson Harbour. When it left, three names had been added to the passenger list: Emmanuel Price and two of his friends.

13

The date was set for Lisa's and Michael's wedding. It was five months now since Michael had been so vindictively set upon. Fortunately he had the strength of the healthy young, and his body was, for the most part, recuperating remarkably. He was being obstinate about using a stick at his wedding.

Sion laughed till he had tears in his eyes. 'You want to go down the aisle arm in arm with your best man then? They could get the wrong idea, boy! I tell you now it's either your stick or nothing. I'm not holding your hand. Lisa can do that on the way back!'

The chapel, decked out for a bride, with flowers and garlands, was packed to witness the community's first wedding – especially after such protracted plans. There was a distinct smell of camphor in the air. Clothes from the old country, packed into boxes upon departure, had barely been opened since, for these were not Sunday best clothes, these were the very best, never–to-be-used clothes. Some of the younger adolescent girls with an eye to the sly coquetry of handsome Argentine soldiers had dared to use drops of eau-de-Cologne; too frivolous to use on the Sabbath but just right for a wedding. Naturally enough, rhea feathers on a magnificent collection of ingeniously shaped hats were the order of the day. And crowded into the back seats were the purveyors of those feathers, Chief Kitchkum, his son Francisco, his wife Maria and ten of his braves, agog with wonder at this curious ceremony, so different from theirs.

Lisa wore the dress her mother had made out of linen sheets and homemade lace to absolute perfection. On her head she wore a little lace cap decorated with flowers. Gripping the arm of her father, who was fairly bursting with pride, they waited at the doorway for Will Fiddler and Mrs Jenkins on the harmonium to strike up the popular Wedding March from *Lohengrin*.

Bron, the bridesmaid, her cheeks as red as the dress she was wearing, her eyes lowered shyly, stood demurely behind her friend. In four weeks she would be following the same route, but this time with their roles completely reversed, when she would walk down the aisle and Sion would be waiting for her.

Michael, in his best suit, shining boots, complete with a newly polished stick, stood nervously before the podium and the Reverend Jenkins. He glanced occasionally at Sion, his best man, standing stiffly with high starched collar and who from time to time surreptitiously touched his waistcoat pocket to make sure the ring was still there.

The opening chords of the march signalled the bridal walk down the aisle. Myfanwy sat in the front row with an excited young Bethan clinging to her skirts and a slightly embarrassed Tomos, who felt this was all women's stuff. She turned to gaze on her beautiful daughter, and, though smiling with sheer happiness at seeing her handsome husband and Lisa on his arm looking so like him, her throat ached with stifled sobs. Silent tears trickled down her cheeks for the lost child who should have been bridesmaid.

Fortunately it was high summer, and by the time the newlyweds and the packed congregation had spilled out of the building the tables had been laid in the square and were already groaning with products from the town's kitchens.

Michael, Dafydd and Sion made their speeches. Lisa and Michael cut Maisie Jones's cake. She was particularly delighted because – as a result of Michael's injuries – her cake mix had been properly matured, as had Will Fiddler's parsnip wine, Herbie's potato brew and Lanky Evan's beer.

Even those who waged a holy war against alcohol were quite happy to be drinking, in some instances copiously, the products of nature, the parsnip, potato and elderberry; being simple products of the land they were regarded as harmless and therefore sin-free. Beer was different; that really was a sin.

Blod nudged Myfanwy with a conspiratorial giggle. 'See Martha Evans over there. She can't abide beer drinkers, alcohol being the work of the Devil. But watch. Give her ten minutes and she'll be paralytic on Will's parsnip wine.'

'Doesn't she know it's alcohol?'

Blod grinned. 'If she does, she's not saying – she likes it too much.'

The dancing that followed was further fuelled by the army camp's generous contribution of Argentinian red wine. By five o'clock the Reverend Jenkins himself was sporting bright red cheeks, and even the most pious bigots were past telling the difference between parsnip wine and the alcohol-fortified wine of the country. As for the chief and his group, half of them had fallen asleep and had to be revived with jugs of *maté*. But it was three Argentine soldiers who contributed the most impressive party piece to the celebrations. One of them suddenly produced an instrument that looked like a concertina.

'Go on, play it,' Tomos and Huw encouraged. They knew the soldier, who was in fact teaching them Spanish. The young man rose, grinning, indicated his two comrades and muttered something to Tomos who announced, 'Ladies and gentlemen, our three friends by here are going to give us a sample of what they are dancing in Buenos Aires. This instrument . . .'

'It's a squeeze box,' somebody shouted.

'No. It's called a *bandoneon*,' said Huw, 'and these two, Felix and Santos, are going to dance!'

A loud ragged cheer was followed by a scramble for ringside seats. Felix made a comic feminine curtsy and pretended to throw back his hair, much to everyone's amusement.

'*Yo soy la morocha*,' he lisped.

Huw laughed. 'He says he's the brunette.'

The *bandoneon* struck up the first tango rhythm that anyone south of the capital had heard. As for the dance – of course it was funny danced by two men but slightly shocking to the older members of the audience if the body contortions were to be taken seriously.

Bron whispered to Sion, 'They don't really dance like this – men and women, do they?'

He laughed. ''Course they do – in Buenos Aires – not the posh people, the immigrants. Like us.'

Bron giggled 'Never! Bit rude! Can you see the Reverend Jenkins doing this?'

'Not easily, no.' He put his arm round his bride-to-be. 'Never mind about him.' He bent down and whispered, 'When are we going to dance it then?'

She shot him a sly glance. 'Any time you like. Tonight?'

Feasting and dancing over, the wedding procession, to the music of Will Fiddler and José the soldier with the *bandoneon*, walked up the rising pathway to the newlyweds' house, now all finished and furnished.

In an orderly queue they lined up and placed their simple gifts, homemade or secondhand, on the living-room table. The Indians had never witnessed white people tying the knot before and stood watching, totally bemused. Young Bethan was now old enough to join in the older children's games with Elin and Francisco and a dozen more.

Hours later, when everyone had returned, leaving the young couple to begin their new life, Myfanwy and Dafydd, exhausted but happy, stole out of their shack for a walk along the riverbank. It was a warm, balmy Patagonian night with moonlight lending enchantment to pasture and grassland. A million stars lit the sky and all was silent save for the River Chubut racing down to the sea.

With arms about each other's waists, her head resting lightly on his shoulder, Myfanwy sighed contentedly. 'What a day it's been, Dav. I was so proud of you both, *cariad*. Our lovely daughter married – in Patagonia!'

Dafydd kissed the tip of her nose. 'Nearly as beautiful as her mother she was.'

'Tomos will be next.'

'Oh?'

'Walking out with Angharad Davies, he is.'

'Serious, is it?'

Myfanwy laughed. 'As serious as any young man can be.'

'Hey, he's my son, so he'll be like me.' He turned her to face him. 'And I was serious – still am, my lovely girl.' He drew her close and kissed her, not a peck but a long, lingering embrace, like a young lover again.

Sitting on the riverbank, they talked not about the family but about the ever-current difficulties in the community's economy.

'The wedding has been good for us all – taken our minds off the problem of survival, but wait till the next general assembly,' Dafydd sighed.

'At least Price is out of the way. Can you imagine, Dav, what it would have been like today with him around?'

'Aye, not good.'

Pensive for a moment she turned to him. 'D'you honestly think it's only the poor harvests that make the community so dissatisfied? I mean, is that it, or is it Patagonia in general?'

'Who can tell, but, one thing's sure, there'd be a lot less grumbling if we could grow enough wheat to sell.'

Myfanwy rose from the bank and stared at the flowing river. 'There's so much water, surely – surely . . .'

'Surely what?'

'Surely we should be able to get the water to those dry crops. Look! See how good the crops are nearer the bank. Dav, why can't we dig long trenches that stretch out like fingers so the river water can flow into them and water this desert. See – the riverbank is so much higher than the land, water would flow down easily.'

For several minutes Dafydd pondered, then beaming he turned to her.

'You brilliant girl! D'you know, I think it could work.'

'Tomorrow morning then. Nothing to lose, is there?'

'Tomorrow it is.'

Myfanwy's idea was circulated and by mid-afternoon several trenches had been started. It was hard work, as the further they were from the river the drier the soil. It took graft and muscle from men and women alike. Finally at the end of two weeks the last clods of soft earth at the river's edge were removed. A loud cheer went up when at last the ribbons of Chubut water ran through their desiccated crops. Within a week water was visibly plumping those thousands of green shoots that had either appeared dead on their barren land or had not even emerged. A new spirit of eager industry was born.

The brick houses were almost complete, and settlers moved in as and when the domiciles were ready. There was a feeling of permanence now, of a real community.

When Dafydd received the latest directive from the capital a Senate meeting was called.

'It's from President Sarmiento. He's keen on education.'

'Aye, Spanish,' Blod interjected.

Dafydd handed the letter to Sion whose Spanish had become nearly fluent. The young man took a few minutes to digest the information.

'The government is making three points,' he said quietly. 'First, Spanish will be taught throughout the day, so all textbooks will be in Spanish. You have permission to have Welsh classes after school and at weekends. Second, we are sending you three teachers because the classes have grown and your present teacher knows no Spanish. Third, your community will be sent two doctors. All will take effect from the end of next month."

As Sion sat down all eyes turned to Dr Williams.

'I'm sorry – I hadn't mentioned this.' The pink-faced doctor looked rather nervously around the group. 'I have been advised to do a c-c-course in Spanish medicine, er – Dr Rawson's suggestion, in a hospital in B-Buenos Aires.'

'And do you intend to stay there?' Glyn asked.

When he stuttered, 'Um – well, n-n-no. I'm pretty sure I shall come back. I mean I'm sure the capital will hold little attraction for m-me', it was clear to all that the doctor had given a great deal of thought to the privations of Rawson compared with the easier life of a doctor in the capital and that he would probably never come back.

'But', he added 'I shall be staying here w-when the two doctors arrive for a couple of weeks overlap, so don't worry', followed by a little nervous laugh.

Blod threw her hands up. 'Worried? Why should we be worried, Doctor, particularly if the ones they send are as good-looking and as good as the last one we had? Yes indeed, we'd be very fortunate – so long as we can understand each other.'

Dr Williams shut up after that.

It was agreed that at the next general assembly plans would be made for an annual *eisteddfod*, a weekly *cymanfa ganu* and a big celebration on St David's Day.

'It's the only way we can ensure our children and our grandchildren remain true to the land of their fathers.'

Dafydd and Myfanwy were having a drink of tea in the kitchen of their newly finished brick house within the cluster of the new Rawson community, near Lisa and Michael.

'Honestly, Dav, sometimes you are like a kid believing in Santa Claus! The government doesn't give a damn about the Welsh language nor its people. P'raps Dr Rawson likes us – but we are here in a Spanish-speaking country – immigrants – no matter what they tell us. For God's sake, get that into your head. In a couple of generations our grandchildren will be totally Argentinian. They'll marry Argentinians. There will be very little left of the Land of My Fathers.'

The colour was rising in Dafydd's cheeks. 'Then it will be up to us to keep the old country alive and well, won't it? That's why there will have to be emphasis on Welsh classes after school, choirs and *cymanfas* at weekends and regular poetry practice for the *eisteddfod*!'

It was time to let the subject drop. 'Another cup of tea?' she smiled.

An official letter arrived for Dafydd. It was marked 'personal' and was from the office of the Governor of the Falklands, Mr William Robinson. Dafydd stared at it for several minutes before daring to open such an alarmingly high-powered communication.

From the stove Myfanwy called, 'Go on, open it – can't bite.'

Not responding immediately, he finally opened the thick parchment envelope and read the contents. Without saying a word he sat at the kitchen table, head lowered and passed it to Myfanwy who, unable to control her curiosity, had wiped her hands on her apron and left the cooking.

It was a shocking letter. It contained a damning report on the condition and administration of the colonists in Patagonia by Mr Dafydd Rhys – who, it said, behaved like an uncrowned despot. It listed the severe shortages for every human need. The total impossibility to cultivate a desert had resulted in famine conditions as serious as tribes in Africa. Worst of all, there were more than forty signatures testifying to these dreadful conditions.

Myfanwy's hands shook as she thumped the pages down on the table. 'As witnessed and sworn to be true by Manny Price. There's his signature! A swine, that's what he is – a lying swine! Well, he can't get away with this, can he? Come on, Dav, get your boxing gloves on! Think of Lisa – think of Michael!'

'All right, calm down, there's a good girl. I'll go and see Glyn and the Trehearnes. See if we can't work out a way to deal with this. Don't want to call a general assembly – too disrupting, especially now the crops are coming on a treat.'

Ever since Myfanwy's brainwave the crops were flourishing with their never-ending water supply even in the driest temperatures. From this first real success it was clear to see that wheat was going to be their most abundant yield. Now they would never starve.

'Pack of bloody lies – that's what this is.' Trevor Trehearne waved the document in disgust.

Blod took it, put on her glasses and perused the signatures.

Her face broadened into a smile. 'Lying bugger! Have you been through these names? Hughie Williams is in form one, I know his mother. He's six. Eirlys Jones, she's eight, in form two.'

Dafydd nodded 'Maybe Blod, but that still leaves thirty-eight.'

Glyn fetched the citizens' register. Two hours later they found that all the names were of the community's children.

Being an honest man, Dafydd did call a general assembly and made public the document.

'Tell the Falklands Governor what he did to young Michael, why don't you?' someone suggested.

Glyn shook his head. 'It's proof we want, isn't it? Can't accuse without that.'

Though the settlers were shocked at the lying effrontery of Price and the forging of names, there was no doubt that the criticisms regarding the quality of the colony itself found sympathetic ears.

Lanky Evan rose to his feet. 'Look, about these freeholds and Argentine citizenship. Now we've more or less got our new houses, has anybody got their freehold yet?'

Dafydd had heard the rumour about the Reverend's little deal with the authorities, a freehold in exchange for Argentinian citizenship, but proof could only come from the man of God himself, who at this moment was keeping his flushed cheeks lowered and his lips closed. It was well known and had been frequently observed that the Reverend gentleman kept company with the Argentine officials who were constant visitors to Rawson, and Argentine generosity and accommodation had been one of his main points in last Sunday's sermon. Right now there was a muffled silence, and perceptibly all eyes focused on the Reverend who squirmed uncomfortably in his seat on the podium.

Unable to answer for God's representative, Dafydd replied, 'Evan, we all accept, I'm sure, that we have our new houses thanks to the Argentine government. May I suggest therefore, the choice of freehold and citizenship, when it is offered, is a matter for the individual conscience to decide?'

He paused and, remembering his conversation with Myfanwy, added, 'We are a proud people, and, though difficult to accept, it may be the only option long term.'

'But only if we stay here in this God-forsaken bit of desert.' It was Aneurin Jones from Tredegar. 'There are other options. There's Canada and South Africa where we wouldn't have to bother with foreign citizenship. Still be British, wouldn't we?'

'What about the Midwest?' shouted another angry voice. 'At least they speak a language we can pretty well understand, and there are acres and acres of wheat-growing fertile soil ready for the asking.'

'And the governments will give us assisted passages for a start.'

Another heated exchange born of political frustrations and arduous living brought Dafydd to his feet. Despite months now of successful agriculture, ideas like these could gather momentum and spread like an epidemic.

'Friends, listen to me, please. Our little community is growing, and despite the problems we have faced we are all beginning to put down our Patagonian roots, proving that we Welsh can survive where others would have given up. But survival isn't enough. We have to grow, and for that we need everyone – and I mean everyone.'

He looked at the sea of anxious faces, knowing he had to talk them away from a further emigration.

'Aneurin mentioned South Africa.' He paused. 'There, it's true, you would be part of the British Empire, but not being rich and not being members of the landed gentry of England, have you thought why the British government is inviting you there? Do you think it is because they have taken pity on our struggle to create a Welsh community away from the cruel inhuman restrictions of that very government in Westminster? Do you think they are suddenly feeling sorry for the misdeeds and corrupt legalities they have showered thoughtlessly on our old country; corruption that satisfied a lust for power and filled their coffers at our expense?'

Dafydd paused. He could feel the perspiration on his top lip. His cheeks were hot with the anger his words were kindling in his own heart. 'No!' he thundered. 'No! Once again the working man is going to be used as a bulwark, perhaps as gun fodder – who can tell – against the Dutch Boers in South Africa? British soldiers have already felt the Zulu spear. The Boers are strong and want their independence from a foreign colonial system. Do you want to be the first in the firing line just to save an Empire that rejected you? Just to give English capitalists free access to the diamond and gold mines, to make them rich on your blood? Think about that, my friends, carefully.'

Dafydd sat down, leaving a somewhat stunned assembly silent and thoughtful. They had never before seen such passion from their appointed leader.

As was usual after community meetings Dafydd and Glyn, like the old friends they were, confided in each other their hopes their fears. Bron was now happily married to Sion and Lisa to Michael, Lanky Evan was marrying Vanw ap Morris, Herbie and Idwal's sister, next month, and a few more likely nuptials seemed to be on the horizon.

'I hope to God nothing else will go wrong.'

'Look,' said Glyn sensing Dafydd's anxiety, 'we've drummed that lying crook Price out of Patagonia, and, if they've got any sense, they'll do the same in the Falklands.'

Dafydd grunted.

'So what's the problem, Dav?'

'What he said about me, I suppose – not very complimentary.

Makes me wonder if there isn't some truth?'

'*Iesu Mawr,* you surely can't believe that little *cachu,* can you? Come on, boy – without you we'd sink. The community looks to you – for pretty well everything And, good God, after your speech tonight you'd could have got me and everyone else at that meeting marching with pitchforks against the British government.' He huffed. 'There's not many will take emigration to South Africa seriously now, you can bet.'

Smiling, he clapped his old friend on the back. 'Well done, Dav, and well done, Myfanwy, with her special Rawson irrigation system.'

14

They had never seen such a bumper crop of wheat, nor indeed of any other crop. The result of the sudden easy fertility meant more abundant milk supply from livestock, and that in turn meant dairy produce demand was amply supplied by the small enterprises selling cheese and butter – for the most part controlled by the community's women.

Dairy produce was not part of the indigenous food chain of the Argentine, but there was developing a growing consumption of these products that had started with the local soldiers. The time had come to make money out of their produce; to show Buenos Aires the Welsh settlers were not cap-in-hand beggars.

Outside the planned Senate and community meetings there were often small informal gatherings in one or other of the houses in Rawson's new settlement. The question of transport to the harbour was the topic for discussion tonight at Blod's house. Trevor had built a dairy shed on their land for his wife to make butter and cheese that she was already selling to locals and soldiers. There were others doing likewise, and in this year of plenty there was a surplus. Already some of the army boys were taking quantities home to their parents.

'And they're coming back for more,' Blod smiled proudly.

'But we'll have a glut of it soon – so we have to find a way of getting it to Buenos Aires to sell in their shops,' her husband added.

'So where's the problem?' Myfanwy was helping Blod hand round slices of *teisen lap*.

'Keeping it fresh.' Blod sat down. 'See, we've only got the short wagon ride to the coast to worry about, then it goes straight into the ice room on the boat, but if it's hot – well,' she shrugged, 'hopeless. By the time it gets there the butter's like a river and the cheese is a bit like . . .'

'My feet,' said Trevor grinning.

'Exactly!' his wife responded.

Glyn looked thoughtful. 'Look, why don't we see if the ship could let us have some ice blocks all packed up that we put in our wagons. They've already got ice wagons on freight trains, haven't they?'

'Aye, same principle.' Dafydd turned to Sion. 'We need our Spanish speaker. Sion boy, ask the Lieutenant how we can get the ice blocks, will you?'

'And he's a good one to ask, too,' Blod interjected. 'He says his mother loves our cheese, so p'raps he'll help.'

Sion nodded. 'Should be easy enough. They ride to the coast nearly every day.'

'Where are the railways? That's what I want to know.' Trevor stirred sugar into his tea.

Sion huffed. 'Not here for sure, but they've got a line from Buenos Aires going north and more planned.'

'For us in the south p'raps?' asked Myfanwy

The young man shook his head. 'I doubt it.'

'Who is providing the money for all this?'

'Three big English companies with their own engineers and architects.'

Dafydd rose from the table.

'So are they going to provide cash to make life easier for the Welsh in the south?' He paused and smiled ruefully. 'Can a leopard change his spots?'

It was an exciting moment in the community when three covered wagons equipped with ice blocks, insulated as well as they knew how and packed with dairy produce, lumbered out of Rawson. The ice was so heavy that spreading the quantities of produce into three wagons made it easier for the horses.

Meanwhile reaping machines had been drawn over abundant golden fields, while all the community's available labour force stacked the wheat into sheaves ready for threshing and another exportation to the capital. One visiting expert had already tested the quality of this new Patagonian wheat and was singing its praises so much he was convinced it could be entered for worldwide competition. This was indeed a moment of triumph for the settlers and served as reminder and encouragement to those who were still contemplating another emigration that, once tamed, this patch of Argentina had plenty to offer.

With his passion for politics Dafydd had been able to follow the rising of the Communards in Paris through journals and pamphlets collected from the boats that came into the port. He had established a personal connection with a Cardiff-born master who whenever docking for a few days, rode down to see the new community, largely because his own son was thinking of emigrating. During these visits Dafydd and the master mariner would parley on every aspect of republican politics about which they saw eye to eye and, not least, the law separating church and state introduced into France.

The level of religious fervour that seemed to persist in the community despite physical hardship and difficulties was something for which Dafydd could find a tolerant respect but no comprehension. He had spoken briefly to Glyn about his impatience with this blind religious belief in, as he saw it, nothing better than a lottery and where no questions seemed to be asked.

The Cardiff master had loaned him a copy of Charles Darwin's book *The Origin of Species*, which was of particular interest, as only forty years before, the author himself had ridden across Patagonia, used a *bolas* to catch rheas and eaten roasted armadillo. Dafydd felt, therefore, he had a personal connection now with Darwin.

Strolling along the riverbank one evening with Glyn, Dafydd said, 'See Glyn, after reading Darwin it seems to make more sense, that we – us humans – are no more than just another cog in the machine of evolution.'

'What's that got to do with belief then?'

'Well, we've got more intelligence than animals for a start, so I suppose once the thinking process began we asked questions about how we came to be here and how the world happened.'

'But that's God, isn't it?'

Dafydd was silent for a few moments. He knew what he was about to say would be shocking even to his closest friend.

'There may not be a God.'

Glyn stopped in his tracks. 'What?'

'Have you thought there may not be a God? That we may have created God – like children create magic and fairytales? Every tribe, every religion on this earth has a God – even an idol – because there was no other way to explain the wonders of the world, was there? And we were confused.'

Glyn smiled, 'Not as much as I am now. So, right, you reckon religion could have been created by a confused bunch of . . .' He paused. 'See what you mean, but – we've got to believe in something, haven't we?'

'What sort of things?'

'Well, chapel, church, the Bible, life hereafter.'

'Religion has been written down for us by men of power, Glyn– to make sure we are kept in our place. Like we'll put your rents up if you don't come and pray in English in our church, right? These are ruthless men who use religion to satisfy their own greed for power and money.'

'But that was just in Merthyr, mun.'

'No, not just Merthyr – in Ancient Rome, when the Emperor decided to go Christian. He did it because it would be easier to control his Christians.'

'But I want to believe in something, Dav. Got to; frightening otherwise.

'We all want to, but when religion is organized by the powerful it becomes political and dangerous. That's where I go my own way.'

'Which way's that?'

'For a start, it's not about sin and punishment, which is all old Jenkins talks about.'

'He loves it, doesn't he?'

'Life's a bloody punishment with the chapel – don't do this, don't do that. Forgive us our sins . . . Why can't they tell us to go and enjoy something for a change?'

Glyn laughed. 'Can't do that, Dav! Do it, but don't enjoy it. Wonder to me how we've managed to keep the birth rate going in Wales!'

'Jenkins probably prays for forgiveness before and after,' Dafydd quipped.

'Does Myfanwy know you're turning – what's the word – atheist?'

'No, Glyn, and I don't know. I'm searching, keeping my options open.'

'Aren't you worried about the hereafter?'

Dafydd chewed on a blade of grass. 'D'you know what my old dad used to say? We make our own heaven and hell on this earth.'

Glyn sighed. 'P'raps he was right. Anyway I know which one we've got here.'

'Aye, me, too, and we've got to make it better with or without an Almighty.'

They strolled along in silence for several minutes, then Glyn suddenly laughed loudly. 'I was wondering how good God's Welsh was.'

Dafydd grinned. 'Now that, Glyn, may be the problem. He could understand the landlords better in English than us tenants in Welsh.'

Though making light of a troubling dilemma, Dafydd felt more at ease with the world, knowing that at last one European country, France, had decided against this unholy matrimony of religion and the state. Now perhaps there was a chance for real thought.

'Are you coming to chapel, Dav, or are you going to sit with your nose in Mr Darwin's bible all night?'

Myfanwy stood at the door with Tomos and Bethan dressed in their Sunday best. He smiled, touching her hat as he passed.

'Where d'you get that feather?'

'The chief gave it to me.'

'Beautiful. D'you know, I think you women only go to chapel to show off your hats and whatever else you've run up.'

She gave him a playful tap on his shoulder.

'What about me, Dadda? D'you like my new frock?'

Dafydd laughed. 'Lovely! Just like you, Bethan, *cariad*. Women, Tomos! Beware! Come on.'

It was a special harvest service tonight.

At last some kind of future seemed assured, but Dafydd was oblivious to the fear, fire and brimstone that spewed again, with predictable regularity, out of the Reverend's mouth into the ears of a flock who listened, fearful of the wrath of a vengeful Almighty should they be foolish enough to deviate from the straight and narrow. Stifling a yawn, he wondered where love had disappeared to, love from the Almighty? It had recently been in short supply, and punishment had seemed His principal characteristic.

Thinking of Darwin, Dafydd tried to transpose the situation into an animal kingdom where the preacher gorilla warned the others about a fearsome big god-creature called man who had a gun to shoot them should they stray out of the jungle.

As they left chapel it began to rain so the congregation hurried home. There would be no loitering tonight, for here the skies could throw down severe but usually short downpours. They were thankful their wonderful wheat crop was safely packed into newly erected corrugated tin, open barns ready for threshing the following day.

It must have been about three in the morning that Myfanwy, unable to sleep with the noise of increasingly heavy rain, made her way downstairs to brew some tea. She peered through the window, made thickly opaque by torrents of water crashing down into bricks and earth. Suddenly there was an urgent banging on the door. Grabbing a shawl, she opened it barely an inch – fearful lest the rain should batter its way into the kitchen. An agitated Michael with lantern aloft quickly slid into the dry room, creating pools of water within seconds.

'Quick, Myfanwy, get Dafydd. It's the river – flooding further down. I'm getting everybody rounded up.'

The mighty river was savaging its way through banks and fields of cultivation, taking with it rivers of mud. Roaring like a mad animal, the flood was uprooting bushes, trees, everything that stood in its way. While the Reverend Jenkins intoned prayers to the Almighty, the men, already out of their houses and waiting for the capricious river's continuing onslaught, saw their first homes, empty wooden shacks now, crushed under water.

'Thank God, the wheat's sheaved up and dry,' Trevor Trehearne shouted to Glyn, a shout that could barely be heard above the roaring river. They were standing near the new barns.

'Don't think we can chance it. Come on, lads , a human chain – we'll shift the sheaves to shelter higher up.' Dafydd, with a dozen more, passed their precious commodity back along the chain as quickly as they were able while rain hammered into their eyes, bombarded their faces and stung the skin of their hands. It was an impossible situation, for the sheaves became saturated as they passed along the line and no tarpaulins were strong enough to protect against the power of water both from above and below.

'It's a dam we need,' shouted Trevor Trehearne in the direction of the immobile Reverend. 'Ask Him,' he muttered under his breath.

Idwal ap Morris and Lanky Evan were standing lower down near the collapsed shacks.

'Look,' shouted Idwal, 'the bloody bank's giving way up there by the barns. *Arglwydd Mawr*, they'll be drowned! Come on!'

With that, they ran yelling to the men in the human chain, but it was not until they were within a few yards that any sound other than the roaring river and slicing rain could be heard.

It was clear there could be no saving of the precious crop. It was a matter now of saving their own lives.

'Come on, boys,' Dafydd yelled above the angry elements. 'No good – we've done our best. It's gone. We must get back to our homes. Let's hope the river doesn't get much higher.'

They watched helplessly as wheat, grabbed by scavenging water, was transformed into sodden flotsam and carried away, to be discarded further downstream.

No one spoke. Some had tears coursing down wet cheeks. Some were openly sobbing.

Only the Reverend Jenkins demanded attention. 'O Almighty Father, who hast seen fit to punish Thy servants for their sins, we beseech Thee to give us Thy blessing and Thy Holy Spirit, that Thy servants may see the error of their ways and follow more obediently in Thy holy footsteps. Thy will be done, O Lord. Amen.'

A few bowed their heads in prayer. A few said, 'Amen.'

Dafydd felt a knot of distaste in his stomach and privately marvelled that the Reverend, who had never soiled his white hands with manual work, could infer it was the community alone that had transgressed and should see the error of its ways. Dafydd swallowed hard, said nothing but knew he would never comprehend why this cruel Almighty seemed to thoroughly enjoy the misery of his people; in this case a pious God-fearing community.

He thought of his darling lost Bethan and, that night, leaning on the ship's rail, of his solitary prayers to the God in the ocean sky. He could not understand then. He could not understand now. Darwin and the explanations of science were a far greater comfort than the Bible and gave him logic he could follow. From now on, the Almighty, as interpreted by the Reverend Jenkins, was out of Dafydd's life.

That was it.

By the following morning the rain had stopped and in days the river had retreated to old boundaries leaving in its wake a ravaged mud-caked landscape that so recently had burgeoned with life and hope. Despair hung like a palpable cloud over the community. For the moment not even the laughter of children could alleviate their wretchedness.

Men and women huddled in groups to talk, and Dafydd could pretty well guess what the talk was about. Emigration was on the agenda again.

He sat down heavily at the supper table and with Myfanwy's bread on his plate, cut off a wedge of cheese and sighed. 'The time for more peppering-up talks has passed. We've done that.'

'Try again. It worked then, Dav.' Myfanwy slid a chair over to the table to join him. They were alone. Bethan was in bed, Tomos was out courting Angharad, and Gors was snoring.

'Because then we hadn't had a flood and seen our best crop since we've been here, washed away – drowned.' He cut into the cheese. 'We need every family – can't afford to lose anybody.'

'Can Buenos Aires do anything?'

'Well, they can't give us compensation for the weather, but they could build a dam higher up.'

'Ask them.'

'Come on, lovely, use your head. Why should they? We've got to prove our land of Patagonia is rich, fertile and productive, but right now all we have to show for it is acres of sodden fields.'

With her hands cupped around her face Myfanwy replied tartly, 'I'm surprised you don't know, Dafydd Rhys, that floodwaters deposit rich alluvial soil, and come the summer it will soon dry out and the next crop will be even better. So tell them that – see what happens.'

The army did a great job working side by side with the immigrants, clearing up the debris, repairing fences, constructing stabling and generally helping to restore some sort of equilibrium to the community. Argentina clearly did not want to lose her investment.

They were half a mile from the riverbank, scouring the terrain for any usable planks of wood deposited when the flood engulfed the wooden shacks. It was Glyn who saw it first. An unmistakable striped red kerchief stuffed into a knothole in a timber and lodged in so firmly only one edge of the fabric was frayed. Removing it carefully, Glyn took it back to show Michael.

Not to be done out of his moment of glory, Glyn asked Dafydd to convene enough men and women for a courtroom jury so that this case could be laid to rest. He had no idea if the procedure was correct, and, frankly, who cared so long as they could see justice being done?

Within an hour the chapel – which had survived the flood – had become a courtroom, with about fifty members of the community waiting expectantly for this first taste of their own legal system at work. Glyn, well used now to addressing his public, took on the mantle of prosecuting lawyer, judge and policeman with consummate ease.

'Well, as the local detective policeman round here, I looked at the wood in which I found this evidence very carefully, and without doubt it came from the shacks on the left-hand side – I could see that, by the way the water had dumped them together in one place. The right-hand side went in a different direction.' He continued, 'Now a certain person, who left us for the Falkland Islands, had a shack on the left-hand side, did he not?'

Heads nodded. Glyn had not enjoyed himself so much in a long time. He called Michael as prime witness.

'Will you please tell us whether or not this was the scarf you saw on one of the men the night you were so brutally assaulted?'

Michael, going along with the serious mood Glyn had created, looked at it carefully. 'Aye, that's it – the one with a hat was wearing this striped scarf to cover half his face. It was tied across – only his eyes were showing. It was getting dark, so I couldn't see them properly.'

The young man looked glum for a moment with the disturbing memory of it all and imperceptibly touched his leg. Though his bones had been put together and had knitted, he still limped when tired.

'So you never saw the colour of his hair?'

'No, sir.'

'But he wore a hat when the others did not?'

'Yes, sir.'

'Well then, I think we can claim, though this is circumstantial evidence, that the crime committed upon Michael Edwards was led by the same man who also deceived the Governor of the Falklands, namely Mr Emmanuel Price. May I have a show of hands please from those who agree with the verdict of guilty.'

All hands were raised.

'Good. The case for the prosecution will submit this evidence to the Governor of the Falklands, if indeed the man guilty of this criminal assault is still at large there. Case closed.'

Glyn sat down, glowing with the power of something achieved. Bron and Rhiannon waved to him from a back seat. They were proud of him, never for a moment thinking he could have risen so well to the occasion. Since coming here he had managed to read a few slim books and pamphlets on rudimentary law and had often wondered whether it was it too late to study properly. For him, perhaps it was, but what about Huw? Always a very bright boy, he had gone back to school since coming to Patagonia. Winifred Howells had personally given up her time to give him extra lessons.

'Your Huw should go to college, Glyn,' she'd said often enough.

But that cost money they didn't have. Maybe he could be articled to a firm of solicitors, even qualify as a clerk? His Spanish was pretty well perfect now. They would have to think seriously about the boy's future. With his brain he shouldn't be wasting his time on manual labour.

As the devastated community filed out of the *ad hoc* courtroom it was clear to see that this piece of legal theatre had been just what they needed. It had restored belief in their own worth again.

15

Change was in the air, some welcome, some not. Lisa was pregnant – much to the delight of Michael and the prospective grandparents.

Tomos had married Angharad, a quiet pretty girl from Carmarthen, and for the moment neither of them was sure about remaining in Rawson.

Huw, encouraged by his parents, was writing to companies of English lawyers in Buenos Aires who were looking for articled clerks. His old teacher, Miss Winifred Howells, helped him compose letters in English, though he would have had no problem with Spanish. Huw and Tomos were still like brothers – brothers who had shared the trauma of a near-death experience in the pit all those years before, back in Wales. Though Tomos dreaded the idea of losing his best friend, Huw had brains and couldn't be expected to spend the rest of his life in Rawson.

'Don't worry, I'll come back as your very own Welsh-speaking solicitor,' he joked.

However, right now life was not much of a joke. Lisa miscarried at three months, but the doctor told her she was young enough to have plenty more, and it was no doubt one of nature's rejects and that she should think about another in a few months. According to the Reverend it was the will of God again. Nothing new there, thought Dafydd.

The crops were flourishing but there seemed to be more than usual activity among the troops, for suddenly their numbers grew.

'They are on an Indian hunt – all over,' Tomos told his father. 'Indians attacking the troops, they say.'

'Not our Indians surely? Lovely people they are.'

'Military orders, Dad; to hunt out all Indians who are anywhere near us for fear of attack.'

'Rubbish! Can you see Chief Kitchkum attacking us?'

Tomos shrugged. 'The Araucans could attack– like before.

They want to make sure we are unharmed.'

'And you know why, don't you, Dav?' said Glyn later, when Dafydd had disclosed this latest army intelligence. 'Huw told me – he's friendly with Fernando, the Sergeant.'

'Go on, why?' urged Dafydd.

Glyn lowered his head. 'They are waiting for a Chilean invasion, that's why, and they're afraid Indians would join forces with the Chileans against Argentina. They've never liked each other.'

'With Patagonia as the battleground. Jesus wept, Glyn, are we to be frontline battle-fodder for yet another empire?'

Glyn grimaced. 'All I know is, they are Indian hunting, so we'd better warn the chief.'

'Aye, and say nothing about Chile's supposed territorial ambitions or half the community will leave.'

Chief Kitchkum, Francisco and a couple of well-liked braves made regular calls on the community's households selling their wares; feathers, petticoats, ponchos, dyes, a variety of leather goods and carved trinkets. In certain households barter was the *modus operandi* and after refreshing *maté* and Welsh cakes, punctuated with a mixture of Spanish and English conversation, the Indians would depart with enough bread for several days.

Sitting in Myfanwy's kitchen on one such visit, the chief warned of Indian reprisals against any white settlers. There were dozens of small Indian tribes whose families had been deliberately murdered, with no provocation it seemed, by the troops. Revenge and slaughter of both soldiers and settlers alike appeared to be the objective. So far the army had not touched the Tehuelches.

Elin, Glyn's girl, looking more and more like her big sister Bron, had delivered Bethan safely home after Welsh classes, and in no time Francisco joined them for a game of bat and ball in the field behind the house. Suddenly the back door burst open. Tomos, breathless and white-faced, stood panting.

'Quick, Chief, hide! The army's doing a house-to-house Indian search, mam. They'll be here in about ten minutes, and they'll shoot first!'

Tomos rounded up the children playing in the field, while the Chief grabbed his scattered goods. Elin hid the *maté* cups in the deep sink, and Myfanwy pushed the chief and Francisco into an upstairs cupboard, which she locked.

One Indian crawled under the big double bed into a nest of blankets, the other clambered on top of a high water tank where he was completely invisible. By the time the Sergeant marched to the door Elin had put the cups away, Myfanwy was peeling vegetables for supper, and Bethan was playing with her whip and top by the back door. Apart from the household's palpitating hearts, the kitchen was as normal as any other day. Tomos had remained chatting to the Sergeant whom he knew through Huw, hoping to deflect the search.

The Major, newly arrived in the camp and determined to leave no stone unturned, followed the Sergeant into the kitchen. Like an inquisitor he marched in, and Myfanwy's heartbeats raced frantically through her body. He began examining artefacts small and large that are found in the most usual of kitchens, questioning the provenance of each one. Tomos had gone upstairs with the Sergeant, and Myfanwy, alone with Elin and Bethan, pared the vegetables with trembling hands. If they were caught impeding the army's duties she knew they would be in serious trouble, to say nothing of their Indian friends. But when the Major's hawk eyes fell on a small Indian carving of a horse that Francisco had just made for Bethan and which she had forgotten to hide in the panic, despite feeling faint with fear she knew she must act quickly.

So did the Major.

Recognizing its Indian origins, he picked it up and, without thinking, the child ran to him.

'Do you like my horse?'

He smiled. 'Very much. Who gave it to you?'

'My friend Francisco.'

'And who is he?'

'Chief Kitchkum's boy.'

'Really? And when did he give you your little horse?'

Myfanwy whispered to the child in Welsh. 'Don't say any more, there's a good girl.'

Myfanwy's smile was as gracious as she could muster. 'When my eldest daughter married a couple of years ago,' she put her arms around Bethan, 'the little one here was far too young to remember, and of course you were not here at that time, were you? The carved horse was part of a wedding present from our Indian friends.'

'So you are friends to the Indians?'

Myfanwy took a deep breath. 'Of course we are. Had it not been for the local Tehuelches coming to our rescue and teaching us how to live in your wild country I doubt if we would have survived.'

Outwardly appearing calm, Myfanwy could feel the pulse in her throat beat wildly, and with a sudden nervous twitch in her top lip it was difficult to hold a frozen smile. The Major was about to put the horse in his pocket, no doubt as evidence of an Indian presence, when Bethan wriggled out of her mother's grasp, stood before him and held out her hand.

'That's my horse if you please, Señor,' she said sweetly in Spanish.

'Of course it is, but I like him, too. May I not keep him?' He held the carving just a little higher than the child's reach.

Thinking it was a game, Bethan giggled. 'No, Señor.'

'And how long have you had him again?'

Myfanwy's heart missed a beat. She opened her mouth to answer for her daughter, when the Major interrupted sharply. 'No, madam, she will answer for herself this time.'

Myfanwy need not have worried.

'Ages and ages, Señor,' the little girl lisped and again thrust her hand forward. 'Please.'

No match for the power of persuasion in the child's eyes, he handed over the carving, clicked his heels marched out of the kitchen and called to his Sergeant who, having finished upstairs, was inspecting the outside of the house with Tomos.

Several hours later, the chief, Francisco and his two comrades left the house as stealthily as trappers, for no one could be sure that the army was not keeping an all-night alert.

The Indians always left their horses tethered together outside Rawson, but earlier in the day the animals had been spotted by an army patrol and deliberately unleashed to roam into the arid wastes, never to be seen again.

★

The community was growing in number. Many more Welsh immigrants had arrived, which upset the *status quo* of the original pioneers. So much had been done, so many hardships had been endured and so much achieved, facts that seemed to escape the newcomers.

'They take it all for granted. Want this, want that. Where's this, where's that? They don't know the half,' Blod grumbled. And she was not alone.

So when the new families decided to go upstream further inland to start a second community in Gaiman, an old disused Indian settlement, the Rawson Welsh were relieved and actively encouraged the exodus.

Spanish being the new *lingua franca*, by government decree, a school and teachers were immediately offered to Gaiman's new community, leaving them to their own spiritual and linguistic needs. Nearly twenty miles away from Rawson, and too far for Glyn's surveillance, they appointed John Hughes, a big burly sheep farmer from Cardigan, as their custodian of the law, brawn being preferable to brains.

'That's sensible anyway,' Blod conceded. 'He's big enough to bump a couple of heads together with one hand, that one.'

However, it was agreed that the old system of a Senate with elected members would continue, with Dafydd, who had been re-elected chairman several times over, at its head. Of course he was well liked, but in fact no one else wanted the job.

There were other reasons, too. What was the point in becoming involved in a community if you were not sure that you would remain there? The uncertainty of life in Patagonia made for an uneasy truce with the land. The problem of bad harvests had, after so much trial and error, been pretty well resolved. The climate was generally good, and it was a vast country with plenty of acreage for all, but it was unpredictable – not only the river but the Argentine government and its insistence on military service, the subtle pressure to become Argentinian citizens – and now Spanish in schools. This was felt keenly, particularly when preservation of the Welsh language had been a reason for emigrating.

At the annual general meeting in the chapel hall Dafydd

announced dates for the *eisteddfod* now to be held twice a year. It was a necessary focus for children and parents alike. After school, Miss Howells gave Welsh classes and coached writing and poetry. Will Fiddler rehearsed with the choir, and, to his great surprise, a couple of the soldiers joined.

Despite all Dafydd's arguments, despite the developing social activities burgeoning through words and music, despite a very real Welsh identity flowering in this Hispanic world, forty good people were about to leave for Canada.

Dispirited, and with a personal sense of failure, Dafydd was quiet over supper.

'Stop worrying, will you? You did your best – can't force people to stay.' Myfanwy pushed an extra potato his way.

Bethan, a bright little button and as feisty as her big sister, soaked a chunk of bread in the gravy left on her plate. 'Eirlys Lewis doesn't want to go, Dadda. She cried in school today. She says Canada's horrible.'

Dafydd sighed 'No it's not horrible, *cariad* – just different, and we are sorry they're going.'

'Is Canada bigger than Wales?'

'Much,' Myfanwy replied as she cleared plates from the table.

A wicked grin spread across the small features. 'Oh no it's not, because Wales is even bigger than Patagonia!'

Dafydd raised his eyebrows in mock amazement. 'Is it, indeed? How do you work that out?' Her parents exchanged amused glances.

'Because – because Wales has got lots of mountains.'

Dafydd nodded. 'Quite right – so?'

Bethan took a deep breath. 'So if God squashed all the mountains in Wales really flat, flat like pancakes,' she brought both her hands down on the table with a resounding smack, 'Wales would be *huge*, wouldn't it? Biggest country in the whole world.'

Dafydd looked at the eager little face without a flicker of a smile. 'Yes, Bethan, I take your point. Trouble is, it's very hard to squash a mountain.'

'Why, Dadda?'

'It's what they are made of – too big and strong. They've grown out of the earth. Never squash them.'

Myfanwy chuckled. 'Like us, Bethan *fach*. We are just like our mountains. Can't squash us either.'

'Big John' as he was now known, Gaiman's law-keeper, was living alone in his small brick farmhouse with several head of cattle, sheep and horses, for company, almost halfway between the two townships.

During the months since his appointment Glyn had established a monthly informal get-together with Big John over home brewed beer and cheese when they discussed the general problems of law-keeping and law-breaking, which to be fair to the communities, were minimal. Most of the disputes arose out of family quarrels over land, particularly after bereavement, but in most cases disagreements were solved locally because few wished to involve the Argentinian judiciary. The big man took his duties seriously and patrolled the vast stretches of land with dedication. Sessions between the two keepers of the peace usually ended with Dafydd, Blod and other members of the Senate dropping in, giving advice and generally throwing in their two penn'orth, based on years of experience in Patagonia.

So regular and punctual was Big John's arrival at midday on the first Friday of the month that when he failed to turn up after a year of the arrangement Glyn was concerned – especially as weather conditions were perfect.

When Dafydd dropped in during mid-afternoon, Glyn was outside keeping a watchful eye on the road, questioning drivers of horse-drawn carts and solo riders on the whereabouts of Big John.

'Funny he hasn't let me know,' said Glyn as the sky darkened.

Though there was no official postal service as yet between the two communities, it was relatively easy to fetch and carry letters between the two villages through tradespeople. It was now dusk, and Glyn felt uneasy.

'Could it be Indians, Dad?' Huw asked.

Glyn shook his head. 'Don't know. Could be rustlers, though. Coming down from the north I'm told, and Big John's got plenty to rustle.'

Between them Glyn and Dafydd rounded up twenty armed men.

'Now, remember, we stick together – no wandering off on your own. It could put us all in danger.'

Taking careful notice of terrain *en route* for any visible signs of Big John, it took the posse two hours to reach his land. Glyn led the way, then as he approached the wooden gate to a large paddock he stopped and called back.

'Dismount here! The gate lock has been forced. Now, for God's sake, go carefully. Spread out in a long line – we'll sweep the field up to the house over there.'

The small brick house was in darkness.

Half an hour later they knew something was wrong, for there were no animals and adjoining gates were open. A few harnesses lay around and evidence of animal feed, but where was Big John? The house was unlocked; doors suspiciously open. They moved first around the perimeter with a stealth they had learnt from the Indians.

'Could be a trap. I'll go in – keep me covered,' Glyn whispered.

Big John was propped on a chair and lay slumped semi-conscious over the table, a severe gash on the back of his head.

It took several men to put him on a horse and ride as quickly as they could back to Glyn's house. The new Argentinian doctor put stitches in the head wound, dressed it and slowly the big man came round. They made him comfortable with pillows and eiderdowns on the floor, Blod and Rhiannon attending to his physical needs with bowls of soup.

By morning he was able to recount what happened. An early riser, he had been feeding the animals in the field next to the house when three men approached asking him for any odd jobs. They spoke English, but he couldn't tell if they were Americans or Argentinian.

'We had a nice chat, and I turned to attend to one of the cows. Next thing I remember is lying over the table with a terrible pain in my head. I tried to get up – must have passed out again. I remember you putting me on a horse – and that's all.' The big man was pale and spoke slowly. 'Good job you came to find me, Glyn boy– God knows, I could have been dead by now.' He tried to smile. 'They gave me a hell of a thump.'

'Aye.' said Glyn. 'The bastards must have dragged you back inside after they thumped you.'

Glyn and Dafydd were determined justice would be done by Big John. The rustlers had to be found, especially as their victim would recognize them.

Through Sion they contacted the Argentinian judiciary, for this could no longer be a small domestic matter. Once the men were caught, they were assured that justice with full compensation to the victim would be delivered.

Certain they would strike again, Big John described each of the men in detail. Huw designed a pamphlet with this information, in Welsh, Spanish and English, which was then distributed in the two communities.

Dafydd and Glyn realized the difficulties in establishing the rustlers' origins, for so many new immigrants from Italy and Germany had now arrived in the Argentine and were drifting down to Patagonia. Rustlers and others of dubious morality could find easy pickings among the relatively naïve newcomers. There was a palpable wave of unrest. Ever watchful, some attempted to patrol their land at night, some corralled the animals close to their homes, some took on more dogs, but tension was high.

Within a couple of weeks news came that men matching the description Big John had given had been seen. Losing no time, Glyn enlisted the help of the army. The three men were arrested near Porth Madryn, waiting for sea transport to take them – anywhere, it appeared. Having no suitable prison, the army locked them in huts under constant surveillance. A judge was brought down from Buenos Aires.

'This is a big day for us, Dav,' Glyn said quietly as they sat in the tense silence of the packed community hall.

'Big John will get compensation for his loss, and those buggers will get a sentence – prison in Buenos Aires, that's what the Sergeant says.'

They rose as the Spanish-speaking judge entered with his clerk and sat on the podium, followed by the prisoners, escorted by three soldiers. The rustlers, confident, hard, swaggered in with half-smiles on their faces.

Big John sat in the front row and glanced at his powerful hands clenched in an imagined retaliation.

Sion was translator from Spanish into Welsh, though in truth many were able, albeit reluctantly, to speak reasonable Spanish by now.

Glyn read his statement and passed it to the judge who, after careful examination of the document, questioned him and a couple of the men whose signatures verified the statement.

Big John was next. He recounted the events from meeting the men and his subsequent attack. The judge pretended to read his statement in Welsh with furrowed brow, but quite obviously he did not understand a single word. He skimmed quickly through the Spanish translation.

When asked to identify the rustlers, the big man spoke out clearly. 'They are the men who stole my livestock and who attempted to murder me, your honour.'

'Are you sure you recognize them?'

'No doubt, sir.'

'It was early morning. You had your back to them. You were struck from behind, on the head and became unconscious. It could have deranged your memory.'

'No, sir! I recognize them.'

'I maintain you could not have seen them clearly at such an early hour in the morning, and it is only natural that you wish to recognize them in order to claim compensation from the government.'

The assembly, as one, gasped. It was an outrage.

Big John clenched his white knuckles; his cheeks were reddening. 'No! No, sir! I am no liar. I want justice.'

The judge was icy calm. 'As do we all, Señor Hughes, but on this occasion I will not uphold your claim.' He turned to the jubilant rustlers. 'I shall bring no case against you. You are free to go, but I suggest you take yourselves far away from this territory. Case dismissed.'

The assembly rose in total silence, Big John sat stunned, immobile with bowed head. The judge, deliberately avoiding eye contact and glancing neither to the left nor right, walked majestically out of the hall with his clerk. In the continuing silence, the three smug rustlers were escorted down the centre aisle by Fernando the Sergeant and a corporal.

Dafydd, Glyn, Michael, Sion and the men from the posse slipped noiselessly into the aisle, following the rustlers out of the door and into the square, where their military escorts were only too willing to stand back. Sneers turned to fear as the trio were suddenly surrounded by the silent menace of twenty angry men.

Not a word was spoken, until Sion, his hands in a fist, pulled the shirt collar of the one standing nearest to him. 'I'm warning you three, if you value your lives get out of here fast and never come back. We all know who you are, and we'll kill you if we ever see you again. Understood? Kill you!'

'Don't worry, my friends, we are taking them back to the bay. Put them out to sea in a fishing boat.' Fernando the Sergeant spat. 'Scum!'

No one could believe that Big John had lost his case. Was this Argentinian justice? If so, was it not a repetition of what had gone on in Wales when the English appropriated the land and justice was a shallow pretence? For another twenty families this was the last straw. They decided to take up the US government's offer of land in the Midwest.

16

For the time being the troops had given up Indian hunting.

Gradually Chief Kitchkum and his friends assumed their old habits as door-to-door salesmen, bartering for *bara* in many of the homesteads, which was just as well, for they brought some important information to Dafydd and Glyn who were sitting at Myfanwy's kitchen table. As the tall Indian took the cup of *maté*, he said, 'We know where rustlers are.'

Dafydd laughed. 'In the Falklands by now, we hope.'

The chief shook his head. 'No, Señor Dav. They don't go away – soldiers think they on ship – but they hide.'

Glyn leant over towards him. 'You sure, Chief?'

'Plenty sure.' He paused. 'Bad men; they will take animals again. Next time they kill.'

'How do you know all this?'

'We hear them talking – they not see us – same men, Señor Glyn, who take animals from big man.'

'D'you know where they are?' asked Dafydd.

The chief nodded. 'Sure – hide in big caves near Gaiman.' He looked from one to the other. 'Easy catch them. We come with you.'

Glyn frowned. 'Show us where they are, but then you must hide. Can't have you there when we arrest them – too dangerous for you if the army finds out.'

They met on the outskirts of Rawson as night fell. The chief and three of his men led the way with Dafydd, Glyn, Sion, Michael, Herbie, Lanky Evan and Big John all armed, following. The idea was to ambush the rustlers at dawn as they emerged from sleep.

The Tehuelches led them to a thickly foliaged rocky area higher up the valley to a hidden cave where the rustlers had been seen. In the clearing outside the cave mouth was evidence of a human presence – a few cooking pots, empty bottles of wine, scattered cups and the dying embers of a fire. Like trappers, the three Indians and seven Welshmen found their own vantage points and settled in for a long night.

Michael nudged Glyn. 'What if they are not the same rustlers?'

'Chief swears they are – he saw them with the army at the port.'

'What if he's wrong?'

'Arrest them on suspicion – no harm done.'

As red flecks of dawn threw boas of light across the sky the first man emerged from the mouth of the cave. They need not have worried. He was one of the rustlers. The posse remained motionless in the surrounding bushes waiting for the others to emerge and for Glyn's signal. The rustlers came out as hoped.

Glyn gave the signal, and in a flash they were surrounded. They stood frozen in horror, their heads turning furtively left and right to assess the odds. Seven men, rifles raised and cocked, were closing in. There was no way out. Instinctively hands dropped to holsters.

'Don't even think about it!' Glyn shouted as the semi-circle of firepower closed in. 'Drop your guns,' he snapped. 'We are arresting you and taking you back to the harbour where we shall personally put you on a military boat. Perhaps the army will teach you how to earn a living the hard way, not steal the livelihoods of good hard-working men.' He paused. 'And don't even think of making a run for it either.'

Turning back to face the group of six, poised and ready, Glyn smiled. 'We can tie them up now, boys.'

No one saw the fourth rustler because the mouth of the cave was too dark, but suddenly a shot ripped through the air. Glyn fell. The rustlers in a flash grabbed their dropped guns. Dafydd ran to Glyn, kneeling beside his motionless body.

'Shoot! All of you, shoot,' he yelled,

Suddenly Big John threw his weight on Dafydd and like a mighty bear pulled him flat on to the ground, while neatly dispatching a rustler a few yards away who was about to take a direct aim at Dafydd. Chief Kitchkum and his braves had emerged from the undergrowth to lend assistance, though by this time the posse had erased any life left in the three rustlers, while Sion and Michael were in the cave dispatching the fourth.

Kneeling beside his friend's body, his face white with shock, Dafydd put his hand gently under Glyn's head. 'Be all right, Glyn – be all right,' he whispered. 'And thanks, Big John. Thanks.'

'For what, Dav? We were all in it. Them or us, wasn't it?' The big man put a placatory hand on Dafydd's shoulder.

Dafydd covered his face with his hands. 'But why – why didn't I see that fourth bastard? I should have – I should have.'

Big John knelt beside Dafydd. 'Nobody could have seen him – nobody,' he whispered. 'It was black inside that cave. Come on, Dav. Not your fault – not anybody's fault.'

Glyn was bleeding profusely and obviously in great pain, barely able to respond to Dafydd's choked words. 'Taking you back now, Glyn – hold on – hold on – please.'

Herbie, who knew a little about first aid, tore his shirt into strips to plug the bleeding, binding it tightly around the wounded man's body.

'We'll soon get him home. I think it's missed the spine, but it could be the main artery in his stomach.'

Tenderly they lifted Glyn's inert body on to a horse. No one said a word.

Chief Kitchkum put his arm around Dafydd, stunned, sick with fear and disbelief. 'White doctor very good,' he said.

Three of them walked back with Glyn lying on his horse. Herbie tore up more shirts to stem the haemorrhaging wound, while Sion and Michael rode ahead to alert the doctor.

Dafydd tried not to think the unthinkable, of life without his dear best friend, a chosen brother with whom he had shared thoughts and dreams.

Rhiannon, Bron and Elin were waiting at the doctor's surgery, as was Blod, the community's unofficial nurse. Immediately, the doctor saw that his patient could not survive, having lost so much blood, though he tried suturing. It was all too late. The artery was ruptured, shredded, and the blood showed no sign of coagulating. Glyn's pulse was becoming weaker.

Blod looked at the doctor, said nothing but raised her eyebrows in question.

The young man shook his head. 'He could perhaps survive if the bleeding stopped – but it is like a water tap, Señora Blod,' he replied. 'In a hospital with proper apparatus I would try a transfusion. Sometimes it can work – it does with animals – but not always.'

One hour later Glyn was dead and worlds turned upside down.

The shock, the tears – and despair– hung over the community like a pall. Myfanwy spent time with Rhiannon and Elin. Sion comforted his wife who moved in with her mother for a few days just to give each other support, and Tomos, ever faithful, was there for Huw, to talk and to weep.

Dafydd was unable to find words to express his grief and the bitterness in his heart towards the corrupt legal system that, in effect, had murdered his best friend. This was the general feeling. They had been badly let down, and a popular community leader had been murdered as a result.

The funeral was attended by everyone, even by the troops. Big John, consumed with needless guilt that it was through him that Glyn died, was one of the pallbearers, Dafydd another. He listened to the Reverend Jenkins explain it was God's will, that it was the sins of the community that were being punished by Glyn's sacrifice. At that point he felt so angry he wanted to shout out against these insulting platitudes.

Singing rousing Welsh hymns together seemed to him to be an expression of collective emotion, a sharing of joys, of sorrows and of that vital element missing from the Reverend's admonishments – love. If it helped ease the pain of loss believing that the loved one was in a better place, happy and smiling down upon his friends and family, so be it. Though Dafydd did not accept the concept of heaven, it was a gentle way of dealing with grief, but fire and brimstone, never was. His anguish was profound. No one could ever be the brother that Glyn had been, and his death inevitably brought back memories of his lost child and her burial at sea.

It was at Glyn's funeral that Tomos met up again with Evan Jones, a young man with a shock of black hair who, though slightly older, had also been a pupil at Miss Howell's school in Rawson. His elderly mother, a widow, had died so soon after the flood that along with two other families he had moved out of Rawson to higher ground outside Gaiman.

'You got a farm?'

The young man grinned. 'Not me – a trading post and post office – that's what I've got – Chief Kitchkum's older lads, twins they are, working for me, too. I took it over from Edward Jones when he went back. That's not all. You get to know everything that's going on when you have a trading post. Couple of Welsh boys dropped in the other day – been prospecting for gold.'

Tomos's eyes opened wide with amused astonishment. 'Gold? Never! Where?'

'Further on, towards the Andes.'

'They find any?'

'Aye, some have by all accounts – but not much. No matter, there's plenty of land, see, and good soil, marvellous weather, fruit trees, grow anything – enough rain to feed the crops and the animals. And no flooding from this bloody river.'

'So how do you get there?'

'It's a good three-day ride to the plains, then, like I said, once you've crossed the plains, foot of the Andes, there's this valley. They all say it's beautiful. Mind you, I'm only telling you what they told me.'

Tomos grinned. 'We'll have to go.'

Evan Jones gave Tomos a friendly cuff on his shoulder. 'When you do, Tomos, let me know – I'll be there with you. All right?'

It was food for thought.

No matter how Myfanwy and even young Bethan tried, Dafydd barely spoke for weeks and cancelled the monthly Senate meeting. He was lost without his confidant in community affairs. A month, and here he was still silent and morose.

Myfanwy knew she had to do something for all their sakes. 'Dav, listen to me, Glyn would want you more than anyone to carry on strengthening our community. There are so many of us now, and everyone turns to you.' She smiled and said gently, 'There is no one else.'

Standing behind his chair Myfanwy lowered her head on to his shoulder. 'And I know Rhiannon would like you to talk to Huw. He needs his dad so much, especially with all those letters he's written to lawyers in Buenos Aires. Glyn always wanted it for him, didn't he?'

She moved round to face her husband and knelt on the stone floor at his feet. 'Rhiannon is getting help on the land for a share in produce, and she's going to join Blod and Trevor in the dairy. That'll probably be enough for them to live on. But Elin's bright – she's a dab hand at Spanish already. Glyn wanted her to go to the new Sarmiento teaching college in Buenos Aires.'

Dafydd's blue eyes, faded with despair, looked up. 'That'll cost, won't it?'

'Yes, but there's an exam she can take in a year's time. If she passes she can be a student teacher first, then go to college free. Winifred Howells found out.'

Dafydd sat quite still, lost in thought for a moment or two, then slowly rose from his chair and made for the door.

'Where are you going, Dav?'

'Have a chat with Rhiannon about Huw and Elin.'

Stopping at the door he turned back to his wife. 'Thanks, *cariad*.'

Myfanwy sighed with relief. At last he was going to get on with life again.

Sion was voted to take Glyn's place. He was thought to be a natural successor, for apart from being a son-in-law his command of Spanish was an important link with the surrounding world.

As for the young, Elin, Bron and Huw, the healing process after their father's murder began. Glyn's death had made Huw even more determined to work towards an honest legal system.

With Rhiannon it was different. She was a broken woman, her dreams shattered. How often had she and Glyn talked about their old age in Patagonia, of seeing Buenos Aires, of one day taking a trip back to Wales? Those dreams were not to be. She ached now for the familiar comfort of Merthyr, the smell of gorse and the swathes of purple foxgloves on the mountain. What was her future to be?

Huw would go to Buenos Aires and one day fulfil his father's ambitions and become a lawyer, Elin would go off to teachers' college, and Bron would have babies. She would be alone, with no husband. Rhiannon did not see the point in life any more, and it was only her children that forced her to pay a feeble lip-service to living. Her heart was dead, and friends could see her rapidly falling into an emotional decline. They resolved to keep her as occupied as possible. She was asked to gather children from their homes, take them to school, collect them at the end of the day and take them to their Welsh classes. Rhiannon spoke very good Welsh, so Miss Howells the teacher persuaded her to take the younger ones in reading and composition twice a week. Slowly life began to circulate in her veins once more.

It was no surprise that Blod was elected Vice-President. She was the wise woman, the life-enhancer of the township; the one they called on for birth and for death.

The thought of gold in the Andean foothills, as well as a fertile valley with a more temperate climate, fired Tomos's thoughts and his imagination. Naturally enough, he shared both with Huw, Sion and Michael. To be fair, it wasn't the possibility of gold that excited but the valley, which, according to Evan, was there for the picking.

Life in Rawson had not been easy and never would be. These young men wanted an easier, more secure future in which to raise their families. They had done the pioneering with their parents and witnessed first hand the suffering and tragedy that this corner of an untamed land had wrought. They were young people in a hurry now, with skills acquired by trial and error. They wanted quicker results from less crippling endeavours.

Tomos called on his father to discuss the idea further and to report on arrangements for the first expedition.

'Hadn't you better make sure there'll be no Indians on the trail?'

'We've already done that, Dad. The army cleared it a couple of weeks ago.'

'And who told you?' Myfanwy asked.

'Fernando the Sergeant.'

'Sorry, boy, not good enough. You must have assurances from the Captain at least. No point inviting avoidable problems, is there?' He paused. 'Tell you what, we'll go and see the Colonel – tomorrow.'

Tomos's cheeks flushed. 'Look, Dad, I'm not a kid.' Looking at his father he saw the all-too-familiar set jaw and knew he had gone too far. He shrugged. 'Right then! We'll go just to make sure. No need for you to come.'

'I shall be there, Tomos. Not as your father but as chairman of the Senate.'

The subject was closed to further discussion.

The Colonel was friendly and polite, speaking in Spanish and some broken English, 'You may rest assured, gentlemen', he said, 'we have combed the area from Rawson to the valley and have cleared all the Indian settlements. They have been moved north, higher into the Andes.'

'Araucans – any in the area?' Dafydd asked, remembering the last time.

'It is not Araucan territory, Señor. They are nearer the coast.' He pointed to a wall map. 'Here, and quite far away, so don't be concerned. In any case, let us know when you plan to go. The day after you leave we will send a small posse, five or six men to trail you – just for a little extra security' He smiled. 'Which I am quite sure you will not need.'

Dafydd could not have been more relieved. They were to be a small band, Sion, Michael and Tomos.

Huw had just received an invitation to join a solicitor's company in Buenos Aires but not until next April. 'So I can come, too,' he declared jubilantly.

They were sitting together in Sion's house planning what they would need for a couple of weeks away from home. It would take them a good four days to reach the plains and cross to the Andean foothills. It was decided to wait until midsummer, the perfect time for exploring the beautiful valley and even prospecting for gold.

Bron bustled in from the kitchen. 'Huw, what's our mam say about you going?'

'Not much. It'll only be for a couple of weeks.'

She looked at her brother. 'Maybe, but you know how nervous she is now.'

'Yes, but she's got Elin and you, and by all accounts the valley would be a much better option than here, for all of us.'

Bron huffed. 'Well, don't go breaking your arm or falling off a horse. Can't have you losing that job in Buenos Aires.'

Sion laughed. 'Him? Fall off a horse? He's our best rider.'

Huw glared at Bron. 'Shows how much notice you take of me. And the job doesn't start until April. All right, big sister?'

'Please yourself – you always do,' and with a shrug Bron bustled back into the kitchen.

Lisa hated the idea of parting with her beloved Michael even for a couple of weeks. He tried to reassure her, 'I'm going there for us, my lovely, and the children we'll have one day.'

'Promise me you'll be careful – please.'

'Sit down,' he steered her to the settle. 'Now let me explain. We have the Colonel's assurances that the trail is clear – no encampments anywhere near us. They've cleared it. And, what's more, he is sending a posse as a back up just in case. More danger going out for a ride in the pampas!' He put his arms around his wife and planted a gentle kiss on her full young mouth. 'It's only for a couple of weeks, and our future could depend on it. The valley doesn't need to be tamed – not like this – it's waiting there ready for us.'

She lowered her head and stared down at her hands. Gently he raised her chin. 'We have to do something, my love – like living on the edge of a volcano here.'

With a little smile she touched his cheek. 'Yes, you are right. Just me – I don't want you to go that's all. I want you by me all the time.'

He laughed. 'Hey! It's not for a month or two yet – so come on, missus, let's have a dish of that *cawl*. I can smell.'

17

Since Glyn's death Big John had continued his monthly sessions in Rawson to discuss policing, the law and public misdemeanours with Dafydd and Sion.

Tucking into his supper after one of these sessions Dafydd said suddenly, 'I don't know, but there's something different about Big John these days.'

'Oh?' said Myfanwy. 'Like what?'

'Well, he seems in much better spirits, ready to have a laugh again. Looking after himself, too, he is – his hair's cut, his boots are polished.'

Myfanwy interrupted, 'Shaved, clean collar and tie?'

'Aye aye. Seemed anxious to get away bit earlier than usual today.'

She laughed. 'It's a woman – *twp*!'

'No, no! Said something about some Americans – got a ranch, other side of Gaiman, they have.'

'Like I said – it's a woman! You don't smarten up to see a bunch of hairy ranchers.'

'You reckon?'

'Ask him.'

'Don't be so soft.'

'What's the matter with you men?' Grinning from ear to ear she nudged him playfully. 'You leave it to me and Blod, good boy.'

The female grapevine, which spreads rapidly and, like water, finds its own level whatever the terrain, quickly found out part of the current mystery surrounding Big John. Two young American males, one single, one with a wife, had indeed taken a ranch the other side of Gaiman. The wife, Mrs Ethel Place with the pet name Etta, was, they were told, blonde and very pretty, therefore, it stood to reason, a bit 'flighty'.

'Well, that's it then, isn't it?' opined Blod, spreading her elbows on the table. 'She's Big John's fancy woman, no question.'

Myfanwy shook her head, 'we can't jump to conclusions. Could be just social.'

Blod snorted.

'But', Myfanwy went on, 'a few weeks ago by all accounts they threw a big party – nearly all Gaiman was there, and the bachelor boy, Santiago whatever he's called, was playing tangos on his guitar.'

'Tangos? *Ychafi.*'

'And they said Big John danced with her – the wife.'

'That's her then, the fancy woman – this Etta.'

'Use your sense, Blod – not much chance if her husband's around all day. Besides Big John's a bit . . . what d'you call . . . awkward with women, and, fair play, he's got to go there to inspect, hasn't he?'

'Aye, the ranch, not her;. No, I'm sticking to my guns, Myfanwy *fach.*'

While the Rawson women were correct about the basic facts concerning the Americans and Big John's involvement, there was more – much more – to this odd trio.

Big John, usually painfully shy with the opposite sex, had almost overnight developed a passionate infatuation with Etta. He had met her when calling on the farm during the course of duty. It was important he knew what livestock they had in case of rustlers. She would walk him round the ranch chatting happily with her southern American drawl that Big John found mesmerizing. Whenever she said 'Beeug Jahn', and smiled so prettily, his stomach lurched. He wanted to touch her blonde hair as they walked through barns and pigsties. He wanted to stroke her sunkissed arms as he held open the gates of the paddock for her.

After the third visit she said with a disarming smile, 'Beeug Jahn, ah hev a special surprise f'you tiday.' And she curled her little finger beckoning him inside. To be fair he would have followed her beckoning anywhere. On a small carved table in their best room she had put out two cups.

'Now – you jes' wait while ah bring you a beeug surprise, Jahn boy.'

He was jelly and had to remind himself she was a married woman, though today there was no sign of her husband.

She was wearing a blue blouse that was so low cut two firm mounds of palpitating flesh were already halfway out. A full skirt fitted snugly round her small waist. He could not take his eyes off her as she pirouetted into the kitchen and emerged seconds later with a jug of steaming coffee and a plate of small cakes.

'Heeya, Beeug Jahn, coffee and cookies foh the best law man in town', and she giggled delightedly.

He had never tasted coffee before and soon realized what he had been missing all his life. Gazing at Etta and her trim little body made him realize what else he was missing.

As he was leaving she casually took his arm. 'Now, Jahn – ah may call you that?'

'Oh, Mrs Place, *fach*, you can call me whatever you like.'

She giggled for a good ten seconds. 'Oh, Jahn, ah lurv the way ye talk! Sorta Indian and tribal and foreign. Now we ah hevin' a paahty next week – to be all friendly lahk with ah neighbours, and you gotta come.' She moved closer to his big frame and gazed up at him with her baby blues, 'Weeil ya come?'

He was lost.

'I would,' he croaked, passion having drained his voice away, 'I would be truly honoured to accept your invitation, Mrs Place.'

'Gee, that is so good', and she jumped for joy like a child, which he found enchanting. Squeezing his arm she added seductively, 'Beeug Jahn, you can call me Etta.'

He rode in a daze back to his ranch, muttering her name. 'Etta, Etta, Etta.'

Sitting at his table later that evening he took pen and paper and tried very hard to compose a poem for his idol. But after several hours all he came up with was 'Etta, Etta, with you I'd feel much better', so he decided poetry was not for him.

Dancing with her at the party was like a dream come true. He could hold her lithe little body close, especially when she tried to teach him the new tango that aroused in him a complex of emotions and physical longings, albeit under the watchful eyes of Mr Harry Place. Regretfully, as he rode home, Big John concluded that, as he was an honourable man, in the end she was a married woman, lovely but out of his league.

However, one morning very soon after the party, when he paid the ranch his regular courtesy call, he found pretty blonde Etta sitting alone on the veranda and in tears, with a noticeable increase in the flow as soon as he stepped closer. Gently he knelt down by her side.

'Oh, Etta, Etta, *fy nghariad i,* what's the matter? I cannot see you, beautiful girl, in tears like this.'

He put his arms around her and drew her blonde head to his manly chest, patting her like a child.

'There there, come you, lovely, come you. Tell Big John what happened.'

He pulled out a spotlessly clean white handkerchief – his mother had said he should always have one on him – and dried her brimming blue eyes, kissing away the tears. His knees were beginning to feel the strain, so he lifted her carefully out of the rocking chair to a settle close by and placed her on it with extreme care – she was so delicate, she reminded him of his mam's best china dog. He sat beside her and was soon comforting with warm kisses. At last their medicinal value took effect, and her tears began to subside.

Taking deep breaths between fewer sobs, she told him, 'We had a little difference of opinion and – and – Butch – he jes' walked out and rode away, taking Santiago with him.'

'Butch? Who's he?'

She opened her big brimming blue eyes and gazed into his. 'Why, that's Harry.'

He was enslaved. 'You mean your Harry – Harry Place?'

'Yes, Beeug Jahn,' she simpered. 'Like ah said, he's not really Harry Place. See, he was a butcher once and admired a cowboy called Cassidy, so they always called heeum Butch Cassidy. But he stole a five-dollar horse, did a spell in prison and escaped. I guess he's been on the run evah since.'

'And Santiago?' He dabbed Etta's eyes.

'He's on the run, too. 'S'not his name either. They call him

Sundance Kid. The youngest in his family, see, so they called him Kid and he did time in Sundance prison.'

'And do you know how long your husband will be away?'

'First of all, he's not ma husband. I ain't married to heeum, and, second, he's gonna be gone till sundown – at the earliest.'

Big John knew that as an officer of the law he should be turning them over to the Argentine legal system. But then he knew at first hand how unfair that could be. And, no doubt about it, his lovely Etta would also be implicated. He would say nothing; simply enjoy being with his only love while Butch and Sundance were away.

He had until sundown, and it has to be said Etta made up for whatever Big John lacked in experience in the art of love.

That was how it started.

For the next few months Butch Cassidy and Sundance were frequently absent for days at a time. Big John did not ask what the duo were up to, better not to know, though Etta said they were off buying more livestock – which could have been true for they had a thriving selection. However, he could not contemplate the thought of this lovely slip of a woman being left on her own in such isolation with no comforting male body to lie beside her. As she was unmarried, he could furthermore dismiss his conscience and attend chapel on Sundays with an easy heart for the Almighty.

The ranch being on Big John's regular route, whenever Etta was alone and could see him, she would leave some token tied to the gates at the end of the long drive. Sometimes he forced himself to make a routine call when it was evident both men were at home. This was a self-inflicted punishment, for to see his lovely Etta and not be able to touch her was a torment worthy of hell itself.

Whatever the problems, life for Big John had taken on an entirely different meaning. Whether awake or asleep, Etta alone occupied his thoughts. In his head he wove elaborate schemes to kidnap her and prise her away from those two criminals. The trouble was they had made themselves well liked in the locality. Only he knew the truth and could say nothing for Etta's sake.

Savouring every moment of this delicious torment, Big John had never been so happy.

*

Early one quiet morning a few weeks later, Chief Kitchkum's twin boys, not more than sixteen years old, who worked with Evan in the trading post, burst into Gaiman on sweating horses that they had whipped into a frenzied gallop. The boys, in a state of sheer panic and terror, were immediately taken into a house where they were given soothing words and cups of *maté* while Big John was summoned.

Slowly he pieced together the horrific events of the morning, his heart heavier with every detail. Two Americans had come into the trading post and asked Evan at gunpoint to open the safe. With voices still shaking with fear, the twins between them retold the events of that morning.

'But Señor Evan he say nothing there.'

'They not believe him.'

'We say he tell true.'

'One Americano, he push us with gun to back of shop.'

'The Americano say we must stop crying or we never see our mother again.'

'We frightened.'

'Señor Evan he hold big Americano's wrist with the gun and hold it so hard pistol drop on floor.'

'But Señor Evan he trip on floor and big Americano take pistol out of his boot and shoot Señor Evan here.' Slapping his chest, the boy began to shake and sob once more.

'We can do nothing,' said the first lad. 'Our Señor Evan – lie there in blood. He is dead. But Americanos make us wait in shop until they are gone or they kill us, too.'

Big John put his hands on the sobbing boys' shoulders. 'All right, boys– all over now. You did well for coming to tell us. Now can you remember what they took?'

'All food in shop, Señor – meat, *bara*, flour, everything.'

Though there were a few American ranchers scattered in the area, Big John knew it had to be Etta's companions if past history were to be taken into account. He had no evidence and did not wish to find any, for to imprison them would be to imprison Etta.

With a murder on his hands he was duty bound to inform the army. A message was dispatched immediately. The two boys were taken back to their parents, a posse went to the trading post to see if there was anything they could do for young Evan, while Big John rode off purportedly to question all the Americans in the area ahead of the army.

He made straight for the ranch. Etta was on the veranda and ran to meet him.

'What you doin' heeah, Beeug Jahn? The boys are sleepin'. They won't wanna see you heeah today – not your usual day to come by, is it?' She appeared tense and nervous and spoke rapidly.

Placing his arm clumsily round her waist he led her back to the veranda and sat her on the rocking chair. 'Wait here,' he said firmly. She opened her mouth to reply. He raised his index finger indicating silence. She obeyed.

He crept round the back of the ranch to the stables and was left in no doubt that these two had indeed committed the crime. Stacked in crates in a corner were sacks of provisions, hocks of smoked ham, salted beef and barrels of butter, ready to be buried in the earth for preservation. Each item carried the trading post's stamp.

Returning to a perplexed Etta still sitting rigid on the chair, he said quite calmly, 'I know what they did, and it will be a murder charge. The army will be investigating the movements of all Americans in the district. There aren't more than about six, and you'll probably be first because you are nearer. Now listen to me and do exactly as I tell you.'

She nodded and put her finger in her mouth like a child.

'As soon as I've gone, wake them up and send them away, *pronto*. They should go north, Chile, Bolivia, anywhere. Got it?'

Tears filled her eyes. 'Oh, Jahn boy, what shall ah do?'

'Do? Stay here, with me, that's what you do! Tell those two you'll look after the ranch till everything dies down. Once they've gone, ride down to my place, you know where it is. You got to be quick. You must not be here when the army comes. Understand? Nobody will find you there. I'll be back in a couple of hours.'

She nodded. 'Thanks, Jahn boy– thanks', and planted a seductive kiss full on his lips. His insides trembled with the stirrings of passion and promise for the future.

He put his ungainly arms round her, 'Oh, Etta, my flower, we can be together at last. Now go on, wake them up. Tell them they are going be arrested for murder, for certain, and they must get away – fast. Go on! Now!'

Galloping away from the only love he had ever known, Big John was fully aware he had committed a serious crime in hindering the course of justice. A young man lay murdered, and he knew the killers.

As the big man disappeared from sight, Butch Cassidy was already mumbling into consciousness from a deep untroubled sleep, watched over by his smiling devoted Etta, whose passionate rosy lips kissed him into a new day.

How many more senseless deaths could the already splintering community take? Tomos was particularly badly shaken, as not only had Evan been a classmate in school but they had plans for the future. Dafydd wrote to the boy's relatives in Wales, for since his mother's death he had been living alone. Even sadder was the fact he had just started seriously courting Eirlys Evans from Gorseinon, also a classmate. All relationships here in whatever stage of development, were taken seriously by both parties. Choice being limited, urban coquetry was not on the community's agenda, so Eirlys had been regarded as young Evan's intended.

After the funeral in Gaiman, there was much gossip surrounding the Americans, who had conveniently disappeared after the murder, confirming their guilt. In any case, Chief Kitchkum's twins had given very clear physical descriptions. Inevitably Big John was questioned.

'I know no more than you,' he mumbled.

'Funny though,' Dafydd replied. 'They must have left pretty quickly. You called on them, didn't you?'

'Well, no. See, they were the last ones. I went to check on the other Americans first, and by the time I got there they'd gone.' Big John was not a good liar.

'The woman, too?'

'Aye, the woman, too.'

That much was true. Big John's little flower Etta had never graced his hearth nor warmed his bed as arranged. She had vanished with her man, leaving Big John and his conscience in shreds with no soft little body to hug in recompense.

But Dafydd guessed the truth and knew that if he pressed Big John he would have had a full confession. It was obvious he had given his American fancy a timely tip-off, long enough for the trio to pack up and run before the army arrived. Was he expecting her to go to him? There could be no excuse, Big John's behaviour was totally out of order, especially for a community law-keeper, but slowly Dafydd came to terms with his own conscience. If he were to turn him in, what then? Arrest? He had already suffered at the hands of a corrupt legal system. The criminals were probably in Bolivia by now anyway, and eventual capture was certain. Nothing could have prevented young Evan's murder and nothing would bring the boy back. Finally if Big John had not deliberately put his large bulk between a rustler's intended bullet and Dafydd, he, too, would surely have died. It was an act of remarkable courage, and Big John was too good a man to lose. Dafydd would therefore do nothing and say nothing.

He wrote in his diary, 'The raw force of nature has no conscience.'

He wondered whether Darwin would have approved.

In the months that followed, Big John's personal appearance suffered such a severe deterioration that Myfanwy was obliged to say, quite smugly, 'See! I was right, wasn't I?'

18

It was only after assurances of safety from the army and the Colonel himself that the young men – still keen to explore the valley and with, of course, the attractions of gold prospecting – set another date. It had to be said, their families and friends were full of misgivings.

'Use your sense, Tomos,' said Myfanwy sharply. 'It's been rustlers, then Indians, then Americans – out for blood. If you ask me, you want your heads read to even think about it now.'

'Look, Mam, we'll be four – all armed. What's more the army will be doing another big recce over the area before we go. They've promised, and they'll be sending a small detachment behind us on the route as a follow-up.'

'And why, because they know it's not safe?' She sat down at the kitchen table with a look of defiance.

'No, Mam. Don't you see, the country needs to expand – go west – develop new communities. From what we've been told –'

Myfanwy put a hand to her head. 'Do you really think we don't know all about the eyewash yarns governments spin, Tomos *bach*?'

'It's not the government this time, Mam, it's the men who have actually been there; a lovely valley better and easier for us than here, all of us. I know Huw wants his mam and Elin there.'

Myfanwy folded her arms on the table. 'Beautiful or not, I don't like the idea of you boys going so soon after,' she paused, 'after all that's happened.'

'But, Mam, it's because of all that's happened the army's going to look after us like babies.'

Myfanwy rose from the table with a sigh of exasperation. There was no persuading her son once he had made up his mind.

*

Having gone over the route with the army – even the detail where they would pitch camp each night, to and from the valley – arrangements were made for the small military detachment to set out along that precise route twenty-four hours after the boys set off.

The young men intended to be absent for about two to three weeks, no more, but that did nothing to placate tearful wives and families who saw them off at dawn.

It was a relatively straightforward route, sometimes a rocky track, sometimes a well-trodden path several feet wide cut through bracken and bushes, but mostly through rough wild terrain. Before them, always, were the distant Andean foothills forming a dramatic backdrop, their irregular peaks covered in snow. *En route* there were clearings where small tributaries of the Chubut trickled lazily over outcrops of rock forming deep pools, perfect for fishing.

They stopped by a stream in open country at midday. For young men they were remarkably well organized; Sion collected kindling for a fire; Huw looked after thirsty horses; Michael and Tomos caught fish. After a filling meal combined with their personal larders of bread and cheese, the four young men began to speculate on life as it could be in the beautiful valley, how everything would grow in that fertile soil.

'Just think, all that healthy livestock we could rear,' said Tomos as he gulped down mouthfuls of running water from the river.

'Aye, and all the fruit and vegetables we need. No problem with irrigation there, boys,' Huw added.

Sion gathered the empty plates. 'Perhaps the government would give us raw materials to build again,' he said.

'We are talking transport here, aren't we?' Michael was crouching on the grass dousing the fire. 'We'd need a road first – for the supply wagons.'

Tomos wiped his wet mouth on his sleeve. 'Cement, sand, bricks.'

Michael poured water on the stubborn embers 'As I said, it's proper transport we need.'

'Like a railway?'

Tomos untethered his horse. 'Aye, Huw *bach*, when pigs can fly.'

At the end of that first day they had talked endlessly of the possibilities that could lie ahead in what seemed at this moment an

El Dorado, certainly when compared with the life they were living. They had been told of a shallow river near the valley with plenty of silt that, when gathered in a pan and washed properly, had left many prospectors with gold nuggets.

But prospecting was a half-mythical dream laden with rumours, like the crock at the end of the rainbow and not something they were taking too seriously.

Tomos called out, 'Hey, Huw, you might find enough nuggets to buy out that law firm in Buenos Aires.'

'Oh yeah!' came the reply, 'It's those flying pigs again!'

By the third day they noticed a distinct change in the landscape. The grass was greener and abundant; foliage was lush; instead of Rawson's arid heat the weather was temperate with a gentle warm breeze. Pushing his hat back off his forehead Michael pulled his horse to a halt and whistled. '*Duw*, it's like being in Wales again,' he whispered, his eyes misty.

Sion had galloped ahead and stopped on a hillock to take in the terrain.

'Come here,' he called back. 'The plains they talked about. Look! There they are! We're getting nearer, boys.'

At sundown they stopped to check the map given to them by Fernando the Sergeant. He knew the route and had marked places for their overnight camps. Michael read his instructions. 'River on the right and a steep rock face in front of you. There is a small clearing surrounded by bushes, with one tall tree standing alone in the middle.'

'Well, this isn't it,' said Sion, taking in the surrounding landscape. 'This clearing is much too big. We haven't got there yet.'

Huw dismounted squinting into the sunset. 'Maybe not, but there are plenty of rocks, a stream and some good grass for the horses. In fact,' he squatted on a stone, 'I bet this space has already been used as a camp if these bits of burnt wood are anything to go by. And, look, a carved toy by here. Strange.'

'Nothing strange about that,' said Sion. 'If this place has been used before – by Americans looking for gold – perhaps, they could have made a fire, stopped the night, carved a toy for one of their kids and dropped it.'

Tomos yawned. 'Well, the horses need a rest, for sure – been galloping for hours, non-stop. My backside, too.' He grimaced. 'Poor old Bess is sweating like a pig.'

Michael folded the map. 'You've got a point there.'

It was agreed for the sake of both horses and men they would rest and pitch camp where they were.

Hours later, after supper and the laughter, jokes and yarns, they each pulled out sleeping bags made out of folded quilts and *carthenni*.

'Better to keep this fire going. Might have a visit from the Patagonian leopard!' said Sion with a broad smile.

'Shut up, Sion. Not true. Lot of old stories.' Tomos retorted, as he tried to find a comfortable patch for the night. 'Plenty of firewood there anyway,' he grinned.

'I'll get some more – better be on the safe side.'

Michael heaved himself up from a tump of grass. 'I'll give you a hand, Sion. Need to water the rhubarb before *cwtching* up for the night anyway.'

'Want any help with the wood?' asked Huw

'No, better you stay here – with the horses. We'll be over in that woody bit.' Sion pointed to thickly foliaged woodland some fifty yards away across a flat open strip that lay behind large boulders, which made a natural boundary to their impromptu campsite.

Tomos and Huw barely had time to tether the horses when Sion and Michael came stumbling back ashen-faced. 'Get on your horses! We've got to get the army, for Christ's sake,' Sion commanded hoarsely.

'Indians – dozens of them.' Breathlessly Michael attempted an explanation.

'No firepower – knives and darts. They know we're here some-where. And they'll be coming out of that forest any minute now,' said Sion. 'So we'll make a barrier of fire between us and them – they won't come through that. Bunch together what kindling you can – quick for Christ's sake! Two bunches each, light them and as soon as they start coming out of that forest we'll chuck them. Spread out and we'll do a shoot-out long enough to make a getaway!'

'And, remember, we don't take the same route. Dodge about,' Michael ordered.

Crouched behind the tall boulders Sion called quietly, 'Here they come, boys. Now get your torches. Two each. Keep them out of sight, and chuck when I tell you to. Then it's shoot to kill – horses and away!'

Dozens of painted Indians swarmed silently out of the woods armed with knives, *bolas* and sheaves of darts. They were visible only by the white paint on their faces and bodies and the intermittent shafts of moonlight that lit the landscape.

Sion gave the signal. Eight flaming torches of long thick twigs and branches were hurled over the boulders to form a flaming barrier between them and the advancing army. Momentary pandemonium from the screaming Indians gave the seconds needed for pistols cocked at the ready.

'Fire, and quick – away! Don't look round, and don't stop!' Sion barked.

Huw and Tomos mounted their horses, firing random shots across the boulders, and sped into the night. Three more rounds and Michael leapt on his horse, followed by Sion who was now felling Indians who had circumnavigated the fire barrier and, armed with darts and spears, were ready to aim with deadly accuracy.

Ahead Huw and Tomos galloped along a meandering route as Sion had instructed, for safety's sake. They would get back to the main pathway in a few hours to reach the army encampment, less than a day behind them, they hoped. Huw led the way.

Two hours had passed since taking flight from the attacking tribe. As there had been no further danger and they were on an open track, Huw steadied Caradog, his horse, for a rest.

Tomos drew alongside. 'No sign of Michael and Sion then?'

'I'm not really surprised,' said Huw. 'There must be a dozen different ways to avoid the main track, and this isn't the one they've taken. We'll meet up with them at the camp, sure to be.'

'So, which way then?'

The moon was clear in the sky now with no clouds to darken its luminescence. 'We should be making for the main track again, so it's south-east.' Huw frowned and thought. 'That way,' he said, pointing.

They followed narrow trails that took them through wooded bush country, shrouded in foliage, never the most comfortable terrain to traverse in moonlight.

Half an hour later Huw slowed down for Tomos to ride alongside. 'What's the matter?'

'I think we are being followed,' Tomos whispered. He had observed movement in the trees and bushes running alongside them.

'Animals, birds, they are.'

'They don't carry anything silver, do they?'

'Moonlight, boy.'

'Aye, moonlight shining on a weapon, Tomos. Come on, let's get out of here quick.'

A canter became a gallop but only for a few minutes.

'Jesus! Tomos, look! A ravine – goes on for miles – no way round it. We've got to jump. I knew it! This is what they are bloody waiting for.'

Tomos put his head in his hands. 'Better leave me here, – she'll never do it. She's small – Bess hasn't got half the strength of Caradog.'

'It's not strength the horse needs for this. It's agility and pluck. Bess has got both. Look, it's narrower here than further up – about fourteen feet.'

'Aye and how many hundreds down?'

'Nobody's going down. Come on, Tomos. No option, boy! We're cornered. Take a run up and keep your body as flat as you can. Get your head next to hers, and talk to her, coax her. Quick! I'll go first.'

Huw's big sturdy Caradog took a run and leapt, clearing the ravine effortlessly.

His friend had been right. Tomos could hear the rustling in the bushes coming nearer. His body shaking, his heart palpitating, he did as he had been told and lay flat on Bess, merging his body on hers, as one.

He put his head on her mane and whispered, 'Come on, my lovely girl. Save both our lives. You can do it – you can. Now come on!'

He gave her a run, but she stopped suddenly on the brink of the ravine nearly throwing her rider.

'Again!' shouted Huw from the other side.

Tomos, shaking like a leaf, could think of better ways to die. With his head flat against hers, he whispered again, 'Come on, Bess – you can do it. Good girl. Come on, for both of us. Ready now. Come on, girl!'

She seemed to know this time what was expected of her, for she took the run-up at a wild gallop. Just as they reached the edge of the ravine an angry troupe of Indians burst out of the bushes behind them, shouting, running, hurling spears, that in the comparative dark missed horse and rider. Bess, smelling danger, did not stop this time. She made an almighty leap across the ravine while Tomos, his eyes tightly shut, hung on to her mane for dear life. They flew in the air over the deep chasm below, never daring to look down for fear gravity would lay claim. He knew that with one well-aimed dart in Bess's hide, they would both plunge to their deaths. Miraculously Bess made a perfect landing on the other side. Tomos slid heavily off her sweating back. Animals and men were exhausted, but they were safe.

The two friends, still trembling, threw their arms round each other in silence, knowing how near to death they had been – and a savage one at that. Tomos nuzzled his head in Bess's mane to dry his tears while whispering his eternal gratitude. They rode on slowly and in silence until well out of range of the danger that patrolled the ravine's opposite bank. At the first stream, they stopped, and both men and horses assuaged that special thirst bred of fear.

'I reckon we should be somewhere near the army detachment by dawn,' said Huw.

Tomos plucked a blade of grass. 'Wonder where Michael and Sion are.'

'They'll have taken a different route. He had the map, didn't he?'

'P'raps they went back the same way.'

'They could be there already then.'

Back on the original track again, by dawn they looked for any sign of the military. Tomos spotted smoke curling up in the distance, but never sure if it signified friend or foe they gave the area a very wide berth until Huw saw a uniform.

Hungry and exhausted, they recounted the events to the Major in charge. The boys were glad to find Fernando, who made sure they were fed and rested after their ordeals. The story of the horses leaping the ravine brought admiration, hugs and sweet titbits for the horses, especially to Bess who was so much smaller than big Caradog.

'D'you know what, Bess?' laughed Tomos. 'You've got more men spoiling you than any other girl I know.'

It was decided to wait another six hours before the detachment of twenty fully armed men would set off in search of Sion and Michael, just in case they turned up. Meanwhile they learnt a few unpleasant facts from Fernando as they parleyed in his tent. There was a reason why the Sergeant had marked so precisely where they should pitch camps on the trail.

'You see,' he said, looking from one to the other, 'the army has been – uh – clearing the Indian villages.'

'You mean destroying and killing. Women, children, too?'

He shrugged, 'Well – yes – people get killed. Not good, but we have to make a safe route to the west.'

'Oh God!' murmured Huw. 'We pitched camp on the site of a village you had destroyed.' He looked at Tomos. 'The kid's toy – charred wood, remember?'

Tomos sighed 'Aye, I remember. Stopped in the wrong place then, didn't we?'

The detachment with Tomos and Huw set out back on the trail once again, hoping they would meet up with their old friends.

They were now approaching the clearing where they had been attacked, Tomos and Huw riding at the back of the detachment with Fernando.

'Sergeant, stay with the two men while we inspect the site.'

'But, Major,' said Huw, 'can't we go with you?'

'No, you stay here – please.'

Fernando could see fear on the faces of the two boys. 'It is very possible', he said brightly, 'Sion and Michael go back another way.'

Ten minutes later their worst fears were realized. The bodies of Sion and Michael were found in the undergrowth. They had been felled by tipped darts and horribly mutilated.

The two boys were struck dumb, at first with disbelief, then profound grief, followed by a torment of conscience that had they not ridden ahead their friends could have been saved. Trembling, they watched as the bodies, covered in blankets, were carefully lifted on to stretchers and laid on saddles for the journey back to Rawson.

They had lost their good friends.

Their sisters were now widows.

Fernando was as devastated as the two young men. He grieved with them, like a brother.

How many more lives would this land devour?

19

They didn't want Lisa and Bron to see the bodies of their young husbands, but nothing would stop them. Lisa fainted and was taken to her parents' house. Bron was hysterical and had to be sedated. The community was in deep shock. Sion and Michael had been there from the start, from the moment *The Mimosa* sailed into harbour on that wind-lashed day all those years ago. They had shared in the joys, the traumas, the problems and the pain. They had been truly the sons of Rawson.

In later years nobody remembered details of the funeral, for a numbing pall had descended like a cloud on the community. Nobody spoke very much, and when they did it was without spirit, even when at work They had ceased to be simply a community sharing the same space, they were a family and the pain of loss was everyone's, to a greater or lesser degree.

'With those two boys gone we seem to have lost our *hwyl* Blod,' said Trevor Trehearne to his wife.

'Aye aye, but, just for now, isn't it? Life will come back to us – in time love, even to those poor girls.'

Lisa fell silent, her spirit broken. She would stand enveloped in her parents' arms, a grieving trio without words. As for Bron, she had lost both her father and her husband. The bond between mother and daughter was never stronger. Huw grew in emotional stature and slipped with ease into his father's role as head of the family.

Minds were confused, perplexed. Life had changed and would never be the same again. Tomos knew he wanted to fulfil his dream of living in that beautiful valley, but it seemed an impossible dream now.

Huw was more than ever determined to study law in Buenos

Aires, and next year Elin would be a student at the teachers' college. He would make sure of that.

As for Bron, there was no future, like Lisa. Every day the two young widows relived in their imagination the pain their husbands had suffered.

Nothing helped. Not even when Fernando told them the tipped darts that felled Sion and Michael would have rendered them immediately unconscious before the mutilation.

Blocking their minds to avoid thinking, hard and constant work in the fields with crops, in the pastures with livestock, was a minimal solution. They worked all the hours of daylight and dreaded the moment each day when darkness forced a return to lonely hearths and memories.

In the months that followed the double tragedy, religion was a solace to many, and to others comfort came from a personal spirituality rather than the rantings from a pulpit. For his part Dafydd turned away even further from religion declaring, 'The Devil made Patagonia as like his own place as two peas in a pod.'

The Reverend Jenkins, on the other hand, appeared to have a direct line of communication with God's mind and therefore knew not only why tragedies occurred but God's reasons for punishing humankind and precisely the sins that provoked divine anger.

'If He made us in His own image, He must be having a bad time of it up there' was Dafydd's wry response.

For him the answer to the present tragedy was purely political and very firmly in the hands of the Argentine government and their extermination policies towards the native Indian tribes. It was a subject for many late-night discussions between Fernando, Tomos, Huw and Dafydd. Despite being a soldier, Fernando had a liberal attitude and agreed that there should be talk with the Indians and a sharing of this vast land. And the government could not justifiably appropriate without something given in return.

'Diplomacy is the only answer,' Dafydd said glumly, wondering if ever the word entered the minds of those in government.

This year the only consolation was in the promising wheat harvest. Not only was it a bumper crop but also the quality, according to an agricultural expert sent down from the capital, was outstanding, and it would certainly be entered in the annual worldwide competition for wheat held in Buenos Aires.

When the news came through that Welsh Patagonian wheat had won the coveted prize and cup, it was just what the community needed. Plans were made immediately for a memorable day of festivities while the weather was still warm enough for outside entertainment.

A celebration lunch would be followed by a *cymanfa ganu*, with Will Fiddler's choir demonstrating an expanding repertoire. Women cooked, voices practised, handicrafts were carved, sewn, forged and knitted for the dozen stalls allocated. The community had a spring in its step again, and life became worth living. At last they had been touched by success, and, after all the sorrows and the heartache and desperation of past years, this was indeed a moment of triumph.

The central square was decked with bunting and flowers; tables were laid out in rows ready to accommodate enough food for the tribes of Israel. The day arrived, bright warm and sunny, which the Reverend privately felt was a direct result of the hours he had spent on his knees praying for good weather. Best frocks and suits were taken out of the wardrobe, and the small newly formed brass band played the traditional airs that they had been practising with a grim determination.

Chief Kitchkum, Francisco and a few of his companions set up their own stalls, selling ostrich feathers, leather hides, moccasins, cotton petticoats, ponchos and rugs. The dairy wives piled their tables high with cheese and butter. Three bread stalls took centre-stage. A large notice hung above them: 'BARA MADE FROM THE BEST WHEAT IN THE WORLD.'

It was a time for laughing and congratulations; a time when no one thought for one moment that life in the old country could have been better. Even Lisa and Bron lost the look of sorrow in their young faces and joined the singing and sense of enjoyment. There was one man who had never left Lisa's side since Michael's murder, who had been caring from the outset and who had helped with crops and livestock despite having his own to cultivate.

Lisa had often said to Myfanwy, 'Honest, Mam, I don't know what I'd do without Herbie.'

Naturally the Reverend proposed a prayer meeting to 'end the day in sober reflection'. He made the announcement after the choir had performed brilliantly and before the dancing was to start. It was to be a new dance called the polka. Several Welsh, living in Gaiman, had been taught the dance by recent German immigrants. It seemed to have a wholesome family appeal and therefore did not offend even the narrowest of minds, though, it has to be said, the Reverend remained tight-lipped at the idea of such abandoned enjoyment – so unrelated to the Bible.

As a dance for two people, it was so much more seemly than the tango that remained *ychafi*, a phrase uttered frequently with a purse of the lip by Blod and many others.

When the piano, fiddle and accordion struck up with the current rage, Dafydd put his arms around his wife's waist and whispered in her ear, 'Let's join in the dancing, but don't expect me to come to his prayer meeting. I've got a headache,' he grinned.

Myfanwy knew nothing could persuade Dafydd once he had made up his mind. He could be as stubborn as a mule. Quickly she tried to think of excuses for his absence. 'But, Dav, what'll they say?'

'For once I don't care. I refuse to pay any more lip-service to something I doubt and certainly never through the ministrations of someone I don't respect.'

'Oh, Dav, how can you say that?'

'Look, *cariad*, what use was he to Lisa over Michael, eh? Came to see her a couple of times to pray for his soul, that it be forgiven all sins, and hers too. Spent her time on her knees with him, she did. No! She got love and support from family and good friends. We gave her love – that's what counts, doesn't it – love? A word that doesn't enter that one's head!'

Myfanwy sighed. 'Trouble is you've got Lisa thinking the way you do.'

'No, no! Nobody tells our Lisa what to think. She wants to know, asks questions, works it out for herself.'

'Aye, and comes to your conclusions.'

'She's seen sense then, good! Anyway the Druids got it right, don't you think – nature, spirituality?' He grinned. 'Go on, tell him I'm an old Druid – a Darwinian one, of course!'

Despite herself, Myfanwy laughed, as her husband spun her into a polka.

When Herbie ap Morris took Lisa in his arms for the first time to dance he realized how much he loved this girl. A wise man, Herbie knew she was still in love with the memory of Michael, but there was no rush. He could and would wait.

Once again, despite the prize-winning wheat harvest, there were too many imponderables to make for an easy relaxed life in Patagonia. No one minded hard work, but it was a constant nagging fear of the unexpected that hovered like a question mark over the brightest dawn. The western valley was always an El Dorado option, but since Sion and Michael had been so brutally murdered it was taken off the subjects for discussion. Tomos dared not even mention it as a future possibility. Meanwhile Bethan, a fluent Spanish speaker now, correcting her parents at every opportunity, was doing very well at school and wanted to do precisely what Elin was doing. She would go to Buenos Aires, to teachers' college.

It has to be said that the idea of losing Bethan depressed Dafydd, though he knew logically that all birds fly the nest and that he couldn't keep her for ever. But emotions and logic were an impossible mix.

'Stop thinking of yourself, Dav.' Myfanwy scolded. 'I'm going to miss her, too – but think of her. She'll be a teacher – what she wants to be – more than we could have done and more than we could have done for her back in Merthyr.'

'I know, I know. You're right as usual, but not seeing her little face around – that's all.'

Dafydd received a letter from Señor Guillermo Rawson announcing a visit with no reason given.

'Funny he hasn't said why,' said Myfanwy, putting the letter back in its envelope.

'I suppose he wants to make sure the government's money has been well spent and is reaping the rewards of investment.'

'Aye, and visiting the school making sure the lessons are taught in Spanish. Wonder how long he'll stay.'

'A few days, sure to be. He's going on to Gaiman. No doubt Big John will be organising *cawl* and *bara brith* for him up there.'

Older now but with an enduring attachment to his favourite little colony, the dignified statesman was received with public ceremony in 'his' town. The tables were set out, the band played and the choir sang, conducted by Will Fiddler who was ever developing his considerable musical skills as a teacher.

Señor Rawson was shown the well-cultivated acres, the new ranches and farmsteads, the herds of livestock that grazed on land that had been wild and barren. He remarked on the particularly good health of the children, the sole epidemic having been whooping cough. The old politician doctor was plainly delighted, and before leaving Rawson for Gaiman he took tea privately with Dafydd and Myfanwy speaking in his adequate English but with Tomos as interpreter if needed.

The statesman, who had put on weight, sat down heavily in the comfortable chair offered to him. 'Now, Señor and Señora Rhys, the first thing I bring is my sympathy and sorrow for the losses you have suffered, both personally and as a community. Your deputy leader, the young man who ran the trading post, the rustling, and the recent murders – too much – and such a small community.'

He took out a large white handkerchief and dabbed his perspiring brow. 'When I heard the terrible fate of your son-in-law and Señor Sion, with whom I communicated on so many occasions, I was so very – saddened. I feel for the two young widows and hope that one day they will rebuild their lives.'

Dafydd nodded. 'Yes, Señor Rawson, it has been very difficult. No sooner do we grow as a community but people want to leave – and they do – to America or Canada on assisted passages given by those governments. You cannot blame them. A prize for wheat doesn't compensate for a difficult life.'

Before the old man could answer, Tomos asked in his good Spanish, 'Señor Rawson, several of us would like to explore the lovely valley in the foothills of the Andes, but how can we? The Indians are angry their villages have been destroyed, and unless we go under an armed army escort no one will dare try it again. My friend and I were lucky to escape when our comrades were murdered. We shall be trapped here, Señor, until your government talks to the Indians and comes to some sort of agreement with them. They have inhabited this country for thousands of years, and killing them, which is what the army is systematically doing, is murder, Señor, and no solution.'

Tomos paused for moment, cheeks flushed. 'And that is the reason we were ambushed and my comrades were butchered,' he snapped, 'because the army had destroyed their village and slaughtered their women and children only weeks before.' He paused again, looking steadily at the old statesman. 'We cannot live like this, sir. Your government must find a diplomatic solution.'

Dafydd and Myfanwy were taken aback at this unexpected political outburst from their mild-mannered son. Tomos waited for a response with slight apprehension.

The government minister slowly took out from his pocket a sheaf of papers. 'The Indian question is not my department, but I shall pass on your views, never fear.' He took a deep breath and sighed. 'What you have said, my boy, is absolutely right. There has to be another solution. The Indian policy is one that has disturbed – no, angered me – for years.' He looked at the nervous young man over his glasses. 'You have the makings of a politician.'

'Thank you, sir,' Tomos nodded, shy but pleased.

'Here', with a little smile the elder statesman waved the papers, 'is part of the answer. A compatriot of yours has proposed a railway line from the coast to run inland through the Chubut Valley.'

Dafydd looked at Tomos. 'And has the government approved?'

'Oh yes, Señor Rhys. We have agreed on all aspects of finance. Labour will be supplied by new immigrants from your native land and others. Arrangements are all but finalized, and the official announcement will be made very soon.'

Tomos beamed. 'When, sir?' he asked.

'Within a year, we think.'

Myfanwy looked at Dafydd. 'What about the river?'

Dafydd nodded to her briefly. 'Señor Rawson, the railway is wonderful news, but we cannot build a railway to be flooded. We need a dam first, Señor. We need protection for our homes and our crops.'

The old man shook his head. 'That will not be necessary for the railway, Señor Rhys. Look!'

He opened up a map showing the proposed route of the new railway line. 'You see', he said, tracing the trajectory with his finger, 'how the railway line avoids the flooding areas. Your dam will have to come later. But', he smiled, 'a little more good news to tell your people. From next month you will all have title to your land.'

When a letter arrived from the capital announcing the imminent arrival of an Argentine Governor to the newly established Chubut Provinces of Rawson and Gaiman it was a blow in the solar plexus for Dafydd. He sat down at the kitchen table, white-faced, the letter falling from his hands. Myfanwy clearing away dishes picked up the letter, read it and said nothing. She looked at him carefully. He was staring into space, his face furrowed and lifeless.

'It's the end, isn't it, the end of our little Wales?' His whispered words seemed to be drawn out of his body slowly and painfully; words he could barely utter.

Sitting quite still staring into emptiness, 'The end of the Senate,' he murmured. 'The end of me.'

He rose from the table and angrily squeezed the letter into a tight ball in his clenched fist and threw it on the fire 'A bloody town council, that's what we'll be – nothing more. All the fighting, persuading everybody to stay – to be steadfast – see it through – to support our new Wales. And what for – cleaning things up – taming the wilderness – losing loved ones – just for the Argentine government to lay claim to it?'

Myfanwy knew his anger would lead to a bout of depression. She remembered the month-long silent despair after Glyn was murdered and thought frantically how she was going to deal with him this time. Bustling about the kitchen, more to fuel her anxiety than clearing up, Myfanwy noisily pushed a chair under the table.

'Dafydd Rhys, are we going through all this again? When will you get it into your head that we are foreigners and our children – most of them born here – are Argentine nationals. How could we ever have expected a little Wales, when the Argentine was paying us to come here? All right, they lied, like all governments, and we did their dirty work for them, but what options did we have? How much of a self-contained Wales would we have had if we had stayed in Wales, tell me? Yes, the children are speaking Spanish in school – and they'd have spoken more English back home. As it is, many of them can speak the three languages now, and even we can get by with Spanish. Look, Señor Rawson remarked on our healthy community – bit of catarrh p'raps because it's so dry – but what about losing an arm or an eye in the tin – and killing chest problems and horrible accidents down the pit? Think back to when we nearly lost Tomos and Huw. The murders and tragedies we have had here could never add up to what it would have been back in the Rhondda. Your problem, Dafydd Rhys, is you. You've been kingpin for years, and now you are not. Nobody can be kingpin for ever – the young grow and take over the reins. So see sense, will you, Dav, and shut up with all this moaning and groaning. This is where we are and where we'll stay!'

She pushed a spitting pan of vegetables off the hot stove. 'Well, I am anyway. You can do what you damn well like!' With head held high she stormed out of the kitchen into the garden.

After several minutes Dafydd did the only thing a man could do. Quietly he walked into the garden and, standing behind her, put his arms about her.

'Yes,' he muttered. 'You're right – as usual.'

Relieved, Myfanwy smiled to herself and turned to face him.

'But you'll always be my kingpin, Dafydd Rhys,' she whispered.

It was time for the half-yearly Senate community meeting, the last one of any consequence. Huw would be translating the minutes into Spanish, an extra demanded by the new Governor of Chubut who would be arriving the following week.

There were many now who wanted to emigrate, land titles or no. Fresh entreaties and magnanimous promises from the United States and Canada, set against another temporary suspension of the railway plans, increased the frustration of being trapped in Chubut. A vote for emigration had therefore been popularly demanded.

It was a packed hall – despite the incessant rain they had had for two weeks turning fields and paths into mud. Trying to persuade any of them into changing their minds about emigrating once they had decided seemed to be a pointless exercise. Dafydd's impassioned speeches in the past had worked, but now so many were incensed about the very idea of an Argentine Governor, in addition to general hardship, he had no heart to say more than a few words – about the grass being greener possibly, that they would be missed in the community and hoped that the countries to which they had been invited did indeed fulfil their promises and, finally, that there would be a welcome should they ever return.

Two hundred and fifty voted to emigrate.

The meeting continued with the frequent trivia that members of the community felt worth raising as an issue. As the talk continued so the light tapping of rain on the corrugated tin roof began to increase. A few heads looked upwards. The tapping became a hammering that continued until it finally developed into a bombardment. More heads turned up to the roof and to their neighbours. Speakers' voices were pitched louder to counter the swelling sound. By now a concerned discussion was emerging in the body of the hall as past experiences were recalled. A few people rose to their feet determining whether they should return to their homes.

It was becoming difficult now to hear anything above the rain on the roof. Suddenly the doors burst open and a breathless Chief Kitchkum and Francisco stood there drenched and dripping.

Voices fell silent as they hurriedly removed their hats. '*Escusa, Señores, Señoras*,' they shouted. 'Señor Davido, Señora Blod – river – very, very high, *mucho inundacion* – dangerous – please all go back your *casas* – take all things – dangerous – big, big water come down here. Quick – quick! We help!'

It took five minutes to empty the hall. People walked in an orderly way to the double doors to avoid a stampede, but once outside they ran like bolts of lightning back to their homes. There was confusion, panic and fear. Children screamed, women cried, men shouted.

The river was throwing torrents of water over the lower slopes of Rawson and was already into the houses. Within an hour, tables, chairs, settles, were floating out to sea, while frantic householders salvaged the deepest drawers, tin baths, the biggest they could find, to put people in, using broom handles as oars to take them to safety on higher slopes.

Dafydd, Myfanwy and Bethan – with only minutes to spare – grabbed whatever was precious and essential, pushing papers, Dafydd's diary and family mementos into an old leather case. They ran upstairs as water forced its way into the kitchen and swept mercilessly through into the parlour, pushing open the front door, with wanton fury like an army of occupation, taking everything that stood in its way, only to abandon it wherever it pleased. They watched helplessly from the comparative safety of the bedroom as their furniture was smashed against walls or submerged in the deepening water. Tears rolled down Myfanwy's cheeks.

'Why, Dav? Why?'

Dafydd opened the window. 'Come on, no time to think of reasons. Doesn't matter. Anything here we can use as a raft?'

'This big drawer – it's oak – it'll float anyway.' Myfanwy pulled at the drawer in the old cupboard they had brought with them.

Bethan, cried as her mother helped her over the sill to Dafydd who stood precariously below them in the oak drawer rising with the swell.

'Don't be afraid, *cariad*. It's going to be all right,' he whispered in her ear.

They had no need for any oars; the force of the water propelled them along. Dafydd grabbed a passing tree branch that he used to steer a safer route through vegetation and half-submerged houses to a distant hillock that still stood as an island of safety above the raging torrents. While they would be safe on this mound, the hazards *en route* were frightening. The river swirled angrily about these makeshift lifeboats hurling them and their terrified occupants into bushes and foliage that lay in wait unseen below the surface. Large families had to arrange a shuttle service, hoisting older children into the top branches of tall trees to wait while they took the younger ones off to safety.

Tomos and Angharad made their escape in the tin bath. Herbie and Idwal, his brother, collected Lisa and Bron in two coracles they had made just months ago for the fun of it. Huw found a tin bath for his mother and Elin, while he made a raft out of the dresser drawer. Men were frantically hacking the shafts off their carts to turn them into rowing boats Though the rain was abating, the river engulfed more houses, and acres of another precious wheat crop disappeared for ever.

Those living higher up were able to wade through the torrents carrying children and babies. Blod had been at a confinement with the doctor when water began pounding open the front door, carrying most of the furniture away. The mother and her newborn were lifted into a tin bath and floated to higher ground. To add to this combined misery, the rain began to fall again, this time with renewed force, not in drops but in buckets.

So far as anyone could tell, families were accounted for. They had lost their possessions, but it seemed that through prompt action the river had claimed no lives. A number of children had been injured, for fragile limbs stood little chance between the force of swirling water and the hard bark of a tree.

On the hill, still well above the flood line, men, old and young, rigged up tented covers out of sheets or anything they could find for shelter. Those who could remember reminisced about *The Mimosa* landing and the beach caves all those years ago. Remarkably Will Fiddler had rescued his fiddle.

They tried, but how could they alleviate the mood of utter despondency that could be read in the eyes of every man woman and child? Groups clung together weeping silently for homes that had already taken years of toil and hardship to build but which were now no more. Once again – they had nothing.

Dafydd and the other members of the Senate walked about talking to the forlorn, soaked, shivering groups, trying to give comfort – as much for themselves as anyone else.

'As soon as the water goes down we'll have our houses, most of us – wet, but nobody's afraid of hard work here. And we'll all pitch in to get everybody on their feet again.'

'Aye, but what about my savings, Dav?' said one weeping elderly woman. 'All in a box they were, under the stairs.'

'How d'you know it isn't still there. Did you see it float out?'

'No.'

'Well, no crying till you know for sure. Come on, *fach*, dry your eyes.'

Rawson, its surrounding homesteads and fields, had all but disappeared, engulfed by relentless torrents of water. On the hill they sat close together uttering few words. No one had the energy, nor the *hwyl*, to say very much. Rain was still falling, but everyone on that hilltop was by now under some sort of awning.

The Reverend rose to announce a service. Myfanwy knew this would be like a red rag to a bull. She watched Dafydd's face set, his body stiffen.

Tugging at his sleeve, 'Leave it be, Dav,' she whispered. 'Please.'

The Reverend, who had been rescued by neighbours, without whom he and his wife would probably have perished, as he could do very little for himself raised his lily-white hands to the heavens. 'O God, our Father in Heaven, we Thy children implore and beseech You to forgive us our terrible sins and transgressions that have caused You in Your infinite wisdom to pour down Your wrath upon us as our just and deserved punishment.'

Dafydd stood up and walked outside the awnings in the rain slowly towards the reverend gentleman. Myfanwy sat transfixed; Lisa, near by, moved and sat beside her mother.

Dafydd, his hair wet, rain trickling down his face, approached the Reverend Jenkins who was about to kneel on someone's coat but stopped, raising his eyebrows in enquiry when he saw Dafydd.

'Could you please list our sins, Reverend Jenkins, and yours, too, of course, so we know how to avoid another disaster?'

There was total silence apart from the sharp intake of breaths. Some were horrified at Dafydd Rhys's effrontery in challenging the man of God. But many, though afraid to admit it openly, were more than sympathetic to his question.

Regaining his shaken composure, the Reverend replied. 'It is up to the Almighty to decide the punishment sinners like us deserve.'

Looking at his ever-obedient flock, he cleverly enlisted their support with an 'Amen'.

'Do you not think it is to do with weather conditions over the mountains – the rising clouds, the winds, the continuing rain?'

'The world is all God's work, Mr Rhys. Nature obeys His commands.'

'So everything good and bad then is all God's work?'

'Do not doubt God knows everything that goes on. He knows.'

'So when our children die and our sons and friends are murdered, this is God's work?'

'Everything is God's work.'

Dafydd's anger was rising. 'Then I put it to you, Reverend Jenkins, that we have a mighty cruel and unpleasant God who seems hell-bent upon our destruction!'

There were audible sounds of shock from the crowd.

'As ye sew so shall ye reap, Mr Rhys. Read your Bible and you will receive the word of the Lord.'

'So what Bible did the native Indians read when they murdered our two boys?'

'They are ignorant heathens!'

'But put here on this earth just like us by God, surely, according to your teachings?'

'It is only belief in the Almighty and His Son that makes us into sober God-fearing human beings.'

'So is that the key to our survival, Reverend Jenkins?'

'Through the word of God we survive.'

'Gorillas and apes survive, too, and they have no idea about the word of God, have they? And do you know, Reverend Jenkins, they help each other, give comfort to each other, protect each other, just as we are doing now. And they don't have a Bible. They don't have a religion. They have a natural instinct to survive just like us. And, what's more, they do not live under the threat of some terrible retribution from a cruel God that, according to you, only sees our sins, our wickedness and never the things we all do in our community to help each other, to give comfort and strength and – and love. That word, Reverend Jenkins, is sadly missing from your prayers. Love.'

The Reverend opened his mouth to speak, but Dafydd drove on. 'According to you and your kind, the sins of our fathers are visited upon us. Therefore that old man with a long white beard in the sky will take from us whatever and whoever we hold close as atonement for those sins. Call that a *just* God?' he shouted.

'Must I believe that God took away the lives of Michael and Sion because of some sins their fathers had committed? No, it was the fault of the army and the government and failure to negotiate proper terms with the natural inhabitants of this land. Must I believe that God took away my child on board ship all those years ago because of some sins I, or my father, had committed? No! It was a severe medical condition my little one contracted brought about by sea-sickness.' He paused, his eyes full with the memory.

'I will never believe that it is our sins that have caused this catastrophe. I will never believe in your God of vengeance and hate and cruelty. I want to believe in a God of love, who loves us for what we are and forgives us for what we are. If that is not to be then I shall go back to the old religion of Wales, of the Druids, where Mother Nature ruled and the wonders of the sky, the sun, the moon, wind and rain, the seasons, the good earth, the promise of springtime and harvest, where birth, death and love were as natural to every man woman and child as drawing breath.'

Dafydd stood quite still, tears mingling with the rain running down his cheeks. His shoulders sagged, exhausted from this verbal attack that had been festering within him for years.

In the silence 'Amen' came from Trevor Trehearne, followed by Blod and several others. It was the superstition of religion, fearing a new terrible catastrophe, that prevented many others from joining in.

Myfanwy rose, followed instantly by Lisa. With heads held high, they walked over to Dafydd, each linking an arm and walked proudly with him back to their patch under an awning. The prayer meeting did not continue. An hour later, when hearts had stopped palpitating, Will Fiddler started playing a selection of favourite folk songs. The singing, as always, diffused all tensions and linked souls together as nothing else could.

The floodwaters gradually subsided, leaving behind thick layers of mud, debris and dead fish with the smell of putrefaction. Household pets, along with livestock, were found floating, bodies bloated, accompanied by wails from children searching for their favourite dog or cat. Bonfires were made to burn the dead animals, and once more the community looked to Buenos Aires for rescue.

Within a few days generous quantities of goods arrived from the capital: blankets, food, clothing, timber and building supplies.

All the houses that were left standing, such as the home of the Rhyses, Lisa's, Bron's and Rhiannon's, would take time to dry out, and nobody was happy with the smell, but for most of them it was upstairs living for the next few months. The government gave each family some furniture to compensate for their loss, but in too many cases nothing could compensate for treasured family heirlooms.

Though the railway was rescheduled with a start date, following this latest disaster the idea of getting out of the Chubut Valley and trekking west was now foremost in the minds of Tomos and a group of like-minded young men. Life in Rawson was no place to live and bring up a family even with the proposed railway. It had become abundantly clear the river needed a dam before anything else, but it appeared not to be on the government's foreseeable agenda.

He asked his mother, 'Would you and Dadda come with me and Angharad to the valley, if it's as they say?'

'We'll see,' said Myfanwy.

'You'll be able to make jam there, Mam – plenty of fruit trees.'

'Like I said, we'll see. You know what your father's like.'

As for Lisa, she was seeing a great deal of Herbie who was fast becoming her right arm. They talked together and appeared to see eye to eye in most things.

'What do you think of Herbie as another son-in-law?' Myfanwy asked her husband, head in a book as usual, as she got into bed.

'Herbie's a good man. Plain to see he thinks the world of our Lisa. Do you think they will then?'

Myfanwy smiled. 'I think you'd better get your best suit out again. Good job you've made peace with the Reverend.'

Dafydd looked up from his reading.

'I haven't made peace with him. He's made peace with the Almighty for me. He hasn't been off his knees since the floods. Eight years older, is he, Herbie?'

'Aye aye, and that's good for her – stop her getting too bossy.'

Dafydd shot his wife a playful glance, 'Like you then.'

*

While Lisa and Herbie were, according to gossip, the next wedding candidates in Rawson, Bron and Herbie's brother, Idwal, were certainly developing a more than casual friendship which had been quietly noted and approved of unanimously by the community – though no one was sure, least of all the couple concerned, whether or not it had a future.

The foursome began spending evenings together, usually in Lisa's house, when it was cold, or else stroll in the meadows in the warm weather.

'Tell you the truth I don't know what to do – well, for the best'

It was one such evening before the two brothers were due to drop in. Bron was sitting in Lisa's kitchen drinking a cup of *maté*.

'So,' said Lisa placing elbows firmly on the table, 'what would you want to do if you weren't thinking of family?'

With a look of guilt and embarrassment Bron lowered her head and raised her big brown orbs. 'Go back,' she whispered, 'p'raps.'

Lisa put her hands to her head. 'Bron! Bron, how could you? What about your mam and Elin and Huw?'

'You asked me what I'd like to do if I wasn't thinking of family, and I'm telling you. Mam's had the idea of going up to Buenos Aires with Elin and Huw. He can find a place for them all. Then when Elin's qualified she'll have a job, and when Huw's a lawyer they'll be well away.'

'Until one of them marries,' Lisa added wryly.

Bron sighed. 'Oh, I don't know what to think, Lisa. Could have been all so – so lovely, couldn't it?'

'Come on, love – it will again, you'll see.'

Idwal with the same shock of auburn hair as his brother, and about a year older than Bron, was continuing to hone his skills as a blacksmith, at the moment a profitable sideline to farming.

The evening went well as always. They discussed the pros and cons of Bron's family's plans.

'I said it would be fine so long as neither Huw nor Elin got married, then it would be a bit difficult for Rhiannon,' said Lisa with her usual authority.

'Well,' Herbie replied, 'that would be up to Huw and Elin. If it was Myfanwy we were talking about she could come and live with us.'

Lisa flashed him a loving smile. 'Thanks, Herbie.' She turned to Bron. 'Go on, tell the boys what you just told me – what you might do.'

Bron looked down at the table, embarrassed again.

'Go on,' Lisa persisted.

'Well,' Bron began slowly, 'I just mentioned I wouldn't mind going back – start afresh.'

Idwal regarded her for a good minute and then said quietly, 'I know exactly how you feel about going back to Wales, Bron – I've had the same *hiraeth*, too.'

Herbie looked at his brother aghast. 'You've never said anything to me.'

Idwal's cheeks reddened. 'Never asked, have you? Anyway it's just an idea – as we're being honest, like.'

Work on the new railway construction into Chubut was now imminent, and at the end of the line another settlement, Trelew, was being planned.

Tomos and a few other young men decided to approach the new Governor about exploring the west once again. Together they wrote a letter asking for government help in mounting an exploratory expedition with a view to establishing a settlement in the valley at the foot of the Andes. Protocol decreed this should be done through his father as chairman of the Senate, albeit a body with token power only.

It was time for plain talking.

With a conniving wink and nod, Myfanwy invited Tomos and Angharad over to supper after chapel. These days Dafydd was not a regular chapel-goer. He went when he wanted a good *cymanfa ganu* – a good sing-song. This was one of his abstaining Sundays, which was a pity, as Tomos observed, because the singing always put him in a good humour.

However, after supper, as previously arranged between mother and son, Tomos took Dafydd outside to the little garden, each with a glass of home-brewed beer.

Taking a deep breath, Tomos pulled a folded sheet of paper out of his jacket pocket and, coming straight to the point, said, 'Dadda, this is a request letter to the new Governor, and we would like your signature and approval as chairman of the Senate.'

Dafydd knew the letter could have been delivered without his seal of approval but was touched by the gesture. He read it carefully while Tomos waited anxiously.

'A good letter, and I don't think you'll have any trouble getting government support – mine, too, for what it's worth – these days,' he added.

Tomos felt he would burst with joy and relief. 'Thanks, Dadda,' he said, putting his arms around his father. 'But we could only think about a new life if you and Mam came with us.'

Dafydd said nothing.

'And Lisa, Herbie and Bethan,' Tomos added, 'if they wanted to.'

Dafydd smiled wearily. 'Too late for your mother and me to start again, Tomos. For you maybe, if this valley is as good as they say, but we've done our bit of pioneering.'

'Of course you have, and I would never ask you unless I had built a home for you. That's what I intend to do, Dadda.'

Dafydd couldn't help smiling at the earnest sincerity in his boy's face. 'We'll see, Tomos – we'll see.'

Activity defined the following weeks.

The Governor gave immediate approval for the proposed expedition, which was quickly followed by equipment in the form of wagons, horses and provisions. Any fears the family had about Tomos venturing once more into formerly hostile territory were partially allayed by the strong military escort they were to have.

From the strength of the community's send-off, it was evident that many were hoping the expedition would bring back confirmation that this beautiful valley – Cwm Hyfryd – really existed.

One evening, just before the expedition was due to return, Dafydd looked up from his reading. 'You know why they got all this government support so quickly, don't you?'

Myfanwy put down her sewing. 'Go on.'

'Chile. You can't have a border with thousands of acres unpopulated – no one there. The Chileans could just march in.'

'Though they aren't quite sure where the border is anyway – which line of mountain peaks it crosses – something like that. Blod was saying.'

'Aye, that, too.' He sighed. 'No government gives anything away for love of humanity. There is always a very good political agenda.'

Myfanwy picked up her sewing. 'You are an old cynic, Dafydd Rhys,' she smiled. 'But you are right.'

Bronzed, fit and bursting with enthusiasm, Tomos returned with the expedition, unharmed and with total determination to make the valley his new home.

'*Cwm Hyfryd* it is, Mam, really!' He grinned. 'We've given it the name now.'

To his parents Tomos carefully detailed the advantages, the soil the climate the absence of a flooding river, the natural abundance of fruit and the huge expanse of land available to all.

Dafydd showed only a perfunctory interest. 'How are you going to get anything going without transport?'

'A road, Dadda – a road right across the plains to the foothills of the Andes, and we start next month.'

'We, who's we?'

'Well, me and a couple of hundred others, I should imagine – there'll be a gang of us from here. Pay's good, too.'

Myfanwy looked anxious. 'What about your land here?'

'No problem, Mam, Angharad will cope with it – a farm girl from Carmarthen, don't forget. Anyway she's as keen as I am to move.'

By the time the road to the Andes was finished Lisa and Herbie had married quietly and were planning to move to the new Trelew and run a lodging house for all the workers the place would attract. Though it was a sad parting, Idwal and Bron finally said goodbye, returning to Wales via Buenos Aires, where the rest of their family, even Rhiannon, had settled very well.

Back home in Rawson, Tomos tackled his father again about moving out to the new Cwm Hyfryd. As last time they were sitting in the garden drinking home-made beer.

'See, we've been able to build simple shacks for families – all helping each other – same as you did here really.'

'No shacks for us this time, Tomos – had enough of shacks.'

'Of course you have. Wouldn't ask you to live in a shack, Dadda, you know that – wouldn't want you to. We are going out there and all pitching in to build our haciendas. I'm going to build one big enough for all of us – Bethan, too, if she wants to come.'

'You know your little sister Tomos – stubborn as a mule. She'll visit, but with her nice teaching job, and the others up there, we won't get her away from Buenos Aires.' He paused, lost in memory. 'I miss her,' he mumbled. He took a swig of beer. 'And I haven't said we are coming yet.' He mopped the froth from his upper lip.

Tomos shrugged. 'There's time enough. Got to build first.'

'So long as you've got a good gang around you.'

'Great boys – Italians they are – from Sicily.'

Tomos had not seen his father look as astounded in a very long time. 'What's the matter, Dadda?' he asked.

Dafydd shook his head 'No Welsh boys?'

'Well, yes – our lot from here – but right now there are more Italians.'

Dafydd put his beer on the wooden garden table and stared into the distance saying nothing, his face creased in thought.

Then he said quietly, 'What happened, Tomos? It was going to be so perfect. We believed we had the makings of our own little state – a beacon for those who had felt oppression to do the same – a self-supporting country – a Welsh island in the middle of the pampas. What happened to it?'

For perhaps the first time Tomos was halfway to understanding his father's almost palpable pain, born of dedication. He put his hand on Dafydd's arm. 'There's evolution in everything, not only nature, Dadda.'

Dafydd sighed. 'Oh, I accept the evolution of society, Tomos, but it's hard, very hard when you have been an idealist, believed so – so fervently in the power of the people to overcome – like the French, the Americans. Ours was going to be a bloodless revolution – remove ourselves quietly from the scene of oppression, and now, now – Wales will disappear from Patagonia; our Senate toothless, impotent; our customs, heritage, values we hold precious will all be diluted into other nationalities. We shall barely be remembered in the history books.' He stopped to mop his brow. 'All those dreams shattered. My life – what has it meant? I have failed, Tomos; an old spent force – that's what I am.'

Tomos had never heard his father open his heart like this.

'No, Dadda,' he replied firmly. 'No – that is not true – not true at all. First of all, don't you realize the other immigrants – like the Italians – look to us to show them, and they have said as much? They all know it was we – we Welsh who tamed this savage land – and with our blood. They know how you pioneers dealt with vicious Araucans when we arrived; the terrible floods, losing crop after crop, homes, possessions washed away time after time – then growing the best wheat in the world. You have made the country. You have made legends in this land. It's you who have made it fit for others. There was nothing – nothing before you.'

Tomos was relieved to see the faint suggestion of a smile on Dafydd's lips.

'Cwm Hyfryd is a ready-made piece of paradise compared with the terrain you were given.' Tomos swigged his beer. 'You trust me, don't you, Dadda?'

Dafydd nodded.

'Well then, believe me when I tell you we are not going to lose our precious heritage nor our language, nor an *eisteddfod*, nor a *cymanfa ganu*. And we all feel the same – I promise you. And as for you, Dafydd Rhys – you are the chairman founder, the one who pulled it together, who gave inspiration to a dispirited people when they were at their lowest. A worthwhile life seems to me – and plenty left for Cwm Hyfryd, Dadda!'

Dafydd sat looking at his glass of beer, saying nothing. It was a warm late spring evening, the pink rays of a setting sun dappling trees and river. They sat in silence for several moments, Dafydd's eyes focused somewhere on the horizon.

'Tell me, Tomos,' he said, speaking at last, 'is this the end of the dream?'

'It's not the end, Dadda. It's the beginning of another. We are going to Cwm Hyfryd to continue what you started.'

Dafydd shrugged. 'I think it is the end of our Welsh Utopia.'

'Utopia is perfection – impossible – but the principles to aim for remain. That's what counts.' He looked at his father, forehead furrowed in thought, and smiled. 'Know what you are, don't you? A political dreamer.'

Dafydd drained his glass. 'Well, I think I'm in good company, and what's life without dreams, eh? Tell you what, though, it is the end of my unconditional belief in a benevolent Almighty.'

'Nothing new there – been coming on for years that has.'

'And it is so liberating, Tomos. No longer do I torment myself that sins, mine and everyone else's, caused floods, caused drought, caused bad harvests, caused untimely deaths of dear ones. No! It's Mother Nature for me, so long as we respect her.'

Putting his hand on his father's shoulder Tomos said, 'You will come with us, won't you – please? We need you, Dadda.'

'Not sure I want to end my days with a bunch of Italians. That was never on the agenda when we left Merthyr. We shall have to think about it.'

One year later, Dafydd and Myfanwy, accompanied by Tomos, left Rawson, bade goodbye to their old Mimosa friends, and with wagons piled high they set out across the new road spanning the plains to Cwm Hyfryd and their son's new hacienda. Dafydd was going with reluctance and misgivings, more to please Myfanwy and Tomos than out of natural inclination.

For his part Tomos was not a little concerned about his father's reaction to the several Italian families living near by and the 'welcome' supper planned between Angharad and his close friends Tino and Bianca Bavetta.

It took a week for Dafydd and Myfanwy to settle into their new home. They were totally captivated by their surroundings, their new ample accommodation and the climate. Fortunately house activity kept them away from the Italian community, and Tomos arranged for some of the Welsh Rawson boys to lend a hand with unpacking. They talked about their proposed building of a much-needed flour-mill cooperative, which they knew would bring them in a steady living wage. All was set fair, but introductions to their Italian community had yet to be got through, for, like it or not, Dafydd and Myfanwy were now part of it.

Anxious to avoid his father showing any signs of prejudice, particularly at the welcome supper, Tomos enlisted the help of Myfanwy.

Without telling Dafydd he took her to meet Tino and Bianca on her own. Communicating easily through a little Spanish and more English, it was obvious they had suffered badly in their native Sicily, fared even worse in New York, where they were herded into meagre rooms and forced to give half their wages to a Padrone, just like landworkers in Sicily. Brazil followed where they were treated like slaves on the coffee plantations. Patagonia was therefore just as much a haven to them as it had finally become to the Welsh.

On the way back to the house, Myfanwy, well aware of the delicate diplomacy that would be required later when Dafydd sat down to eat with the Italians, said, 'Well now, Tomos *bach*, we have to make this work and work well. They are lovely people, those Italians, and when your father knows what they have just told me – I'm sure he'll see sense. But let's get one thing straight. I am not going back to Rawson for Dadda.' She pondered for a moment. 'What's your father's favourite subject, Tomos?'

'Politics. If only he could see himself in a role again – I don't mean a Senate – but something he could organize.'

'Now then, before supper – you tell Tino to talk to Dadda about what's his name, Garibaldi, and why life hasn't been any better for them since he united the country – that's politics, and that'll get him sparking.'

'The sulphur mines in Sicily will grab him, too, Mam, the terrible conditions – accidents – workers treated like animals – no compensation – even worse than Merthyr. Tino's family were half starved working on the land. That's why he went to work in the sulphur.'

'And don't forget New York – and Brazil even worse. That will inflame his sense of injustice. He will understand, I know, and once he gets going he'll fight for anybody's rights, no matter who or what they are.'

'Tino must ask Dadda about how best to preserve the Italian language and customs. He'll like that – give him something else to think about.'

Myfanwy raised her index finger. 'But don't touch God and religion, or there'll be *ffradach*.'

Tomos laughed. 'Don't think Tino's too bothered, but I'll tell him.'

The arranged conversation between Tino and Dafydd went as anticipated, particularly as Dafydd was treated with great reverence as a famous elder statesman which of course he was. Tino, diminutive in stature, with a careworn face, was genuinely in awe of the old pioneer and asked pertinent questions, which pleased Dafydd. By the time they sat down to eat Dafydd and Tino had verbally drafted a rough plan for organized Italian classes, for both language and cultural pursuits, based on the Rawson Welsh model.

Myfanwy looked at her beloved husband across the table and smiled. It was plain to see a burden had been lifted from his shoulders. Here he was, holding court, kingpin again, giving advice, suggesting a committee to run the community, in which of course he would be pivotal. Without even noticing, he was eating with great enthusiasm an Italian dish he had never tasted before.

Tomos leaned over and whispered in his mother's ear, 'No spent force about him, is there?'

POSTSCRIPT

Eighteen-year-old Luis Gonzales opened his heavy-lidded eyes slowly. He could feel nothing. He tried to focus on his surroundings, but images were blurred. Where was he? How did he come to be here, unable to move, lying in a bed?

He remembered being carried flat on his back and the unmistakable whiff of antiseptic. He remembered hearing words in Spanish that said something about going home to the Argentine, to Puerto Madryn.

'Repatriation,' the voice had whispered.

But before? What happened before? Port Stanley, or was it Port William? Luis tried to assemble his thoughts into some sequence of events.

He remembered being with his regiment. There was a battle – that was it – a battle. Why could he not remember detail? He remembered a terrible pain in his shoulder, then his leg. He remembered falling and something heavy holding him down, then, nothing.

For how long did he lie in the world of nothing before he heard voices – English voices – the enemy? He could not see them.

He must be a prisoner – a wounded prisoner. How wounded was he? Right now his body was lying, albeit inert below his neck, but he had just moved a toe on his right foot.

He remembered something else; a light shining on his face and someone taking his arm. He had felt no pain. The Malvinas – that's where he was. War – war with the British!

No one had told them about war; the dry-mouthed terror; the shock at seeing a comrade's head blown off, guts spilling out of a fellow you had just spoken to and the shattering hideous noises; screams of pain, screams of fear, shouts of panic. The noises were still there, in his head. Perhaps time would take them away, like the memory of a nightmare. But the images? Each time he closed his eyes before he drifted back to his numb black world they were there.

Luis wanted to stay awake now. There was someone moving around him. He could see a shadow. There were voices speaking quietly to each other. He hoped one of them would speak to him, say something – anything.

Medical orderlies Colin James and Gary Davies were doing a brief round of inspection before their boss, the medical officer, arrived. They would have to have all the patients' notes ready and any changes written up for the medical officer to read, Captain Morris being a stickler for correct protocol, even with wounded Argentine prisoners due for repatriation.

Colin and Gary each had around twenty wounded prisoners to look after, and all were bed cases in this part of the liner specially converted into a temporary hospital bay. The wounded weren't in bad shape and were sure of survival except perhaps for the young lad in Colin's care. His chances were about fifty–fifty according to Captain Morris.

They were on the *Canberra*, anchored in the shallow waters of San Carlos. Normally a cruise ship, this great white whale had been specially commandeered for repatriation of prisoners of war who had been lining up to board for nearly two days now, hundreds of them, the line snaking round the docks. Colin was glad to be working in the hospital, far from the smelly unwashed bodies crowding on to the decks. They hadn't seen water in ten days, most of them. He wasn't sorry they were due to sail to Puerto Madryn in Patagonia tomorrow, the 19th; then, for him, home, to Merthyr.

He approached the young prisoner of war, their only cause for concern, and quietly took out the sheaf of notes in the tray at the end of his bed. The lad had been drifting in and out of a coma for a couple of days, but to Colin's great surprise he now had his eyes open.

He leant close to the bed. 'Hello, boy,' he whispered, taking his pulse 'Won't be long before we get you home – home,' he repeated. 'Comprendy?'

He did not expect an Argentinian prisoner of war to understand

and was about to move away when Luis replied in broken but perfectly good English.

'Thank you, soldier. Please say what happened to me – why I here.'

'You speak English then? Great. You'll be OK, boy. The doctor – medical officer – will explain it all. Don't you worry now.'

Colin adjusted the drip in the young soldier's arm and placed a thermometer under his tongue. He was glad the medical officer was about to make his rounds. He knew he couldn't handle this one. That was his boss's job, not his, thank God.

Ten minutes later Captain Geraint Morris, the medical officer, appeared. He was a handsome young man with blue eyes and black hair who from his first taste of battle had never stopped regretting leaving his job in the National Health Service for the role of an army doctor. Admittedly this was not on the scale of the Second World War, but pain, suffering and, as he saw it, needless death were the same whichever theatre of war.

Relieved that he was now nearing the end of his term of duty and would be returning to a practice in Cardiff, he smiled affably. 'Anything new, Corporal?'

'Well, yes, sir.' Corporal James handed over the prisoner's medical notes. 'Luis Gonzales, sir', and indicated the bed. 'He's opened his eyes long enough to ask where he was – and in English, sir. He wants to know what happened to him.'

Captain Morris's face clouded. 'Does he, poor chap?' He sighed. 'This is the bit I loathe most of all, Corporal.'

'Yes, I know, sir – but you can do it better than most, if you don't mind me saying, sir.'

With a thin smile, the doctor shrugged. 'Thanks.' He walked over to Luis Gonzales's bed, drew up a chair and said quietly, 'Luis, I am the medical officer – doctor. Glad to see you have come back to us. I believe you want to know . . .'

The young man's brown eyes opened wide, and a smile hovered on his lips. 'I am very glad you come to talk to me. You see, I am starting in medical school in Buenos Aires in October, so I would like to know what happened to me.'

Geraint Morris sighed. This was going to be very difficult.

Speaking slowly and clearly he said, 'Well – you were found underneath several dead bodies of your compatriots at Mount William. You had been shot in your shoulder and your leg.'

Small beads of perspiration lay on the boy's forehead. 'I remember the pain and something heavy on me. I am glad you found me – leg and shoulder important – I play rugby for my high school, and I will in medical school.' He paused for a moment. It was obvious speaking was a strain.

This was Dr Morris's opportunity to change direction. 'So, Luis, your parents – do they work?'

'Oh yes – both teachers – of English – so they make me learn it, too.' He gave a little smile. 'Not good, as they like. But they very happy because I must be doctor – always.' He took a deep breath. 'I am already nearly finishing my conscription year when there is trouble in Malvinas, and I must go. I say to my mother if I will be doctor it will be good experience for me, but she cries.'

The boy had to know. As medical officer Geraint had to tell him the full story. 'Luis, there is more. When you were found after two days, gangrene . . .' He stopped. 'You know – gangrene?' The boy nodded, his eyes wide with fear.

'It had already set in,' Geraint continued, 'but — and this is good – the freezing cold stopped it spreading and it was your fever that kept your blood warm. Do you understand?'

The boy nodded mutely.

'At the base hospital we worked on you for hours. We saved your life, Luis. Your shoulder is healing well, but your right leg above the knee had to be . . .' The doctor paused and looked directly into the boy's eyes. 'Had to be amputated,' he said, the word barely leaving his throat. Amputation had always seemed a medical failure.

There followed the most painful silence Geraint Morris had ever sat through.

Eventually the young man turned his head away from the doctor. 'So no more rugby – no more ski – my life is already changed – for ever – useless.'

Geraint took his hand. 'No! No! You mustn't talk like that.' He was emphatic. 'You will still be a doctor, Luis. That will not change.'

Tears were welling up in the boy's eyes as Geraint quietly rose from the chair, patted the young man's hands and moved on to the next patient.

Before leaving the ward he called, 'Corporal James – a word, please.' His voice a whisper, he said, 'Keep an eye on young Luis. He knows now – a shock – never good especially in his fragile condition, poor little sod. Oh, and see what you can find out about him from the papers we found in his kit.'

'Don't worry, sir, we will.'

Immediately Medical Orderly James took his broad six-foot frame over to the young prisoner of war whose face was stained now with silent tears.

'I know, boy, I know.' Colin, a generous, big-hearted young man, blinked his own smarting eyes as he gently squeezed the boy's arm.

'But I feel my right toe – and the doctor say it is not there.'

'Always happens like that, Luis. You go on feeling the limb for months.'

Colin felt helpless. He had seen so many senseless deaths on both sides in the last few months, and for what? A useless piece of sheep-rearing territory far from home.

Dr Geraint Morris returned to his cabin after this depressing round. He pulled off his white coat and threw it on his bed, the stethoscope falling out of a pocket.

He crossed to the shelf displaying a few alcoholic beverages and reached for the whisky bottle, pouring himself a generous slug into one of the glasses lined up in readiness. He slumped into a comfortable leather chair and downed his drink.

'Bloody fucking Falklands war,' he muttered. 'Why, for Chrissake? Why? To give their sodding sheep a UK passport?'

He poured himself another drink, consuming it just as rapidly.

'Poor little buggers, all of them. No arms, no legs. Only kids they are – and all for pompous political pricks – on both sides. Fuck them. Fuck them all.'

Fully clothed he lay down on the bunk bed, his pager on standby for that inevitable summons to a patient in the early hours. The young doctor had taken as much as he could bear from the senseless negativity of war. He was tired and longed to be back home in Cardiff; a new life, a new start, away from London. Joining the army had been an escape, he knew that, an escape from the debilitating scenario of divorce. There were still fleeting moments of gut-wrenching despair at the thought of Gina and of Paul, his so-called best friend, but time was healing, and war, with its horrors, was a grisly reminder of life's priorities. Geraint was learning quickly, but, for now, sleep.

'Like a ciggy – cigarette, Luis?'

The boy nodded.

'My friend Gary has got some. He'll look after you when I'm not here, don't worry.'

Colin called over to his friend in Welsh. '*Oes mwgyn 'da ti?*' Have you got a cigarette?

With a nod and a grin Gary walked over to Luis's bed.

'*Oes. Mae dau baced 'da fi.*' Yes, I have two packs. Gary fished them out of his pocket. '*Sawl un wyt ti'n moyn?*' How many do you want?

'*Un, dau.*' One, two.

As the two men were exchanging the cigarettes they did not see that Luis Gonzales had been staring at them open-mouthed. Summoning all his vocal strength the young man called, '*Galeses!*' Welsh! 'I, too – *rwy'n siarad Cymraeg.*' I speak Welsh.

The two young men were as stupefied and as open-mouthed as Luis had been. Here was an Argentine prisoner speaking Welsh – admittedly it had a bit of a Spanish 'twang', as Colin remarked later, but speaking the same language as some of the enemy army, and on the other side of the world to the little principality, was something else.

'But – how, Luis?' Gary asked.

Some of the tensions that had been apparent on the young boy's face seemed to evaporate as he explained to them in Welsh that his great-great-grandfather had come to Patagonia from Wales on *The Mimosa* in 1865. The fact he had come from Merthyr, the home town of both Colin and Gary, was yet another extraordinary coincidence.

It was his mother's side of the family, he explained. She had always spoken Welsh to him, and he had plenty of relatives all over the country, though he and his parents now lived in the capital.

Colin lit a cigarette for Luis and put it in his mouth. Allowing his patient just a few puffs, he removed it.

'Enough for now, Luis.'

The boy smiled. '*Diolch yn fawr.*' Thank you.

Colin mopped the lad's perspiring forehead and his flushed cheeks. It was clear his temperature was rising again. Speaking was a luxury his wartorn body could not afford just now. His eyelids looked heavy, and Colin suspected it could be a return of the fever.

'I have papers,' the boy mumbled.

'Yes, yes. Sleep now – tell us later, OK?'

Colin walked over to Gary who was about to settle down for the nightshift at a table in the makeshift ward. 'Don't like the look of our lad tonight.'

'Me neither. But, God, there's a thing – an Argy turns out to be Welsh.'

'Aye, bloody incredible. Wonder if there's more.'

'Have you heard of this Patagonia emigration then?'

'Aye, a bit from my *dadcu*. They never really told us about it in school, did they?'

'Not important enough p'raps.' Gary looked in the direction of Luis's bed. 'I'd better go and cool him down a bit, poor dab.'

'Where's that box with all his belongings kept?'

'Under the bed – why?'

'Doc asked me to go through it – just in case the poor little bugger doesn't make it home, I suppose.'

Gary rose from the table, a thin smile on his lips. 'He's got to now, mun. He's one of us.'

The cardboard box was indistinguishable from all the others into which was packed the artefacts of a young life, letters, keys, comb, a small wooden bear, a photograph of the school rugby team with Luis at the centre.

'*Duw,*' said Colin, 'looking at him now – never think it was the same boy.'

'But he isn't, is he? Nobody's the same after war – leg or no leg.'

As Gary ministered cold compresses to the young man's flushed cheeks, Colin, following instructions, continued delving into the cardboard box. At the bottom, wrapped around carefully in a waterproof material, he found a thick copybook, pretty old by the look of it. Carefully he opened the first page. What he saw took him so completely by surprise he was forced to sit down. It was written in Welsh in a beautiful copperplate hand and read, 'This is the diary of Dafydd Rhys born in Merthyr, who emigrated to Patagonia in 1865 aboard *The Mimosa*.'

He walked over to Gary who was noting Luis's temperature again.

'Think those compresses have brought it down a bit.' Gary looked up at his friend. 'What's the matter, Col? Seen a ghost or something?'

'In a way, yes. Come and have a look at this.'

Thumbing through the brown-edged pages, an unbelievable story began to unfold; of their own compatriots, simple ordinary people, and their struggle for survival against ferocious odds and about whom they knew so little.

'Whew! I'm gobsmacked, Col! This must be his great-great-great-*dadcu* then, Dafydd Rhys. Who's going to believe us?'

Colin shrugged and shook his head. 'I can hardly believe it myself. And from Merthyr, too. To think, over there on the edge of life and death is his Argentinian great-great-great-grandson who we've shot up! It's like bloody civil war, mun.'

'Welsh on his mam's side – that's what he said, didn't he?'

'Got to be – not many Gonzales in Merthyr.'

'If he's awake I'll ask him.'

Leaving Colin to continue reading Dafydd Rhys's diary, Gary strode over to Luis, applied more cold compresses and took his temperature. The boy looked up and smiled weakly. Gary gave him a reassuring grin.

'Don't worry, boy. We'll get you home.'

After recording Luis's temperature on the chart at the end of the bed, Gary whispered, 'What was your mam's Welsh family name before she married your dad?'

'It was ap Morris.'

'Sleep now. We sail tomorrow morning, so you've got to be fit to meet your mam.'

With lifeless eyes and a look of disbelief, the young man mumbled, 'Perhaps.'

Colin took the diary back to his cabin and spent most of the night reading it, leaving Gary on duty.

It was 18 June. The ship's turboprop engines lumbered into action for the journey to Puerto Madryn where her cargo of prisoners would be discharged. For those seriously wounded, Argentine medical staff had been alerted, and transport would be standing by at the port.

When Colin came on duty Dr Morris had already started his last round, with Gary in tow supplying the latest information on the wounded. Looking at his notes at the table in the middle of the ward Dr Morris turned to Colin.

'Corporal James, I'm still not happy about Luis Gonzales – very unstable. Better try to cool him down – blanket baths throughout the day. Once we get him on shore it's up to his own kith and kin.'

Gary shot a swift but knowing look at Colin.

'Yes, sir, and, sir, remember you asked me to go through Gonzales's cardboard box?'

'Oh, did I? Find anything?'

'Do you speak Welsh, Dr Morris?'

The young doctor huffed. 'Not very well – I can read it better.'

Gary smiled. 'There's a treat in store for you then, doctor.'

Quickly they told Dr Morris about the diary and their Welsh-speaking prisoner. Handing him the fat diary, Colin added, 'We didn't know much about this Patagonian emigration, did you, sir?'

The doctor opened the first page. 'I think a relative of mine went out with the first lot but came back. That's all I know. Lived in your neck of the woods, Merthyr, so the story goes.'

Carefully he flicked through the first few pages. 'My God, what a find this is. I'll have a chat later with our Luis if he rallies a bit. Rhys his Welsh family name?'

Colin shook his head. 'It's ap Morris, sir, on his mother's side.'

The young doctor looked so astonished Gary laughed.

''S'all right, sir, you're in the clear – it's ap Morris.'

Clutching the diary, Geraint Morris fairly raced back to his cabin, his head spinning with remarkable coincidence and possibilities, for he, too, was originally an ap Morris. At the grammar school his name had become the good-natured butt of schoolboy jibes, and he had been known as Appendage Morris, Appalling Morris, Apprentice Morris and, finally, when he was off to medical school, Appendix Morris. Not wanting any confusion at St Bartholomew's, he had abandoned the 'ap'.

The end of the war and coming home had a positive psychological effect even on the dispirited troops of the losing side. For the injured the prospect of seeing family, particularly their mothers again, was remarkable. Luis's temperature, too, had dropped and stabilized.

'C'mon, let's make you smell a bit better for your mams and girlfriends or they'll walk away!'

Colin and Gary joked their way through the ward, shaving, washing, combing hair and cleaning fingernails. The atmosphere of celebration and good spirits despite injuries was like Christmas.

As they steamed into Puerto Madryn, the patients, clean and presentable, Gary said, 'Col, why did we have to have a war to end up like this? Shooting the crap out of each other – and now we're laughing together?'

Dr Morris came into the ward dressed in his army captain's uniform with a last-minute checklist for the disembarkation of wounded. He carried sheaves of notes to hand over to his Argentine counterparts waiting on the dockside and briefly bade farewell to each patient. Colin and Gary stood by, ready to hand over their charges, and watched him converse with Luis who was leaning back against the pillows, his young face at last showing signs of animation. Handing him back Dafydd Rhys's diary, the doctor gave the young Argentinian a reassuring pat on his arm.

As they were steaming into harbour, Dr Morris joined Commander Briggs on the bridge.

'So, Dr Morris, I dare say you'll be glad to get back to the UK?'

'Well, yes, Commander, eventually. I'm going to be remaining here for a week or two; here and Buenos Aires.'

The Commander's eyebrows shot up to his hairline.

'Good God, man – fraternizing with the enemy so soon?' He gave a silly high-pitched laugh. 'Or sussing out enemy territory for next time, eh?'

'No enemies where I'm going, Commander.'

'Really?'

'It's a research project combined with other, er – relative factors,' the doctor added with a smile that disclosed nothing.

The Commander grinned. 'Full of mystery, you bloody Welsh!'

SOME AUTHORS WE HAVE PUBLISHED

James Agee • Bella Akhmadulina • Tariq Ali • Kenneth Allsop • Alfred Andersch
Guillaume Apollinaire • Machado de Assis • Miguel Angel Asturias • Duke of Bedford
Oliver Bernard • Thomas Blackburn • Jane Bowles • Paul Bowles • Richard Bradford
Ilse, Countess von Bredow • Lenny Bruce • Finn Carling • Blaise Cendrars • Marc Chagall
Giorgio de Chirico • Uno Chiyo • Hugo Claus • Jean Cocteau • Albert Cohen
Colette • Ithell Colquhoun • Richard Corson • Benedetto Croce • Margaret Crosland
e.e. cummings • Stig Dalager • Salvador Dalí • Osamu Dazai • Anita Desai
Charles Dickens • Bernard Diederich • Fabián Dobles • William Donaldson
Autran Dourado • Yuri Druzhnikov • Lawrence Durrell • Isabelle Eberhardt
Sergei Eisenstein • Shusaku Endo • Erté • Knut Faldbakken • Ida Fink
Wolfgang George Fischer • Nicholas Freeling • Philip Freund • Carlo Emilio Gadda
Rhea Galanaki • Salvador Garmendia • Michel Gauquelin • André Gide
Natalia Ginzburg • Jean Giono • Geoffrey Gorer • William Goyen • Julien Gracq
Sue Grafton • Robert Graves • Angela Green • Julien Green • George Grosz
Barbara Hardy • H.D. • Rayner Heppenstall • David Herbert • Gustaw Herling
Hermann Hesse • Shere Hite • Stewart Home • Abdullah Hussein • King Hussein of Jordan
Ruth Inglis • Grace Ingoldby • Yasushi Inoue • Hans Henny Jahnn • Karl Jaspers
Takeshi Kaiko • Jaan Kaplinski • Anna Kavan • Yasunuri Kawabata • Nikos Kazantzakis
Orhan Kemal • Christer Kihlman • James Kirkup • Paul Klee • James Laughlin
Patricia Laurent • Violette Leduc • Lee Seung-U • Vernon Lee • József Lengyel
Robert Liddell • Francisco García Lorca • Moura Lympany • Thomas Mann
Dacia Maraini • Marcel Marceau • André Maurois • Henri Michaux • Henry Miller
Miranda Miller • Marga Minco • Yukio Mishima • Quim Monzó • Margaret Morris
Angus Wolfe Murray • Atle Næss • Gérard de Nerval • Anaïs Nin • Yoko Ono
Uri Orlev • Wendy Owen • Arto Paasilinna • Marco Pallis • Oscar Parland
Boris Pasternak • Cesare Pavese • Milorad Pavic • Octavio Paz • Mervyn Peake
Carlos Pedretti • Dame Margery Perham • Graciliano Ramos • Jeremy Reed
Rodrigo Rey Rosa • Joseph Roth • Ken Russell • Marquis de Sade • Cora Sandel
Iván Sándor • George Santayana • May Sarton • Jean-Paul Sartre
Ferdinand de Saussure • Gerald Scarfe • Albert Schweitzer
George Bernard Shaw • Isaac Bashevis Singer • Patwant Singh • Edith Sitwell
Suzanne St Albans • Stevie Smith • C.P. Snow • Bengt Söderbergh
Vladimir Soloukhin • Natsume Soseki • Muriel Spark • Gertrude Stein • Bram Stoker
August Strindberg • Rabindranath Tagore • Tambimuttu • Elisabeth Russell Taylor
Emma Tennant • Anne Tibble • Roland Topor • Miloš Urban • Anne Valery
Peter Vansittart • José J. Veiga • Tarjei Vesaas • Noel Virtue • Max Weber
Edith Wharton • William Carlos Williams • Phyllis Willmott
G. Peter Winnington • Monique Wittig • A.B. Yehoshua • Marguerite Young
Fakhar Zaman • Alexander Zinoviev • Emile Zola

 Peter Owen Publishers, 81 Ridge Road, London N8 9NP, UK
T + 44 (0)20 8350 1775 / F + 44 (0)20 8340 9488 / E info@peterowen.com
www.peterowen.com / @PeterOwenPubs
Independent publishers since 1951